ACKNOWLEDGMENTS

Many thanks to my writing posse and support group: Laura Alford, Laura Butler, Susan Sands and Tracy Solheim. You ladies are trusted advisors and wonderful friends. I can't thank my editor, Cassie Cox, enough for her assistance with all my books. I would have nothing without the love and support of my family. I love you all.

CHAPTER 1

Ty Bloodworth had been in a daze for the better part of three months. He inhaled deeply and closed his eyes while he waited for the object of his desire to appear. All the things he savored with that one breath captured everything he loved about the woods. Nobody understood why he chose to live alone tucked in the forest instead of in the free wheeling dorms near the fly shop, but at twenty-four, he'd had enough of communal living.

He sucked in another breath of cool morning air and could almost feel it clearing out all the dust in his lungs. His friends said it was too quiet, but had they listened, really listened? The birds called to loved ones, back and forth from above and all around. The bugs croaked a different melody from the ground. Squirrels, when they scuttled about the forest floor, sounded like a speeding jaguar leaping on its prey.

And then he heard it, the sound he'd been waiting for while holding his steaming cup of coffee and wearing nothing but a pair of shorts. The gravel crunched under her mile-eating stride. When she cleared the curve, he let his free hand rest on his stomach and tried to wipe away the ache. He felt the clench in his gut, the adrenaline rush he felt just before reeling in a big fish. Jill Jennings probably wouldn't appreciate being compared to a fish.

He felt himself lean forward in anticipation, ushering the moment of eye contact to fruition. He wasn't disappointed by the wait. She was beauty in motion, although she'd probably hate that description as she pushed herself up the steep incline. Sweat made her thin shirt cling to her stomach muscles as they twisted with every step. Her quadriceps quivered, almost in tune with his thundering heart. She wasn't the biggest fish he'd ever seen, not with her elegant build and slight frame, but she was the most magnificent.

Conflicted by his overwhelming attraction while still attached to his girlfriend back home, Ty avoided Jill most of the time, at the restaurant where she worked and whenever she came to the fly and rafting shop to visit her roommate. He didn't even try to ignore her here, outside his door when he could watch her move and admire everything about her that had caught his attention from the very first glance.

She looked up, her head swung in his direction, and a line of irritation graced the delicate space between her dark brows. She glanced down at the path, but not before she landed on a rock that had fallen from the stony overhang at some point and came to rest in the road. Her ankle buckled and she went down hard, her leg crashing against a boulder lining the road. Ty heard the crack just seconds before her scream. He was at her side in a flash, grabbing her shoulders as she thrashed around on the ground, filling her chestnut hair with gravel and dirt.

"It's broken," she huffed through clenched teeth. "Damn it, it's broken."

Ty noticed her eyes hadn't filled with tears, but the tawny color had almost disappeared around her enlarged pupils. She was dangerously close to shock.

"I'm going to pick you up and carry you to my truck," he said.

"No, no, no," she whispered, as if speaking loudly would make the pain spread throughout her body. "Call an ambulance. I don't want to move."

"I don't think either one of us wants to wait forty minutes for an ambulance to come from Del Noches. I'll be careful. Put your arms around my neck."

After one uncertain look, she cinched her fingers around his neck and he lifted her into his arms, careful to support, but not grab her injured leg. Once he got the door open, he kicked his fly vest to the floorboard and gently placed her on the backseat. She used her arms to inch across so Ty could close the door before he raced inside the cabin for his keys, wallet, and cell phone.

He tried to drive with consideration for how every bump and turn felt as she braced herself with her arms and breathed heavily through her nose. "You okay back there?" he asked as he studied her face through the rearview mirror. She'd gone deathly pale and her pupils were still enlarged.

She let out a groan when the truck bounced over a rut in the gravel. "I will be once we get onto the blacktop."

"We're almost there." He gunned the engine when they leveled out and he could see the pavement ahead. "Is there anyone you want me to call? Your family?"

"No. Not yet." She held her lips tight and her head leaned back against the seat. "I'll deal with them later."

Ty could only wonder why she didn't want her family around when she'd obviously broken her leg and lay writhing in pain. He knew her dad was her coach, but beyond that, he knew very little about the girl in his backseat, other than how she'd occupied his mind for most of the summer.

He passed an RV, a huge tractor, and a carful of tourists on the two-lane highway before pulling under the emergency overhang for Del Noches General. He hopped out, ran inside, grabbed a wheelchair, and lifted her from the truck as delicately as he could. He wheeled her in, oblivious to his state of half dress.

"I need some help here," he said to no one specific when everyone seemed not to notice the girl whimpering in pain in the wheelchair with her leg lying at a very unnatural angle. When the nurse stood up and looked over the partition and down at Jill, she dropped her clipboard and bounded around the counter.

"What happened?"

"I broke my leg," she managed before her eyes fluttered closed.

"She's going into shock." The nurse grabbed the wheelchair and ran her into the back. Ty stopped at the doors she'd disappeared behind and wondered what he should do. He walked back to his truck, fished his cell phone out of the cup holder, and called Tommy Golden at The Golden Rule fly shop.

"Tommy, it's Ty."

"Don't tell me you're canceling this afternoon with the Allgoods."

"I'm not. Listen, I'm with Jill Jennings at the hospital. She broke her leg running on the road outside my house."

"Shit."

"Yeah. They just took her back and I don't have any way to get in touch with her family. Is Olivia there?"

Tommy blew out a breath loud enough for Ty to hear. "She's out with a group, but I know someone who'd know. Where'd you take her? Westmoreland?"

"Del Noches." When Tommy groaned, Ty explained, "It's a bad break, Tommy. She was going into shock. I don't think she'd have made it all the way to Westmoreland."

"Her dad's going to have a fit."

"Yeah. Can you make some calls? I don't want her to be here alone."

"You leaving?"

He looked down at his bare feet and chest. "No, not until someone else gets here. But tell them to hurry."

"Will do," Tommy said. "I'll be in touch."

Ty knew when Jill's father arrived. Picking him out as a track coach wasn't hard, not with his lean figure and the gold windbreaker synonymous with the local college. His dark hair, the exact color of his daughter's, was beginning to streak with

Mending the Line

Christy Hayes

DEDICATION

To our friends in south central Colorado. Thanks for making us feel welcome.

OTHER BOOKS BY CHRISTY HAYES

Angle of Incidence
Dodge the Bullet
Heart of Glass
Misconception
Shoe Strings
The Accidental Encore
The Sweetheart Hoax

Golden Rule Outfitters Series
Guiding the Fall, Book 2
Taming the Moguls, Book 3

Kiss & Tell Series
A Kiss by Design, Book 1
A Kiss by the Book, Book 2
Kiss & Make Up, A Kiss & Tell Novella

gray around the temples and his worried expression turned to suspicion when Ty stood up and approached him as he waited by the nurses' station.

"Mr. Jennings?" Ty asked.

Gary Jennings assessed Ty from toe to head. Ty stood at least half a foot taller than Jill's dad. Despite his height advantage, Ty felt put in place by Gary's disdainful stare, especially since Ty stood shirtless in a pair of flip-flops he'd found in the back of his truck. "Yes?"

"I'm Tyler Bloodworth. I brought your daughter in."

"*You* did? From where?"

"She fell in front of my place on Vista Road just north of the Lower Fork."

"Vista Road? What the hell was she doing up there?"

Ty lifted his shoulder. "Running?"

The nurse returned and told Gary he could follow her through the double doors. Gary didn't even say thank you, or goodbye, or glance in Ty's direction before hurling himself through the doors.

Ty's cell phone rang as he walked to the parking lot. "Yeah," he said when he recognized Tommy's shop number on the display.

"Jill's dad should be there soon."

"He's already here. Thanks for the warning."

"Lyle said he'd be upset."

"Lyle?" Ty rubbed the spot on his chest that continued to ache from not knowing how Jill was doing. The nurses wouldn't even give him an update because he wasn't family.

"Lyle Woodward. Friend of Jill's; he lives in Hailey."

"Oh." Friend didn't mean boyfriend, but that didn't help Ty's mood. Of course, he wasn't exactly one to cast stones considering he'd yet to cut ties with Dana. "I'll be in later for the Allgoods."

"Last group of the season for you, my friend. You're one hell of a fishing guide. If you change your mind and want to come back next summer, you let me know."

"I just might," Ty said. He'd been thinking about it since

the first moment he saw Jill. "I'll let you know by the end of the first semester."

"Hell, kid. I thought I was pissing in the wind. What happened to Wyoming?"

"I like it here," he said as he took one last glance at the hospital entrance where the real reason he'd come back was hopefully getting the help she needed. "More than I thought I would."

CHAPTER 2

Ty slept like the dead. After nine solid months at school with an apartment full of frat boys and their girlfriends mingling about at all hours, the quiet had lulled him into the kind of sleep he longed for while studying for finals. Ty rolled over and glanced at the clock through the one eye he dared to open against the sun slanting through the shades. Almost noon and he could have easily slept for a few more hours. As it stood, he only had seven minutes before his stepmom or one of his sisters bounded into the room demanding he rise and join the living. Like clockwork, they knocked at twelve on the dot.

"Ty? Are you getting up?" Gabby asked through the closed door. He grunted an answer that could have been yes or could have been no. With a headful of chestnut curls, his middle sister poked her head inside and scowled at him with the same expression his stepmom wore when she was irritated. "Mommy said to get you up."

"I'm up, I'm up." He leaned onto an elbow and tried to pry his eyes wide.

She held tight to the doll cradled against her side. "Mommy said up meant out of bed."

"Maybe to her it does." He finally got his eyes to function

and stared at Gabby. His five-year-old half-sister wore a bright yellow sundress and a hot pink sweater. "You're wearing two different shoes."

"I know," she said, and if she knew how to roll her eyes, Ty felt sure she would have done so. "I can't find the matches, so Mommy said I could wear these. She said it was a fashion statement."

Ty thought of his stepmother, the shoe designer, and smiled. "She would know." Ty pulled back the covers and stifled a grin as his sister squealed and hid her eyes.

"Don't look, Baby," she told her doll. "Ty's naked."

"I'm not naked," he said and popped her on the butt before she scooted out of his room. "I'm wearing boxers, aren't I?" he asked the bathroom mirror before relieving his aching bladder. He grabbed a shower, took his time shaving, and brushed his teeth before dressing in his usual t-shirt and cargo shorts.

He looked around the room, tossed the comforter over the bed to make it seem as if he'd made his bed, and realized he was stalling. It was his life, he told himself as he descended the stairs of the old farmhouse his dad had called home since he came back to Sequoyah Falls almost twenty years before. Ty could barely remember living with both his parents in the one level ranch on Third Street.

He could smell something simmering on the stove before his feet cleared the stairs. Lita stood in the kitchen wearing an apron, a thin white shirt, snakeskin heels, and capri pants the same color as her middle daughter's sweater, chopping vegetables on a cutting board. "'Bout time you got up," she said. The scolding tone of her voice didn't match the dazzling smile she barely tried to hide. "Sleep well?"

"Like a baby." Ty rifled through the crammed refrigerator and scowled at the six packs of yogurt and gallon jugs of apple juice and milk. "Where's the adult food?"

"Rumor has it there's some in the back. I'm making shrimp stew for dinner tonight and your dad's going by the new bakery in town for dessert. Your mom and Bryce and the twins are coming, and so is Cal."

"All this for me?"

"The prodigal son is home, at least for a few days." Lita waved the knife in his direction. "We're not allowed to spoil you rotten?"

"Spoil away." He pulled out the milk, grabbed a bowl from the cupboard, and almost sighed when he spied a new box of Frosted Flakes in the pantry.

"I thought you wanted adult food?" Lita asked.

"I forgot how great it feels to be a kid."

She set the paring knife down and grabbed his shoulders from behind when he plopped at the bar to eat his breakfast. "We've missed you. Your dad is so glad to have you home. He's a little testosterone challenged in this house."

Ty shoved a spoonful in his mouth and spoke around his food, something he'd have gotten in trouble for at his mom's house. "Even with me home, the odds still aren't good."

"Yes, but you're both bigger than the rest of us. That has to count for something."

"Where'd the rug rats go?"

"The girls are having a tea party on the porch with their stuffed animals. Gabby said you're invited if you put some clothes on."

"I wasn't naked!" Ty said, his face hot.

Lita only laughed. "It's so good to have you home, Ty. We've missed you."

"It's good to be home. I wish I could stay longer, but I've got to head out day after tomorrow if I'm going to make it to Colorado on time."

"Colorado?" She tilted her head and her enormous gold hoops swung like pendulums into her hair. "I thought you were going to Wyoming this year?"

Practice with her, Ty reminded himself. If he could pull the story off with Lita, he might stand a chance with his dad. "I'm going back to the Lower Fork."

She wiped her hands on a towel and leaned on the counter. "Does your dad know?"

"No."

"I didn't think so," she mumbled under her breath.

She came around the island and plopped a knee on the barstool next to him. Ty concentrated on fishing the last flakes from his bowl and not on his stepmother's steely eyes. It didn't matter that she was only thirteen years older than him. She could yield parental guilt like the best of them.

"Why do I get the feeling you don't want to tell him?"

Ty shrugged and filled his bowl again. He got up to retrieve the milk from the refrigerator and avoid eye contact. "I guess I don't."

"You think he'll be upset?"

He looked at her with one sharp glance.

"Of course he will." She stood up and placed her hands on his shoulders. If it weren't for her heels, she wouldn't have been able to reach them. "It's your life, Ty. Tell him. If you make him feel like you're keeping it from him, he'll get upset."

"He's going to be upset regardless."

"Maybe, but if you hide it from him, he'll be hurt." She backed off and went around the counter. "I'm glad I hadn't already made a reservation. The girls can't wait to go out West."

"You'll love it there, Lita. The air is so clean, the people are nice, and there's a lot for the girls to do. There's a dude ranch midway between Del Noches and the Lower Fork that offers horseback riding and has a kids program. They'll hold a cabin for me if you let me know what week you want to come."

"I'll talk to your dad after you talk to your dad."

He slurped up the rest of his milk and rinsed the bowl in the sink.

"Just leave it," Lita said. "I've got to empty the dishwasher."

"I'll empty it," Ty said.

"You could, and I'd appreciate the help, but I think you'd better go to the shop and talk to Jesse."

"He's working. He won't want the interruption."

"Ty," Lita scolded. "You won't be an interruption. Go." She pushed him out of the kitchen. "Talk to your dad, see your friends, and come back hungry."

He turned around and flashed a smile. "I'm always hungry."

The raft shop was quiet, but that didn't mean Ty had an easy time finding a parking spot. He squeezed his truck next to the trash bin and figured his dad wouldn't put a call in to have him towed. He didn't recognize the girl at the reception desk with a nose ring and dreadlocks; she must have been a new summer hire. She smiled and lifted her brows. "Can I help you?"

"Jesse around?" he asked.

"He's in his office. Can I tell him who's here?"

"I'll tell him myself."

She seemed a little unsure about letting a stranger into the back, but Ty just waved her off and rapped on the office door. His dad looked up from the computer and hopped to his feet. "Ty! I didn't know you were coming down."

At 42, his dad wore contentment like a blanket around his shoulders. He'd be hard pressed not to love his life with a beautiful wife, three little girls, and a thriving business. He wore his light brown hair shaggy and Ty spotted a few hints of gray in his day old beard. His uniform of cargo shorts and t-shirts—nearly identical to Ty's—hadn't changed in years. The grungy look hid a shrewd businessman with a predilection for making cunning investments. "Figured I'd come by, let you give me a tour of the new building."

"Now's a good time. All the groups are out, so the changing area is deserted." He slapped Ty's shoulder and led him out of the office. "Did you meet Desiree?"

Ty nodded to the girl. "Sort of."

"This is my son, Ty. He's just home for a few days before he heads out to Wyoming to guide on the North Platte."

"Cool," she said. "I've heard there's great water on the Platte."

"I'm a fishing guide," Ty explained. "The only water I'm interested is the kind where trout like to hide."

She looked at Jesse and shook her head. "Where'd you go wrong?"

"Beats me," Jesse said with a smirk and led Ty out the back door. "Here she is."

The log building was huge and held both the raft storage and changing area. The structure was a big improvement from the original barn.

"I like the way you've used the space," Ty said.

Jesse led him through a door to the back part where rafts were stacked on shelves. "I've got this corner saved for the fly shop. You won't need much space and the arrangements can be done through our front desk or you could set up a counter here by the back door."

Ty could see it. The fly shop they'd talked about for years, working side by side with his dad building something of his own. He'd spent six years at school getting degrees to hang on the wall and he figured out that what he wanted out of life was no farther than his home away from home. "I love it. Dan did a good job. I really like the open ceiling and exposed beams."

Jesse slapped Ty on the back. "That was your idea. Saved money, too, except for the beams." He let out a contented sigh. "Just think, this time next year, we'll be working together."

"'Bout time," Ty said. He peeked his head in the changing area, remarked about the roominess and stall placement before heading back outside. They both turned at the sound of the bus rounding the corner. "Morning group's back."

"You'd better bug outta here before they disembark."

"Dad, I wanted to talk to you about something."

The bus pulled in front of them and hissed to a stop. "Better hold that thought 'til later. I'll be home around seven. Lita tell you about dinner tonight?"

"Yeah, she did."

"Good. We'll talk then." Jesse greeted the guests as they ambled off the bus. "Have a good time, young lady?"

A sloe-eyed preteen hopped off the steps. "The best!"

Jesse winked at Ty and waved him off as he herded the masses toward the changing area while instructing them to drop their wetsuits in the trough by the entrance after they changed.

Damn, he should have pulled Jesse aside when Desiree mentioned the Platte, but he didn't want an audience for their conversation. If it had to wait until tonight, he'd have even more of an audience.

CHAPTER 3

Jill Jennings grabbed a towel from the gym's meager pile and wiped the sweat from her brow. She'd only done two sets and had used the towel break as an excuse to gear herself up for number three. She only hoped her dad didn't notice.

"Jill?" Gary Jennings called from his station by the leg lift machine. "You coming? You've got another set to do before we hit the yoga ball."

Jill took a deep breath and planted on a smile before turning to face him. Fooling her father into thinking her recovery was going better than expected was quickly becoming as difficult as resuming her training after breaking her leg. Thankfully, members of the Warlock State cross country team started trickling in for their morning workout, and Gary got distracted talking to coach Miles.

"You're here early," one of the girls mumbled as she plopped down on the mat to stretch. "I was feeling sorry for myself before I spotted you looking half done with your workout."

"I wish," Jill said. "I'm about a third done. I've still got pool work."

"How's the leg?" she asked.

Jill averted her eyes. She couldn't tell a lie looking someone in the face. "Better. Getting stronger every day."

It wasn't that her leg wasn't healing; it just wasn't healing fast enough. Her dad was pushing her hard, harder than anyone else he'd ever trained after an injury. He was still mad at her for breaking her leg and forfeiting a chance at the Olympic trials. He couldn't have been more upset than she was that she'd tripped and fallen on a rock while running along her favorite mountain trail. A trail he'd continuously discouraged her from running. *There are too many obstacles on those trails. You can't concentrate on your form when you're always looking down to see what you're going to step on.*

She'd gone anyway, running up and down the winding gravel roads because she loved pushing herself and discovering what was around every twist and turn. She went twice a week, the same days at the same time so she could catch a glimpse of the biggest obstacle in her life: Ty Bloodworth. She wasn't looking down because she was looking into the eyes of the man who'd intrigued her, saved her, and left town without a word.

She had no right to be upset; they weren't involved. Hell, they weren't even friends. But it stung that his boyish charm and that easy aura were the reasons for her fall. Nothing ever seemed to faze him, certainly not a skinny runner with more determination than talent and a penchant for being alone.

He was back east where he belonged and she needed to focus on the future. She'd been a long shot runner before her injury. Now, with a broken tibia and fibula, a plate and countless screws surgically inserted and finally removed, her chance of making any Olympic team seemed more like a pipe dream. The pursuit of it, the golden pie in the sky task of training for another four years when all she wanted to do was move on with her life felt like an albatross around her neck.

"Jill," her dad called from the leg press machine. When he tapped his watch and turned around, she wished for the millionth time in a decade her father wasn't her coach.

"I gotta go."

"Yeah," the girl mumbled.

Gary had the leg press machine set at more weight than Jill's fragile leg could handle for thirty reps. She changed the weight setting and was met with a stern stare. Did he know how much disappointment he could convey with just that one look?

"You won't make any progress unless you push yourself."

"I won't make any progress if I reinjure my leg by pushing too hard."

"It's a fine line, Jill. That's why you have me, so you don't have to worry about being pushed too hard or not hard enough."

Jill began using the machine with the weight she'd set. He couldn't change the weight when the machine was in motion and the noisy pulley system would force him to yell. Gary Jennings wouldn't yell at her in public for fear of spreading rumors that her recovery wasn't coming along as well as he'd led everyone to believe. He signed her up for a race the next month and she'd yet to log any miles in the current one.

She worked methodically through the rest of his routine, concentrating on her breathing and form, blocking out the pain from her leg and the frustration she felt at not being in top shape. Her stamina wasn't the only thing missing. Her passion for the chase and the thrill of competition had dimmed significantly as the months of recovery stretched along during winter. With the removal of the plate and the screws and the dawning of the summer season ahead, she didn't know how to recapture her love of the sport. She'd simply lost the fire that had kept her going these last few years.

Gary shoved a bottle of water in her face and nodded with his head toward the college's indoor swimming pool. "Go change and I'll meet you at the pool."

Her only response was a grunt. She knew she'd face a lecture on respecting his role as her coach at some point during the day. She couldn't muster enough energy to care. She'd agreed to have him coach her and he did a good job before the injury. They skirted around the sticky parts of working together with the solid determination to make the team. It drove them both to overlook the petty irritations and the blurring of the lines between family and coach. Missing the trials and facing a lengthy rehabilitation paled in comparison to the thought of spending the next four years with him on her back 24/7. She didn't think their relationship or her family could survive the pressure of it again.

She toweled off after forty-five minutes strapped to the flotation belt that let her run in the pool without putting pressure on her leg and made a beeline for the locker room. Her dad caught her arm before she could disappear inside.

"Where are you in such a hurry to go?"

"I've got to change and get to work."

"Work?" Gary asked, his forehead a maze of lines.

"The Golden Tap. I got my old job back."

He sighed, one long exhalation of breath that said as much as the sneering look on his face. His expression went slack and his shoulders slumped as if she'd tossed a boulder onto his back. "You shouldn't spend any more time on your feet than you need for training."

"That'd be great, Dad, if I didn't have to earn some money. My apartment doesn't pay for itself and the last time I checked, gas wasn't free."

"All the more reason for you to stay at home instead of moving back in with Olivia. You could ride into the gym with me and God knows as much as your brother eats, we wouldn't charge you rent."

"We've talked about this before. I'm twenty-two years old. I'm not living with my parents."

"You've been living with us the last few months. It hasn't been so bad." He stuffed his hands on his hips. "You act like the only kid your age who does it. You're not."

"People who move back in with their parents are out of options. Now that my leg's recovered, I have options. Tommy let me have my job back—the only job I could find that works perfectly around my training schedule—and you think that's a bad thing?"

"I think you shouldn't do anything right now that'll hinder

your progress. The less time you spend on your feet, and that includes delivering burgers and beer to your grungy friends, the faster your leg will heal and you can get back to serious training." He dragged a hand through his hair. "We've got to start all over again, Jill. This wasn't a bump in the road; it was a full-fledged mountain, and we're not even half way back to where we were before you broke your leg."

They both knew he'd swallowed the rest of what he wanted to say: that where she was before she broke her leg probably wasn't good enough to get where he desperately wanted her to go. "Do you really need me to say it again? I'm sorry, all right! I'm sorry I took it upon myself to do some incline training without asking you first. I'm sorry I was stupid enough to fall and break my leg right before the trials, and I'm sorry I keep being a miserable disappointment to you. Believe it or not, I'm not doing this on purpose."

"You could have fooled me," he mumbled under his breath before shaking his head as if to wipe away the words that still hung in the air between them. "I don't think it's a good idea to go back to work so soon. You just had your last surgery."

"I'm going crazy sitting around the house all day, and I'm sick to death of you and mom paying for everything. Besides, it's not fair to pull out of the lease with Olivia just because you don't think it's a good idea."

"Perhaps if you'd asked our opinion before you signed the lease…"

"I'm an adult and I don't need your permission to live on my own. The only reason I've been at home is because I couldn't use the stairs in the apartment. You control my life for more hours of the day than I do, but I'm not going to let you control everything. Don't you see how dysfunctional that is?"

"Oh, yes. Poor Jill with parents who love her and care."

She whirled around and stomped as best she could with bare feet into the locker room, ignoring the stares from the other girls who'd overheard her fight with her father. She felt the angry tears burn the backs of her eyes and rushed to get into the shower stall before giving in and letting them fall. She damned him for making her feel twelve for the last decade of her life and damned herself for letting him do it.

CHAPTER 4

When Ty walked into the kitchen, Lita was setting the table with plastic plates and cups featuring any and all cartoon characters from his generation and beyond.

"Can I have Captain Firefly?" Ty asked. "He was always my favorite."

She stood up abruptly and clutched her chest with her hand. Ty felt bad about scaring her. "How does someone so tall walk around so quietly?" she asked before resuming her task. "You get to sit with us in the dining room. You're too big for the kids' table."

He'd never actually sat at the kids' table, and watching the girls run into the kitchen, with wet hair smelling of strawberry shampoo, to lay claim to their spots, he felt as though he missed out on something pretty special. "Do I have time for a shower? I stopped at Jimmy Helton's and he wheedled me into helping plant a tree for his wife."

"Just enough. Your dad is on his way and your mom and Bryce and the boys will be here in thirty minutes."

"I'll be back in ten and you can put me to work."

Lita wrapped an apron around his waist when he loped back into the kitchen eight minutes later and tied it from behind. "You can cut the bread when the timer beeps and place it in the warmer in the dining room. If you could stir the macaroni and cheese and mix up a pitcher of lemonade while I shower, that would be a huge help."

"Go." He shoved her toward the back staircase. "Make yourself even more beautiful. I've got this until you get back."

"You're a life saver."

"I'm just a sucker for a beautiful woman who can cook."

"Like father like son," she shouted as she dashed up the stairs faster than she should have been able to in her man-killing heels.

Before Ty could fill the pitcher with water, Jesse walked in shouting for his wife. "Angelita?"

"She's in the shower."

Jesse eyed Ty's apron as he set two enormous bakery boxes on the counter. "That's a good look for you."

"Your wife thinks so."

"She can't help but play dress up with everyone. Thank goodness we have three daughters."

As if he'd summoned them, Jesse laughed as his girls squealed and charged straight at him. "Daddy!" they wailed in unison.

Jesse lifted all three in his arms, quite a feat considering seven-year-old Ella was no lightweight, Gabby brought Baby along for the ride, and Jesse's fingers looked tangled in Brooke's blanket. "How are my girls? Did you have a good day?"

"We had a tea party," Brooke explained. "I spilled apple juice on Baby and Gabby yelled at me. Mommy sent her to her room and now she's mad."

"I yelled at you because you spilled juice on Baby's new dress," Gabby said and shoved her three-year-old sister.

Jesse dropped the girls to their feet and stared down at them with disapproval and mischief in his eyes. Those girls had him wrapped around every one of their fingers. "No fighting or I'll send you both to your rooms."

Ella shrugged at Ty. As the oldest of the three, she felt a

kinship with her half-brother. "They'd deserve it."

Ty decided distraction was the best medicine. "Who wants to help me in the kitchen?"

"I do!" they all yelled at once. Jesse slipped up the stairs in search of his wife.

Ty let Ella stir the noodles on the stove under his watchful eye, gave Brooke the pitcher and a wooden spoon after setting up the step stool so she could reach the sink, and asked Gabby to hold the bread he'd just removed from the oven so he could cut it. He leaned down and sniffed Gabby's hair after marveling at the smallness of her hands. He could hardly believe the beautiful girls who chattered around him were his sisters, growing up in his house with everything he'd ever wanted as a child: two parents madly in love and siblings to hang out and fight with on a daily basis. He didn't begrudge his dad his wife and kids, but he sure did feel an empty pang of regret that he hadn't had the same experience growing up.

The doorbell rang out like a warning bell, for before Ty could turn off the fire under the noodles, move the knives from within the grasp of little fingers, and help Brooke off the stool, his half-brothers Brody and Quinn barreled into the kitchen holding out their motorized robot dinosaurs and making roaring noises. Their exasperated parents followed closely behind.

"Sorry," his stepfather said with a case of beer on his shoulder. Ty figured Bryce Jenson said those words rather frequently in the wake of his twin sons. "No need to announce our presence." He slapped Ty on the back before opening the fridge. "Where should I put this beer?" he asked.

"Try the garage fridge," Ty suggested. He turned and offered his mom a quick, but hearty hug. She smelled like she always had: Italian sauce from her restaurant and peaches from her soap. He could pick his mother out blindfolded.

"I'm sorry I couldn't visit when you came by the restaurant today, honey," Kerri Ann said. "Frank had to get a filling and we were swamped."

"I should have known better than to show up at

lunchtime," he said. "I figured I got out just before you put me to work."

"You only get a few days off before you leave. I wouldn't make you work at the restaurant."

"You had no problem putting me to work when I was younger," Ty said.

"That's when you were eating me out of house and home. Now," she said, blowing her blond bangs out of her eyes, "I have double the trouble to look forward to."

Someone who didn't know his mother better would have missed the twinkle in her eye as she watched her sons chase the screaming girls through the house and out into the backyard when Bryce opened the back door. Kerri Ann was happier than ever since she married Bryce Jenson and gave birth to his twin partners in crime. He intended to teach the boys everything he knew about causing trouble in Sequoyah Falls.

Lita and Jesse came down the steps moments later, and Lita and Kerri Ann took charge of the kitchen. Jesse opened wine for the ladies and grabbed three beers for the men, who were ordered to watch the kids outside. When Ty's grandfather, Cal Bloodworth, came whistling around the corner of the house, all five kids circled his legs. Although Brody and Quinn weren't his official grandkids, he treated them like they were. He reached down and cradled Brooke in his arms while the twins resumed chasing Ella and Gabby.

"There's my boy." Cal gave Ty the best hug he could offer with Brooke snuggled against his chest. Jesse and Lita's youngest daughter had a soft spot for her granddad. "I heard I missed you today."

Ty took a swig of his beer. "I came by the cabins to see if you needed any help and the renters said you'd gone to Asheville with the Garden Club."

The tips of Cal's ears turned pink. "They tricked me into helping them load some plants up from the big nursery they've got up there. I swear I've never heard so much gossip in all my life." Cal set Brooke down when she began to squirm. "Those are my last renters of the season. They're staying until the end of July and that'll give me plenty of time to get the place cleaned up for you."

"You sure you don't mind me staying there in the fall until I find a place of my own?" Ty asked.

"I've told you to stay as long as you want. I'm thinking of hanging up my hat and retiring for good."

Ty would have been shocked if he hadn't heard his grandfather make that claim for years. He'd never retire.

Before long, they were all situated in the dining room while the kids happily giggled in the kitchen at their own table. Lita's shrimp stew had just been ladled over steaming bowls of rice when Jesse lifted his glass in the air.

"A toast. To Ty, for the few days we have him before he heads out west. To my beautiful wife for preparing such a lovely dinner, to good friends," he nodded at Bryce and Kerri Ann, "and to family."

Ty felt the tug, right in the center of his chest, for what he had and what still felt like a missing piece. His parents were both in love and had beautiful families of their own. His grandfather was content with his life, flirting with the ladies, knowing full well he'd someday be reunited with his true love, Ty's grandmother Ellie. Ty thought of Jill, as he had so many times over the last nine months. He could see her at this table, surrounded by the people he loved the most in the world. He was anxious to return to Colorado and begin the task of winning her over, but he had to win over someone else first.

CHAPTER 5

Jill felt herself relax for the first time in months the moment she crossed the threshold of The Golden Tap. As someone who loved being outdoors, Jill never expected to enjoy working in the dimly lit tavern. The brick wall behind the mahogany bar held shelves of liquor between the neon beer signs that were the main sources of light. High top tables featured votive candles in antique lanterns. The red vinyl bar stools were faded from age and use. The small raised area in the back corner of the one room establishment welcomed anyone with a guitar, a voice, and the moxie to try and entertain a crowd. The Golden Tap wasn't the only bar in the Lower Fork, but it certainly was the favorite among locals.

Tommy Golden came out of the back room and smiled when he spotted Jill just inside the door. His dark hair and ever-present five o'clock shadow were a sight for sore eyes. No one from out of town would have guessed he owned the dive bar. He wore the uniform of the valley—jeans and t-shirts— but something about the way he moved, the way he interacted with people led Jill to believe he'd come from money. The fact that he never talked about his life before his dad moved them to the Lower Fork provided ample fodder for theories. "Are you going to stand there all day or get to work?" he asked.

"Work," she said and strapped on the half apron he tossed her way. "I can't thank you enough for letting me come back."

"I didn't let you, Jill. You earned it. The regulars haven't stopped complaining about the service since you left."

"By regulars you mean Eddie, Shane, and Cody?"

Tommy gave his trademark crooked smile. "The three stooges will be overjoyed you've returned." He straightened the menus on the corner of the bar. "Olivia's thrilled you're moving back in."

"She can't be more excited than me. I've missed your sister."

"I'll sleep a lot easier knowing she's not alone in that apartment anymore."

Jill had to slap her lips closed so as not to mutter that Olivia probably hadn't been alone. What he chose to overlook about his half-sister was his own business.

He tossed her a wet rag from the sink before disappearing out the side door. Jill started by wiping down the tables and refilling the salt and pepper shakers. When she wandered into the back, she got a big hug from Stevie, the lunchtime line cook.

"Look at you," Stevie said. He wore his long black hair in a braided ponytail and an apron covered a concert t-shirt from the year Jill was born. "No more crutches?"

"Nope." She tapped her jeans. "I'm almost as good as new." She picked up a ladle and sniffed at the soup. "Ummm. Your white bean chili is still the best I've ever had."

"And always will be, sweetheart."

"Any changes to the menu I should know about?" Jill asked.

Stevie tapped his finger to his thin lips as he walked through the swinging door to the front of the bar. "Tommy got rid of the pasta salad and replaced it with coleslaw. We've got sweet potato fries as a side and a couple of new dressings." He scanned a laminated menu before clucking his tongue. "That's about it. Most of the changes were in the dinner menu, but you never hang around that long."

"I'm on my second round of training by dinnertime, Stevie."

"All that running seems like chasing your tail if you ask me. All those miles you log and where do you end up?"

Right back where she started, she thought, but didn't say. She'd hoped to end up in the Olympics, but that dream was all but dead. If she'd missed the finish line on her most important race, where did all the miles she ran get her? Right now, standing in the bar where she served lunch and drinks to regulars, she wondered if she was simply marking time until something better came along. If only she knew what that was.

***

"I thought you wanted an authentic, fishing-only experience on your last summer out west?" Jessie asked after Ty broke the news. Everyone at the table stopped eating and stared in his direction. When he said nothing, only stared at his father, Jesse asked, "What changed? You said I'd love the Lower Fork because they're known as much for their rafting as they are for fishing."

"You would love it. I liked it last year and I want to go back."

"You *liked* it. I can't believe you'd go back just because you liked it."

"I want to go back, Dad. Just leave it at that."

"Oh," Jesse said with knowing frown and that damn annoying head tip that meant he thought he'd figured everything out. "I get it. There's a girl."

Ty didn't want to blush in front of his entire family, but he felt his neck heat anyway. "I wouldn't call her a girl."

His dad looked first to Lita with his brows raised, and then to Ty's mom before landing those hazel lasers on him. It was like having a conversation with a three-headed monster. "How old is she?"

"It's not about her age. She's a distance runner and right before I left, she fell and broke her leg." At Jesse's pointed stare, he said, "She's twenty-two."

"Is she why you broke up with Dana?" his mom asked.

Ty cocked his shoulder and tucked his chin down to hide from his family's prying eyes before stuffing a spoonful of stew in his mouth. Truth was, he'd known the minute he laid eyes on Jill that he couldn't be with Dana anymore. But Ty wasn't a cheater, and breaking up with someone he cared about and had dated for over a year didn't happen over the phone. "Probably."

"Why are you being so cagey about this?" Jesse asked. "You've never been shy about girls."

"I'm not being shy. I just..." Ty stood up and excused himself from the table. He walked out onto the front porch expecting his dad to follow. When he heard footsteps on the landing and the screen door slap shut, he turned around and stared at his dad. Ty didn't need to hem and haw with Jesse. He'd understand; Ty remembered how fast he and Lita got serious. His granddad would understand, too, if the stories of his whirlwind courtship with his grandmother were true.

"She's different," Ty explained. "One look at her and I was half gone. Watching her train last summer and then struggle with an injury...she just got to me in a way no one else ever has."

"Are you sure she's still there?"

"Yeah, I'm sure."

"So, you've talked to her? She knows you're coming back?"

Ty sighed. This was the sticky part. "No, I've talked to Tommy. He owns the fish and raft shop. She's still there."

"Could she be involved with someone else?"

Ty met Jesse's stare with one of his own. The hazel eyes he'd seen every morning in the mirror stared back at him from his dad's suntanned face. "I don't care."

Jesse let out a long breath. "Okay. If this is what you want, I support you. I just don't want you to have any regrets."

'No regrets' was his dad's mantra. "The only thing I'd regret is if I didn't go back and see this through."

"You could get hurt," Jesse pointed out.

"Yeah, but I could get lucky." Ty's quick smirk was

automatic and the instinct to do it helped to level his ground. "I'm feeling pretty lucky."

"You just make sure you wrap that luck in a condom."

Ty's grin disappeared with his dad's fruitless warning. "I'm not careless, Dad, and I'm not seventeen."

Jesse rubbed the back of his neck and let out a sigh that sounded like a concession. "No, I know you're not. But an unexpected baby can change everything." He grabbed Ty around the neck and rubbed his knuckles over his scalp. Hard. "Sometimes for the better."

"What are you going to worry about when you realize I've sowed all my oats and end up in a committed relationship?"

"I've got three daughters bringing up the rear. I have a feeling you're just the warm up act." Jesse let go and gave Ty a thoughtful stare. "I thought you were in a committed relationship with Dana. I liked her."

"I liked her, too." Ty thought of his bubbly ex and the way she never quite fit into his life. "I just didn't love her. I'm not going to settle when it comes to the important stuff."

"Good. At least I've gotten through to you on that one."

"Don't worry. You and mom are like a tag team with the condoms. I swear, whenever I roll one on, I can hear you both clapping with approval."

Jesse laughed. "That's probably the last image you want at that moment."

"Exactly, but I get your point. No regrets, no excuses. I want this, Dad. I won't regret going back even if I don't end up with the prize."

"Hell, son, you're a catch and release fisherman. You know the hunt is more than half the fun."

"Yeah," Ty sighed. "But I really want this prize."

Jesse wrapped his arm around Ty's shoulder and led him back inside. "Then go get her."

CHAPTER 6

Jill winced as the suitcase thumped against her injured leg, but she didn't let the pain break her stride. One wince and her mother would whisk her back to their split level in Westmoreland faster than Jill could unpack.

The move would have gone a lot smoother if her dad had bothered to help, but Jill knew he wouldn't assist her in doing something he'd vetoed. He offered some lame excuse of a meeting and left the bulk of Jill's things in the hands of the Jennings women.

"One more run and I think we've got it all," Bobbie Jennings said as she wiped the sweat from her brow with the back of her hand. All the packing, loading, and unloading hadn't wrecked her manicure or messed up her perfectly coiffed bob. Jill was convinced her mother could wrestle cows on horseback and never look worse for the wear.

"I've got it, Mom. Why don't you sit down and take a breather while I bring up the rest of my stuff? Olivia's probably got some soda in the refrigerator."

"Olivia's got better than soda." Olivia Golden pranced up the stairs carrying a six-pack of beer and an orange patchwork purse. She gave Bobbie a hug, hip bumped Jill, and disappeared around the corner to put her beer in the fridge. "I've got soda,

Mrs. Jennings, if you'd prefer that over the beer."

"Considering I'm driving home, I'd better just have the soda. Or on second thought, I'd love a bottle of water."

When Jill made it back with the last box in her hands and a bag slung over each shoulder, her mother and Olivia were chatting on the couch like old girlfriends. Olivia was better suited to be Bobbie Jennings's daughter. While Bobbie's shiny, dark brown hair and fair skin were a contrast to Olivia's sun bleached blond hair and golden tan, their interests and energy level were almost identical. Both loved to shop, gossip, and look their best at all times.

"So it's a done deal?" Bobbie asked as Olivia nodded and sipped a beer.

"Yep. Rumor has it they're going to start building the resort by next spring."

"How do you know this?" Bobbie demanded.

"I have my sources."

"Her source is her brother," Jill filled in the blanks for her mother. "Tommy's leading the charge against the development."

"What on earth for?" Bobbie asked. "Seems like a fancy resort would draw all sorts of people and money into the valley."

"That's exactly what I keep telling Tommy," Olivia said. "He's dead set against it. He says it'll ruin the area and force the farmers and ranchers out of business."

"Hummm." Bobbie took a contemplative sip. "I'll have to ask Gary about this. I wonder if the college has an opinion."

Jill set the box down and let the bags slip from her aching shoulders. Her afternoon workout was going to be a killer after all the stair climbing and box lifting. "It's been all over the papers, Mom."

Bobbie waved a hand in the air. "You know I don't read anything but the living section and the ads."

"Just think about the shopping a big development would bring," Olivia said with a dreamy look on her face.

"Don't forget the restaurants," her mom added.

"And the traffic," Jill pointed out and began tapping reasons they shouldn't get ahead of themselves off on her fingers. "And even more tourists, and the taxes."

"You sound just like my brother," Olivia pouted. "I get enough of that from him."

"I'm just pointing out that there are two sides to every story."

"Yes," Olivia said and stood up to poke around the box Jill had opened. She pulled out a bold chartreuse blouse and held it up to her shoulders. "As long as you're on mine, you can stay."

"I pay half the rent, so I'm staying no matter whose side I'm on." Jill considered the impulse buy Olivia held up in front of her. "You can have that shirt if you want. That color looks awful on me."

Olivia's blue eyes sparkled in delight as if Jill had offered her a diamond. "Really?"

Jill shrugged. She may as well let Olivia have the shirt she'd never wear instead of finding it in Olivia's closet later on. "It's all yours."

Olivia gave her a quick hug and sprinted down the hall to try it on.

Bobbie got to her feet and stepped in front of her daughter. "Well, sweet girl, I guess I'd better head home."

"Thanks for your help today, Mom." Her mother's embrace held everything Jill loved about home, including the unmistakable smell of Shalimar perfume. "I couldn't have lugged all this stuff by myself."

"I hate that I won't see you everyday like before, even though I'm glad you've recovered so well. I liked having you at home. Your dad and your brother are so…well, they're men."

"I'll miss you, too, Mom, but I need to be on my own. I'm only thirty minutes away."

"I know, sweetie. I guess I didn't realize how much I missed you until you came back home."

"I'll be at Sunday dinner like always."

"You'd better be. And bring Olivia some time. I like that

girl, even if your dad thinks she's wild."

Jill let loose a roaring laugh. "She'd love that. Wild Olivia Golden."

"I think it's just an act," Bobbie whispered to Jill.

"You're mostly right, Mom."

"Mostly?" Bobbie's lashes fluttered. "Should I be worried about you?"

"Me?" Jill snorted. "Between workouts and work, I don't have time to even think about being wild."

Bobbie picked up her clutch, but stopped at the doorway with her hand on the doorknob. When she turned around, the corners of her mouth were turned down. "Jill, I'm proud of the way you've come back from your injury. Your dad and I both are, but there's more to life than running. Do yourself a favor and make some time to be wild."

When Jill's mouth hung open and the words she tried to form died on her tongue, her mother said, "You're young, you're healthy, and you deserve to have some fun every now and again. If you get the chance to do something different, something exciting, don't turn your back on it just because you don't have time."

"Okay," Jill finally managed as the door gently closed.

Olivia came out from her room and modeled the shirt Jill had given her. "I love it. Thanks, Jill."

Jill nodded, but couldn't think of anything but what her mother had just said.

"What's wrong?" Olivia asked. "You look funny."

Jill shook her head and smiled at Olivia when she plopped on the couch next to her. "My mom just said the strangest thing."

"What?"

"I think she wants me to be more like you."

Olivia barked out a laugh. "Ha! I knew I liked your mom, but what does that mean, exactly?"

"She wants me to make time to do something crazy."

"Like what?"

"I don't know. But she said I shouldn't ignore an

opportunity to have fun just because of my schedule."

"Sounds like great advice to me. I've never known anyone who works as hard as you who doesn't ever do anything for fun."

"Running is fun." Or at least it used to be. "I enjoy it, or I wouldn't spend every day training."

"I know. I love rafting, but I still manage to squeeze in some fun."

Jill lifted her brows at her gorgeous roommate. "You manage to more than squeeze in some fun. You're a walking party."

"Hey, I'm always on time for work, I'm going to graduate eventually, and I know how to have fun. What's wrong with that?"

"Nothing, according to Bobbie Jennings." Jill looked down at her hands, wrapped tightly together in her lap. She let go and flexed her fingers, willing herself to relax. "I think I've forgotten how to have fun."

Olivia wrapped her arm around Jill's shoulders and squeezed. "That's what I'm here for. You just sit back and let me show you how it's done."

CHAPTER 7

Ty pulled up in front of the cabin he'd rented last summer and eased out of the driver's seat. After two days in the car, the sight of the cottage in the woods brought as much relief as the cool mountain air on his face. He'd enjoyed the drive. It wasn't often a man got to be alone with his thoughts through six states and countless interstate miles. When he drove out last summer, he'd been in awe of the changing landscape and the beauty of his country. This time, his mind was full of Jill.

He knew he'd gambled quite a bit on instinct and an undeniable attraction. He felt pulls of lust and licks of sexual compatibility from other women in his life. He hadn't lived to be twenty-four in a vacuum. He'd never pigeon holed a type of woman as his ideal, for just as soon as he decided he preferred brunettes over blondes, a flaxen haired beauty would catch his eye and blow his theories to smithereens. So he enjoyed them all. Tall and thin. Short and curvy. Boisterous. Loud. Quiet. Shy. There wasn't a category of woman he'd yet to consider not his type.

So how had Jill Jennings, who'd largely ignored him for the better part of the months they spent in each other's space, managed to slither into his blood? How did she give him the kind of tunnel vision that made all others pale in comparison for almost a year? Had he, by making her seem just outside of his grasp, made her out to be more than she was—a flesh and blood human who might not live up to his image of her?

He'd pondered those questions on his drive, the answers to which he felt eager to seek, but not before using the bathroom and getting settled. He found the key under the empty planter right where the landlord said he'd leave it and let himself into his home for the next three months.

The wood paneled walls held the same decorations as last summer: a mounted mule deer, a series of Indian arrowheads artlessly arranged in a display box along the hallway, and an oil painting of a snow covered mountaintop that Ty found strangely appealing above the leather couch. He flung the keys into the empty basket by the door as if he'd never left.

Unpacking took no time at all considering he didn't have to think about where things went. He dumped his suitcases on the queen-sized iron bed, stored his fishing gear in the extra bedroom, and set the meager box of kitchen supplies on the small counter. He needed groceries, but knew better than to go to the store on an empty stomach. A quick stop at The Golden Tap would kill several birds with one stone, including his main mission: information about Jill.

He didn't see her at the bar, but if she had resumed her job at the restaurant, her shift would have ended a few hours ago. He did spot Shane Richards, one of Tommy's fishing guides, sitting at his favorite spot at the bar next to local cattle rustlers he knew only as Eddie and Cody.

"Well, if it isn't the east coast pretty boy." Shane smirked when he saw Ty wedge himself onto the stool next to him. "I heard you were coming back to work for Tommy."

Ty had to force himself not to rub his shoulder where Shane had slapped him in greeting. As with all fisherman, his arm strength was astounding, especially considering his slight frame. "I couldn't spend the summer without you, Shane."

"I thought you were going to work the North Platte this year," Eddie chimed in from the other side of Shane. His brown hair looked as if it hadn't been washed in days and the chaps he wore were coated in dirt.

"I changed my mind."

"It's just like old times around here," Cody piped up from Eddie's right. He took a long sip from the dark beer he was famous for drinking like water. "Everybody's back."

"Who's everybody?" Ty asked as he perused the menu. Not much had changed as far as he could tell.

"Jill's back on the lunch shift," Shane said. "Tommy hasn't had reliable service since she broke her leg and left."

"She's back?" Ty set the menu aside, his hunger forgotten. "Recently?"

"Just yesterday. Looks good as new." Eddie slurped his Coke from a straw. "She doesn't have a limp or anything. My friend, Billy, he broke his leg two years ago and he still walks with a limp."

Shane slapped Eddie on the head. "Do you seriously think Jill got the same medical care as your back woods drifter? Her dad's a big wig at the college."

"What's she been up to?" Ty asked after ordering a beer from the bartender. He didn't want the three of them to get off the subject of Jill.

"The runner?" Shane asked and slapped Ty on the shoulder again. "You always did have a thing for her. I gotta tell you, man, you're barking up the wrong tree with that one. She's laser focused on running."

"I didn't ask for your assessment of my chances. I asked about her."

"She's doing better. Out of the brace. She spent the winter in rehab." He shrugged and tossed the shaggy hair from his eyes in a move so routine, he probably didn't realize he'd done it. "She's back training and back here, which you now know."

"Yeah."

"She hasn't changed enough for you to work your magic," Shane added. "I've never seen a woman so immune to my charm." He looked up with a twinkle in his baby blue eyes that led the girls to him in droves. "You don't have a chance in hell."

"Good thing I'm not in hell," Ty countered with a lift of his arms. "Most folks call this paradise."

"This ought to be entertaining." He leaned his elbows on the bar and shouted to the men at his left. "Hey, guys? You wanna place odds on Ty here hooking up with Jill?"

"You and Jill?" Eddie asked and scratched his jaw.

Cody pursed his lips. "The ice queen?"

"Who?" asked a guy Ty didn't recognize at the table behind them.

"Olivia's roommate," Eddie answered. When the guy continued to look at him with a blank stare, Eddie said, "The lunch waitress." Eddie turned to Ty. "I'll give you 20 to one."

Ty took a sip of the beer and smiled. "Ye of little faith."

"We've got faith," Shane said. "And I hope you do, too. You're going to need some divine intervention. That girl's got one thing and one thing only on her mind, and it isn't a North Carolina pretty boy."

"I don't need divine intervention," Ty said with a lift of his glass. "All I need is time and the Bloodworth charm. I've got plenty of both."

***

Olivia squealed Jill's name as soon as she entered the apartment. Jill had just gotten out of the shower and came running into the hallway wearing only a towel and dripping water. "What's wrong?" Jill asked.

"I've got news!" She flung her messenger bag off her shoulder and onto the floor before grabbing Jill by the shoulders. "You'll never guess who's back in town."

Jill's mind went blank. Who in the world would elicit that kind of reaction from her overconfident roommate? "I give up."

"I'll give you a hint." She let go of Jill to tick clues off on her fingers. "He's a gorgeous fisherman, and he's asking about you already."

The muscles in Jill's body that were so fatigued from her

run suddenly tingled with excitement. "Tyler? He's back?"

"I haven't seen him, but Rob talked to Cody and he's back."

"Who's Rob?" Jill asked.

"He works at the raft shop. He overheard Shane talking to Tommy about how Ty was at The Golden Tap earlier asking how you were and making bets on him hooking up with you this summer."

"He's making bets? About hooking up with *me*?"

Olivia grabbed Jill's shoulders again and gave her a quick shake. "Focus, please. The hottest guy to hit the Lower Fork in over a decade is back and what's the first thing he does? Goes into town for information about you." She rubbed her hot pink nail polish along the sleeve of her bright yellow swim shirt and wiggled her fingers. "I think we've found your fun."

"Why would he make bets on hooking up with me?"

"Who cares?" Olivia asked as she pushed Jill down the hallway and into her room. Olivia bounced on her bed as if she'd come straight from middle school with a love note in her pocket. "I used every trick in my well stocked arsenal to get his attention last summer and he never took the bait. He only had eyes for you. Strange how he never made a move," she pondered while staring at the ceiling, "but, nonetheless, he's back and this time, you're going to be ready."

"He had a girlfriend last summer," Jill mumbled. "Wait!" Her stomach rolled at the excited glimmer in Olivia's eyes. "Ready for what?"

"Ready for anything." At Jill's scowl, Olivia said, "Remember what your mom said, Jill. You can't ignore the chance to have fun. And, sweetheart, I'd bet all the Olympic gold in the world that man knows how to have fun."

CHAPTER 8

Jill would bet Tyler Bloodworth knew how to have fun. What she didn't know was why on earth he'd make bets about hooking up with her. There were so many things about what Olivia told her that sat unsettled in her chest, she found herself unable to regulate her breathing and struggled to keep pace on her short warm up run around the college track. It didn't take her father long to notice.

"Pick up the pace a little, Jill," he called from the starting mark. She lengthened her stride and focused on exhaling. She'd been excited to get out of the gym and the pool and get onto the track. It was the first step toward running on the roads, where she could think and reconnect with everything she loved about the sport, but so far, every step felt like drudgery.

"You look a little sluggish out there. Is your leg feeling okay?" her father asked after looking up from his stopwatch.

"My leg's fine." She took a sip of water from the bottle she'd brought with her this morning. "I thought you said I'd do some road work today."

"You can. I want you to take the Harper trail and loop around by the hospital twice. I'll be behind you in the van."

"Why?"

"Why?" he asked. "On your first run after a major leg

break? I can't believe you have to ask."

"Don't you have a class to teach or something? I thought you were working this summer."

"I am working this summer, but not during our training hours. I've got a class this afternoon." He quickly zipped up the gold windbreaker as a gust of wind slapped him in the face. "You're impatient enough to push too hard. I don't want you running without me, at least not for a week or two."

Jill had to bite her tongue to keep from suggesting he attach a leash and run alongside her. Knowing her father, he'd probably consider her suggestion an option.

"I think one week is enough. You must have better things to do than to follow me in the van."

"You're my daughter and, for now, my only coaching client. I don't have any problem trailing you. Besides, I don't like the idea of you running alone. I'm going to put some feelers out and find you a running partner."

"I don't want a running partner."

"Tough. You need one. You know it's not safe to run alone, unless you want me trailing you day and night."

"Fine, but I get a say in who you choose. I don't want to spend a huge chunk of my day with some dork."

"You'll spend your day running with whomever I can find to match your pace and schedule."

"I'll ask Lyle," Jill suggested as she stretched her quad muscle. "He's writing now, so his schedule is flexible."

"You're an elite athlete, Jill. Lyle isn't even training anymore."

"He was one of your top runners."

"That was two years ago. I've got to find someone of your caliber." He rubbed his forehead. "Our pool of options is the size of a puddle."

Jill stretched out her calf muscle in an attempt to end the conversation. These days, she and her dad couldn't say two words to each other without ending up in an argument. "I'm getting stiff standing here talking. I'm going to go."

"I'll find you along the route. Be careful, Jill. Don't push too hard your first time out."

She turned and walked away without a word. She picked up her pace as she weeded through the parking lot, past the intramural fields, and out onto the street that would lead her toward the Harper Ranch. It was a short loop, only two miles back and forth, but she'd always enjoyed running through the small college town and out to where the Harpers' nervous cows grazed along the wire fence. She normally ran well beyond the property, but she understood she had to take it slow.

Jill tried to settle into her run and find the calm that usually took over her mind during these moments of solitude. She hadn't experienced the kind of freedom she only ever found while training in months. Her muscles began to warm along the residential street, the crunching of the road underfoot sounded sweeter than her favorite country song, and she lengthened her stride as the houses started to thin. She tried to focus on leveling out her breathing, but the air kept clogging in her chest despite her best efforts.

The sound of the van in the distance seemed to snatch all the oxygen from her lungs. The peace she'd been searching for that was just out of reach took a nose dive to the bottom of nowhere. Abruptly, she stopped mid-stride and leaned over to clutch her knees, gasping for air.

"It's too soon," her father said after jerking the van into park and exiting the vehicle. "Damn it, I should have kept you on the track."

"No," Jill huffed, sucking in air as fast as she could. "My leg's okay. I'm just...I..." She stood up and moved her hands to her hips. When she met her father's eyes, the wariness in them almost stopped the words from leaping off her tongue. Almost. "I can't do this anymore."

"Jill." He grabbed her arm and led her to the side of the van, yanking open the door and shoving a bottle of water in her hand. "Take a couple of sips and get your breath back. You're good; we just need to take it slower."

"Did you hear what I said?"

"How fast were you going? You've got to start slow. You can't just jump back into the pace you set before the break and expect to be fine." He gripped his forehead and rubbed in the same practiced move she'd seen him make whenever she screwed up: when she skipped training in high school to see a concert with friends, when she got caught holding hands at the movies with bad boy Brian Mitchell, and countless times since she'd broken her leg and broken his dream.

"You're not listening to me, Dad. I'm done. I don't want to do this anymore."

"Do what? What else is there for you to do?"

"That's just it! I have no idea. Every time I think about my life, I see nothing ahead but weeks of us fighting with each other. And for what? I'm not going to make the Olympic team!" She took a sip to ease her stinging throat. "I'm not having fun anymore. You always told me to walk away when it wasn't fun."

He tucked his chin and frowned at her while making an indistinguishable noise in his throat. "Don't you throw that back in my face."

"What? The truth? I blew it, Dad. I broke my leg at the worst possible time. I missed the boat when all we've done for the last two years, hell, the last six years, was plan how to get aboard. Now I'm floundering in the wake while the ship has set sail. I'm so tired of treading water."

"You're giving up too easily. There's the race next month. You're a long shot, yes, but the trials aren't out of the question. All you have to do is work at it. Get back to where you were."

"You and I both know that where I was wasn't anywhere good enough to make the Olympic team."

"If I thought that, I wouldn't have wasted the last two years training you."

"Good to know you think it was a waste."

"That's not what I said."

"Yeah, I think it was." She capped the water and tried to hand it back. He wouldn't take it, only stared into her eyes, his lips pressed tight. "The harder you try to get me back to where

I was, the more I resent you for pushing me and the harder I resist. I'm starting to hate this sport and I'm starting to hate you. I don't think that's good for either one of us."

"What do you need to get your head in the right place? Because that's all that's going on here, Jill. You simply need the mental fortitude to push past the doubt."

"I need time."

"Time's the one thing we don't have."

She felt nothing but pity when she looked up into his furious eyes. "I'm taking it anyway."

"You're throwing your career away." He kicked at the tiny stones in the road. "Both of ours."

"I'm trying to save our relationship. I think that's worth more."

When she turned away from him and started walking back toward town, he grabbed her arm. "Where do you think you're going?"

"I'm going back to get my car. I've got a job I need to get to."

"Get in the van."

She pulled her arm from his grasp. She felt like a petulant teenager, but couldn't help herself. Her pride wouldn't let her do anything but walk with her head held high back to her life, or what little of one she had. "I'd rather walk."

"You'd rather walk," he repeated. "Fine. Fine. I'll talk to Warlock's coach, see if he can take you on while I find you a new coach."

She spun around and threw her hands in the air. "I don't want a new coach. I don't want to run at all!"

"You're right. Me coaching you isn't working anymore. I'll find someone else, someone neutral."

"Dad, when and if I'm ready to run again, I'd appreciate your help finding a coach, but not now. I'm done training. I'm getting off the hamster wheel and figuring out what I want to do with my life."

He stared at her so long, she thought he was trying to change her mind by the sheer force of his will. "You know what, Jill? That's a great idea. You run back to your dumpy apartment and your pointless job as a waitress, and grow the hell up. But when you realize what you've done, don't come crying to me to get you back in the game. I'm through."

Throwing anger right back in his face would have been so easy, but taking the easy road now wouldn't do anything to help the relationship she was trying to salvage. "I love you, Dad. This doesn't have anything to do with you. All these years I've been training for the school, for my coaches, for you. Breaking my leg and moving back in with you and Mom made me realize I don't have a life outside of running. I don't want my entire life to be about just one thing."

He got into the van, started the engine, and looped around in the road to head back into town. He rolled the window down as he passed her. "Good luck finding yourself," he said before gunning the engine. She had to turn her head away to keep the pebbles the tires kicked up from spraying in her eyes.

Jill told herself the pebbles caused the tears to come on the long walk back to campus. It wasn't that she'd jumped off a cliff without a parachute.

CHAPTER 9

Olivia dragged the cooler containing lunch for eight along the dirt bank toward the waiting rafts. She grunted with the effort and swore under her breath at her brother who left the task for her to complete. When the other end lifted and the scraping noise disappeared, she looked back into a very appealing pair of bluish gray eyes.

"Well, well, well," she purred. "I heard you were back."

Tyler Bloodworth held the end of the cooler with one hand and lazily propped the other on his low-slung cargo pants. "Word travels fast."

"It does where you're concerned." She adjusted her hold on the cooler. "I thought you were headed north this summer. Montana, wasn't it?"

"Wyoming. I changed my plans."

Olivia found it interesting he offered no explanation. She wasn't one to leave a pretty stone unturned. "Because?"

He shrugged his appealingly wide shoulders and shuffled his feet. "Just because."

"Come on, Ty, a guy like you doesn't do anything on a whim."

"A guy like me?" he asked.

"You've got your whole life planned out. Guide here last

summer, finish up your graduate degree, Wyoming this summer, and back to teach classes and start the business with your dad."

"I don't remember giving you an itinerary of my life's plans."

"You told my brother." She shrugged and switched the cooler to her opposite hand. "That's as good as telling me."

"I'll have to remember that."

She watched him squirm as she slowly surveyed his assets. At about an even six feet, he had a rangy build to go along with the loose-limbed gait that was as calm as the ambling river at her back. He'd caught her eye from the very first look last summer, even in his fishing waders, vest, and hat. Olivia found it hard to hide gorgeous.

His blond hair was darker than when she'd last seen him, but she knew it wouldn't take long for the ends to lighten in the sun. His boyish good looks edged just a little toward shaggy with the days old beard and wind swept hair. It didn't help that the t-shirt poking out from his well-worn fleece sported a ragged collar. She'd seen him with his shirt off enough times to lust after the work hardened physique hidden under his clothes.

"You done checking me out yet?" he asked with an irritated sneer that flashed his dimples.

"No. I figure it doesn't really count since you've already called dibs on Jill."

The only thing that saved him from being ridiculously handsome was the half-inch scar over his right eyebrow. It disappeared when they shot to his hairline. "Who told you that?"

"Oh, please. A woman never reveals her sources." She continued on toward the dock, grateful he hadn't dropped the other end of the cooler and left it for her to drag the rest of the way. They set the cooler down together.

"I didn't call dibs," he explained as he stared out over the wide river. "I would never call dibs on anyone, especially Jill."

"Relax, Indiana Jones. She's cool with it."

He whipped around to face her. "You told her?"

"I may have mentioned it in passing."

"Great..." he said through gritted teeth. "Just great."

"Look, you want to keep your plans on the down low, you might not want to go into The Tap and start blabbing about your chances with her."

"I didn't...or at least, I didn't mean to. Shit. She probably thinks I'm an ass."

Olivia knelt down and turned her back to him to conceal her grin. The guy was like putty in her hands. Jill would definitely be thanking her later. "Probably."

***

Ty couldn't tell if Olivia was joking, which seemed ironic considering he'd never met a more obvious woman in his life. Everything about her, from her shiny blond hair, to her pouty lips, to her knock out, wetsuit clad body screamed, "Come and get me, boys!"

He appreciated a beautiful woman, but considering her interest last year, he'd been grateful for his relationship with Dana and his loyalty to her when Olivia zoned in on him like a heat seeking missile. Dana or not, he wasn't interested in Olivia and her insatiable need for attention, not to mention the fact that she was his boss's sister.

Ty left her digging through the lunch cooler and made his way toward the main barn-shaped building that housed The Golden Rule Raft and Fly Shop. He stripped off his favorite fleece as the June morning eased into midday.

He found Tommy Golden in his usual spot behind the counter helping guests sign waivers and directing them to the changing area. Ty appreciated Tommy's hands on approach, but often wondered if the man ever slept. He ran three successful businesses—well, four if he counted the fly and raft shops as separate entities. Tommy ran them together from the same building, a model Ty planned to duplicate with his dad.

Tommy greeted him with a nod while dealing with a nervous family of four wearing University of Oklahoma t-shirts.

"The Rio Grande has class two and three rapids," Tommy explained. "Class two means medium rapids. There's a stretch of class three where you'll hit some high, irregular waves." The woman's face visibly paled. "That's why we've got experienced guides in each boat. They know the river and they know how to navigate the rocks and eddies."

Ty had heard the spiel thousands of times at home with his dad and hundreds over the last summer when he came in to the shop to meet and greet the fishermen who'd hired him for the day. He waited patiently as the family signed, paid, and were shown to the locker rooms. Considering he'd already blown it with Jill, he was anxious to get to work. He felt confident he couldn't do too much damage there.

Tommy stepped around the counter and gave Ty a hearty handshake and a slap on the back. It wasn't a hardship to return to the Lower Fork and work for Tommy. No matter what happened with Jill, he'd get in some good fishing and spend another summer with a man who, at the age of 31, knew how to run several successful seasonal businesses.

"You made it," Tommy said. He adjusted the sock cap on his head. The short ends of his hair were the same color as the coffee he habitually drank day and night.

"Yesterday. I'm ready to go whenever you are."

Tommy scratched his freshly shaven chin. In a place where razors and hairbrushes were considered optional, Tommy's grooming habits set him apart from the masses. "The salmon and stone fish haven't hatched yet, so we're not swamped, but I can certainly put you in the rotation. When did you want to get started?"

"As soon as you need me. I pulled my raft out this year. You still have some storage space for me or am I going to have to lug it up to the cabin every day?"

"I think I can spare some room for a guide who's generous enough to bring his own boat. Let's have a look at her, shall we?"

Ty led Tommy out back to where he'd pulled his truck and

boat trailer.

Tommy whistled through his teeth. "Sweet." He ran his hand along the gray rubber raft. "This is the exact model I was going to buy to add to the fleet. You've saved me the effort."

"She leaves when I do," Ty reminded him.

"Yeah, but that's months from now. I can get one like her for a steal after the season's over."

Tommy pointed to a storage shed at the far end of the property. "You can pull her in there. It's got a combination lock so you can grab her and go whenever you need to."

"Appreciate it." Ty looked out over the river. "Listen, I'm itching to get on the water. Do you have anything this afternoon because if not, I'm fishing anyway. I'd much rather make some money doing it."

"I've got a father-son duo coming in at three. They're beginners and only interested in wading. I was going to give them to Shane, but I'd rather you take them. He's not very good with the newbies."

Ty held out his hand. "Consider it done. I'll get the boat locked up and be back here by two thirty."

Tommy gripped his hand and shook. "It's good to have you back, bro."

"It's good to be back," Ty said and meant it. He'd worried about having regrets, about giving up on a summer spent on a river he'd admired and dreamed of fishing his whole life. The river wasn't going anywhere, and his chances with Jill, as fleeting as they were, seemed even smaller than before now that he knew Olivia had opened her big mouth.

He took a deep breath of mountain air and hopped behind the wheel. It was time to man up and do some damage control.

CHAPTER 10

Jill felt numb. As she delivered food and drinks to the lunchtime crowd, she couldn't focus her thoughts on anything, so she tried to narrow her mind and focus only on the job at hand. A customer at table four needed a soft drink refill, his companion some extra napkins. The three beers for table two were waiting on the bar for her to deliver. The hostess had just sat a group of tourists at a four-top near the stage.

Jill could handle each task simultaneously. She'd graduated in the top ten percent of her class with an accounting degree, so keeping a few tables and their orders straight wasn't much of a hardship. She majored in accounting because math had always come easily to her and she didn't have time to think much about a career beyond training. "Get a degree in something where there's always a need," her father had drilled into her head. His other motto was, "Do your best."

Had she done her best today? It had felt like the best thing for her at the time, but now that she'd unleashed her desire to quit—or take a break—she felt sick with worry. He'd asked her to grow up, but didn't he understand that growing up with him dictating her life for the next four years wasn't possible? She needed to be on her own, make her own decisions about how she lived her life in order to figure out if she really wanted to devote her time and energy to running. Could it be a career or just a hobby that kept her healthy and satisfied?

She could have wept with relief when she saw Lyle Woodward and his stepfather enter the restaurant. Lyle greeted her with a wink and a wave. Lyle would help her. Lyle would listen and understand her doubt and worry. He'd fretted over a similar choice years ago and then happily segued into writing and working with his stepfather on their family's ranch. He continued to run every day for fun. He'd help her figure out if what she did was for the best or if she made the biggest mistake of her life.

"I need to talk to you," she whispered in Lyle's ear after she said hello to Dodge. She loaded her tray with the waiting beer. "Do you have some time after the lunch rush?"

"We're grabbing a quick bite and then going to the ATV place. The big cat's on the blink and Dodge's been eyeing the new model."

Dodge elbowed Lyle while slurping down his Coke. "You can stay and talk. I wanna look around without you breathing down my neck, anyway."

"You sure?" Lyle asked.

"I think I can decide on an ATV without your opinion."

Lyle flashed Jill his toothy smile. "I'm all yours."

"Great," she said. "It should be clearing out by the time you're done with lunch."

Only a few customers were left in the restaurant by the time Dodge had moseyed out of The Tap, leaving Lyle at the bar nursing his sweet tea. The only other person she knew who drank sweet tea was Tyler Bloodworth, but she couldn't even begin to let her mind wander into that uncharted territory, not when she was filled with so much anxiety over her kneejerk reaction this morning.

After refilling drinks and settling their bills, Jill slipped behind the bar and eased her elbows onto the slick surface.

"So what's up?" Lyle asked. He blinked his warm brown

eyes and gave a sympathetic smile that flashed his deep and boyish dimples. He'd never had a serious girlfriend, but he'd certainly dated a fair share of women in his twenty-one years.

"I'm freaking out a little bit."

"Over what?" His eyes narrowed. "Is it your leg?"

"No." She blew out a big breath. "I quit today."

"Quit what?"

"Training. I got pissed off at my dad this morning and I quit."

"Just like that?"

She stood up and tried to be patient. Of course he would think her decision impulsive. She certainly hadn't let on to anyone her lingering doubts and her feelings of being caged. "It's been building for a while."

"How did he take it?"

"About how you'd expect. He told me to grow up."

Lyle shook his head. "I've never understood how your relationship could survive him coaching you. Don't get me wrong," he lifted his hand in a plea, "he's a great coach. One of the best. But he's not my dad and on many occasions, I wanted to kill him. Literally. Run over the man with the van."

"Are you saying this was destined to happen?"

"No. I'm just not surprised."

Jill pulled the empty plate away from him and set it in the bus bin under the counter. "So now I'm freaking out."

"Understandable. It was a hard decision for me to make, and I wasn't in jeopardy of letting a parent down with my choice. My mom always knew about my interest in being a writer. I still get to run, Jill, only now I do it for fun."

"And that's enough?"

"For me it is. But I'm not you. Only you can decide if running for pleasure and not for competition will be enough."

"That's part of the problem. You had your writing to pursue." She looked around the empty bar. "This isn't exactly a career."

"Then figure out what you want."

"You make it sound easy."

"Look, you've done the hard part. You quit running—"

"Took a break from running. I'm not sure about anything."

"Okay, you took a break. Whatever." He picked up a toothpick from the dispenser and popped it in his mouth. "So now that you've taken a break, use the time you normally train and figure out what you want to do."

"It's more complicated than that. What I want to do could involve moving. The Lower Fork and surrounding areas aren't exactly thriving in the accounting arena."

"That depends on what kind of work you want. There's plenty of bookkeeping and account management for a farm or ranch in Hailey. I'm sure Dodge could give you a handful of names right now." He ran his tongue along his teeth in thought. "Westmoreland has the hospital and the college. Hell, Tommy owns four businesses here in the Lower Fork. You could always talk to him if you want to stay."

Jill nodded. She didn't know if she felt better or worse. Lyle had basically told her exactly what she didn't want to hear: the direction of her life was totally and completely up to her. "Well, thanks, Lyle. I appreciate you listening." She came around the bar and gave him a hug as he stood up to leave.

They both looked over as the door to the restaurant opened. Jill sucked in a hasty breath when she recognized Tyler Bloodworth and quickly returned her gaze to Lyle.

"Friend of yours?" Lyle whispered before placing a friendly kiss on her cheek.

"Something like that." She eased out of his grasp and tried to compose herself as her heart fluttered in her chest. Damn it, she didn't need another complication at the exact moment her life was falling apart.

Lyle's hands drifted down her arms and he let his fingers linger in hers before dropping her hands and walking toward the door. Jill eyed him curiously as he slipped outside. He was normally pretty touchy-feely, much more so than any of her other guy friends, but something about the way he'd looked at her with mischief in his eyes made her think he was up to something.

CHAPTER 11

Ty stood just inside the doorway, watching Jill with a look of cool indifference, but his jaw was clenched so tight he could barely force the breath in and out of his lungs. He felt like he'd been punched in the gut. He'd expected to find Jill mad, maybe even a little cold, but never did he expect to find her in the arms of another man.

"We're getting ready to shut down for lunch," she told him.

"I'll take whatever you've got left. Soup, the special." He shrugged his shoulders. "Whatever."

She nodded, but didn't move. He couldn't read the look on her face, somewhere between irritated and unapproachable.

A kernel of apprehension took root in his gut as he tried to shake off his irrational anger. "You okay?" he asked.

"You left before I could thank you." When he stared at her, confounded, she said, "When I broke my leg. For the ride to the hospital. I didn't think I'd ever see you again."

He shrugged because he couldn't tell if she was happy about seeing him again or not. "That was nothing." He glanced down at her legs. She wore loose fitting jeans and an old pair of running shoes. The plain black t-shirt shouldn't have made lust curl in his belly, but logic didn't seem to stop his body from responding to hers. He rubbed his hand over the ache while she stood staring. "How's the leg?"

"Better."

She slid her hands into her back pockets, pulling the shirt tight against her chest. He fought hard to keep his eyes on hers.

"I'll go see what Stevie has in the back. Take a seat wherever you want."

He figured she'd have less of a chance to slip away from him if he sat at the bar. He was about to take the same seat where he'd bragged about his chances with her and thought better of it. He moved two seats down, to the center of the bar, and sat.

She came out of the back carrying a big plastic cup and set it down in front of him with a container of sugar packets. He smiled when he realized she'd brought him tea.

"Sweet, right?"

He nodded and dumped two packets into the mix. "Thanks."

"Lyle says it's not the same unless you sweeten it while it brews, but this is the best we can do."

"Lyle?" he asked.

She jerked her head toward the door as if he'd just left. Her dark brown ponytail swung like a pendulum against her back. Her hair had grown in the time they'd spent apart. "Lyle Woodward. He just left."

"Is he from the south?"

"Atlanta, originally. He lives in Hailey now."

Ty bobbed his head up and down, stalling. He didn't gather his nerve until she turned to leave. "Jill?"

The pleasant flush of her cheeks made her light brown eyes appear huge and inviting. He felt clumsy and out of practice with women, since he'd spent all last summer avoiding her and the school year engrossed in his studies. He worried that when he finally saw her, Jill wouldn't be as mesmerizing, she wouldn't hold the appeal that had followed him like a fog for the last year. He worried for nothing.

"I owe you an apology."

Her brow furrowed. "Umm, you do?"

"I was here the other day and ran into Eddie, Shane, and Cody. I was asking about you—how your leg was—and they seemed to think I was asking for a different reason and—"

"Oh, that." She reached for a rag under the counter and began wiping furiously at the surface of the bar. "It's okay."

"I never meant to insinuate that you were...that I was..." He rubbed the back of his neck and struggled for words to explain without making it obvious he was interested. Well, any more obvious.

"Trust me, Ty. I know you didn't mean anything. Shane thinks any woman who doesn't fall at his feet is gay. He was baiting you when you were just being nice."

"I might have made it seem as though there were more to it than that."

She glanced up at him and his heart gave one long, hard thump against his ribs. She lifted her chin in the air and raised a single brow at him, staring into his eyes.

She gave an uncomfortable shrug of her shoulders. "Don't worry. I'm not holding you to barroom talk. Besides, you've got a girlfriend and I—"

"I don't have a girlfriend anymore."

She blinked once and stared at him.

"I broke up with Dana last year."

"Oh." Their eyes met, held.

Stevie came out of the back with a steaming bowl of beef stew and a wedge of bread. "Last of the stew," he said as he set the bowl down in front of Ty. Ty could have punched him for interrupting what was starting to feel like an intimate moment. "Dishes are piling up in the back, Jill. If you want to make your afternoon training, you'd better get a move on."

Jill looked at Ty and rapped her fingers on the counter. "I gotta go. You okay with everything?"

No, he wanted to say. I'm dying here. "Yep. I'm good."

CHAPTER 12

Olivia sat on the couch munching a bag of chips and washing them down with a diet soda, figuring one would balance the other out. If only she could get the math problem she struggled with to balance. She clutched her chest and shrieked when Jill opened the door and stepped inside.

"What are you doing here?" Olivia asked. "You scared the crap out of me."

"I live here, remember?"

Olivia twisted the sports watch on her wrist. "Not at five o'clock you don't. Why aren't you on your hundredth lap around some track?"

Jill eased onto the couch and slumped back against the cushions. "I quit this morning."

"Quit what?"

"Seriously? Why is that everyone's first question?" She tossed her keys on the coffee table and stretched out her legs. "I quit training. I'm taking a break."

"Didn't you just take a break—literally?"

Jill scrunched up her face, rolled her eyes, and began nervously chewing her bottom lip. "I'm taking a break of my own doing. A mental health break."

"But...I don't understand. I thought you couldn't wait to get out of your parents' house and start running again. What happened?"

"I don't know." She shot to her feet and began to pace around the small den. "I was miserable living with my parents and I thought I'd be better once I got out of the house. I am better, or I was." She gave Olivia a glassy eyed stare. "I've started having doubts about my life. I always assumed I'd pursue running as a career and whatever else happened would happen after I achieved my goals. Breaking my leg changed all that and I'm starting to feel like I'd better have a backup plan."

"So what's your backup plan?"

She sank onto the couch again. "I have no idea."

"Okay." Olivia sat up. "At least you've got your degree." She closed her textbook with an audible pop and tossed it onto the coffee table. "I don't know what possessed me to take a few semesters off school. All I managed to do was delay the inevitable."

"What's the inevitable? Getting a job?"

"Eventually. Right now the inevitable is this class. Remind me again why I chose to get a teaching degree?"

"The same reason I chose accounting. So we could get jobs."

"Oh, yeah." She picked up the bag of chips and offered some to Jill, but she refused. Jill watched what she ate, but she usually gave in and had a few chips. Her not eating them now meant she was seriously stressed. "So get a real job and see how you like it."

"Where am I going to get a real job, huh? I want to figure out what I want to do with my life without picking up and moving to some city. I want to figure it out here."

"So find a job here. I'm sure there are entry level accounting positions in Westmoreland."

"I don't think I need to be in the same town as my parents right now. My dad's pissed."

"Okay, but that kinda limits your options."

"I know. Do you think Tommy is in need of bookkeeping

help with any of his businesses?"

"You think he'd tell me?" Olivia took a swig out of her drink and set the can down. "I'll bet, for you, he'd invent one."

"I don't want him to create some position he doesn't need just to get me through a rough patch."

"How do you know he doesn't need help? The man runs four businesses and he told me today he's taking the lead in organizing the group to stop the ski development. I'm sure he'd be grateful to pass something along to you."

"Does he ever sleep?" Jill asked.

"Who knows? What he needs more than sleep is someone to sleep with. He's such a tightass."

Jill reached over to rub Olivia's leg. "Are you fighting again?"

"When are we not? He won't even let me lead more than one trip a day."

"That's because you're back in school and he wants you to finish your degree."

Olivia scrunched up her face. "So will you talk to Tommy?"

"I guess. I certainly can't sit around the apartment day and night worrying about my future." She rubbed a fist to her ribcage. "I can already feel the pressure building in my chest. Maybe I need to take a run."

"I thought you were taking a break?"

"From training. From my dad, basically. That doesn't mean I can't run for pleasure."

"Who does that?" Olivia shivered in horror. Thank God she'd been blessed with good metabolism.

Jill threw a pillow at her, smacking her in the face. "Speaking of pleasure," Jill said after dodging Olivia's throw. "I saw Tyler Bloodworth today."

"Talk about burying the lead. When?"

"At The Tap." Jill shrugged as if the sight of him hadn't gotten to her. Her cheeks betrayed her indifference by turning a definite shade of pink. It always amazed Olivia how inexperienced her roommate was in matters of the heart. "He's even better looking than I remember."

"What'd he say?"

Jill began picking at a loose thread on the pillow cradled in her lap. "He apologized for whatever he'd said in front of the rat pack, although he never really explained what he said. As a matter of fact..." She tapped a finger to her lips. She never wore much makeup and yet her lips were rosy red. Olivia assumed it was from all the biting her bottom lip endured. "He did say that he may have made them think there was more to his comments than a misunderstanding." She shook her head. "I'm not really sure what he meant, but I do know he's single."

"What happened to the annoying blonde who came to see him last year?"

"She was nice."

"How would you know?" Olivia demanded.

"She came into The Tap once. The place was dead and she seemed a little down. I knew she was in town to see him and I didn't want to get to know her, but when I gave her the bill, she asked if I knew Ty."

"What'd you say?"

"I told her I knew who he was, but I didn't know him that well."

Olivia braced her hands on her knees and leaned forward. Wasn't it just like Jill to hold this kind of information back for almost a year! "Why was she asking?"

"She asked me if I'd seen him with someone, ya know, a girl. I think she thought he was cheating on her."

Olivia sat back against the cushions and pursed her lips. "So she was jealous, but didn't know of whom?"

"I don't remember seeing him with anyone last summer. He'd deflect everyone with the 'I've got a girlfriend' line and I never heard even a peep about him catting around." Jill looked at Olivia. "Don't you think we would have heard if he was seeing someone here?"

"Oh, yeah. No way he could have kept that a secret. Not in this fishbowl."

"That's what I thought." She shrugged it away. "Anyway, he told me he broke up with her last year."

"So *he* broke up with *her*."

"That's what he said."

"Don't you get it, Jill? How much more obvious could the guy be?"

"Obvious about what?"

Olivia shifted so her feet were on the floor. "You said yourself he apologized for the taunting, but not for the substance of what he'd said. Then, he makes sure you know he's available." She slapped her hands on her knees. "He's totally hot for you."

"That's ridiculous. And I'm not interested."

"Okay, now you're just lying."

"I've got too much going on right now to even think about starting something up with a fisherman who's going to be gone in a few months."

"You just told me you can't sit around the apartment day and night, and yet you have no plans. Sounds like you've got plenty of time to start something up with a hot fisherman who's been after you since last year. I wouldn't be surprised if you're the reason he's back."

"That's the most insane thing you've ever said. Stop putting ideas in my head, Olivia. He's just here to fish, and even if he came back for some other reason, it sure wasn't me."

"Why? You're hot, Jill, even though you do everything in your power to hide it. Apparently Indiana Jones thinks you're hot anyway."

"What do you mean I hide it? And who is Indiana Jones?"

"Tyler! He's going to teach at the local college back home. Didn't he get his degree in archeology or something?"

"Economics," Jill answered. "How in the world did you manage to confuse economics with archeology?"

She shooed Jill's barb away with a wave of her hand. "Anyway, you totally downplay your looks." When Jill rolled her eyes, Olivia continued. "You've got great hair. That rich brunette color makes your flawless skin glow, but yet you're not all pasty white. Those big, brown eyes are both sexy and vulnerable at the same time. And even though you've run off every ounce of fat on your body, you still have a decent rack."

Jill looked down at her chest. "Not compared to you, I don't."

"He's not interested in me." Olivia rubbed her hands together with glee. This, she thought, was going to be fun. "He's interested in you. Now all we have to do is figure out how to make the first move."

CHAPTER 13

Jill's apartment sat along a two-lane highway with wide shoulders and very little traffic in the early morning hours. Years of training had made sleeping in impossible and by seven, Jill was stretching in the parking lot and eyeing the route she planned to take. A quarter mile past the local grocery store, she could veer into a neighborhood.

She glanced behind her toward the mountains where a small cabin sat tucked along a curvy road somewhere deep in the cover of blue spruce and aspen trees. She could picture Tyler in his shorts, no shirt, cupping his hands around a hot mug of coffee steaming in the chill of early morning. She shook her head to dislodge the image. Ty Bloodworth was a distraction, pure and simple.

She wouldn't believe the lies Olivia fed her about his interest. She couldn't afford to open her heart to that kind of disappointment. Not when she felt totally rudderless in her life, as if she was floating aimlessly down the river that fed the valley.

She started with a slow, deliberate pace. It always took around a half mile before her breathing felt relaxed and even. She wondered if her rehabilitation would cause that distance to lengthen. Just as she rounded the grocery store, she felt everything click into place: the steady in and out of her breathing, the long, methodical stride, the emptying of her mind. Nothing, absolutely nothing filled her with total peace the way a run could.

Her leg felt strong and healthy. The cool air cleansed her lungs and helped to pump out the anxiety she'd harbored since the day before. She quit the sport she loved, the sport that had consumed her life since the fifth grade when she went out for cross country and had never looked back.

She felt a hitch in her step when she realized she'd walked away from the finish line and was running without a goal in mind. She told herself she didn't need a goal. She didn't need to beat a time or edge out a competitor. She only needed to feel the road beneath her feet, the wind in her face, and the lightness of her heart.

People did this every day. People ran to wake up, ran to keep the extra pounds at bay, ran to relax. She could run for those reasons. As a matter of fact, she mused, this time she'd taken for herself, by herself, was the only thing in recent memory she'd done just for her.

When she let her lungs open and her legs press forward and tried to get her mind to disengage, she started to feel invincible. If she could do this every day, with the sun on her skin and the road beneath her feet, she could live a very happy life. She'd need a job. Tommy worked in his office at the raft shop on Tuesdays. She'd stop by early and feel him out about a job. He might be grateful, he might feel put out, but she'd never know unless she asked.

She rounded a bend in the road and scared a flock of gray doves into the air. The flapping of their wings sounded like tiny bubbles popping. She wondered if she'd see Ty at the shop when she went to visit Tommy. If he'd had a morning job, he'd be pulling back in around the same time she'd be there. She wondered if seeing him was a good idea.

Wise or not, she was attracted. She wanted to sink into those hazel eyes and see what he would do next. She couldn't look at him without images of him shirtless, carrying her in his arms flashing into her mind. She shook her head at the tricks the mind could play. Shouldn't she remember the pain, sharp and lethal, instead of the heat from his skin and the ripe smell of him fresh from bed with coffee on his breath? Yep, definitely attracted, almost needy with it. She quickened her pace and used her hunger to urge her faster.

How long had it been since she'd felt something, anything more than a fleeting interest in a man? So long she could hardly recall. She'd dabbled at romance with Darren in college, but that had fizzled as her running left little time for anything else. She knew it was over when leaving him in bed for her training had filled her with relief.

She'd flirted with Lyle and they'd kissed a few times before realizing they were meant to be friends. Since then, nothing. She was fine with nothing until Tyler showed up last summer, turning her upside down with his smoldering looks and igniting the ugly green monster when his girlfriend came to town.

Now she had nothing but time. Nothing but time to think about him and the long summer ahead.

She ended her run feeling rejuvenated. The cool mountain air had awakened every sense in her body and she felt alive with the possibility of what the future held. She'd done something risky by quitting her training, but at least she'd done something.

She was riding high when she crept back into the apartment, hoping not to wake Olivia, who'd been up late studying. Jill had just tiptoed past Olivia's door when her cell phone rang in her hand. She bolted for her room and shoved the door shut behind her, answering the phone without looking at the display.

"Hello?"

"I thought you'd be up," her mother said. From the sound of her voice, Bobbie hadn't had enough sleep.

"Just got in from a run," Jill confessed. She knew what was coming and had hoped to avoid a confrontation for at least a day or two. "What's up?"

"What's up? What do you think is up?" She heard her

mother take a sip of something Jill knew to be her overly sweet morning coffee. "Your father is fit to be tied."

"I figured as much."

"What in the world is going on? I thought you were happy moving back in with Olivia, getting back to training, and working at The Tap. What changed?"

Jill sighed. It wasn't that she didn't owe her mother an explanation, but she didn't know how to explain her heart. "I don't know. I know I'm not going to qualify for this year's trials. I just started looking at the next four years and I couldn't stomach where my life was heading."

"You of all people know what goes into training for the Olympics. I thought that was what you wanted. Your dad thought that was what you wanted."

"It was. I'm not so sure anymore."

There was a long pause on the other end of the line before her mother cleared her throat and said, "Is this about me telling you to have some fun? Because I didn't mean for you to throw everything you've worked so hard to achieve out the door and be irresponsible. I just meant that you should make time to be young."

"Relax, Mom. This has nothing to do with what you said." She plopped on her bed and toed off her shoes. "When I broke my leg, I thought I was done. I know that sounds overly dramatic, but I thought I'd never run again. Once I realized I would, I took a good look at what that meant. I'm not going to have a shot at this year's team. I know Dad thinks otherwise, but he's being unrealistic."

"He thinks you do, Jill. He really thinks you do."

"No, Mom, he wants me to, but wanting and doing are two different things. I'm not even back to where I was before I hurt my leg. It may take months to get back to that point and then years before I'm in serious contention. That's a long time for me and Dad to train." And fight. What she really wanted to say was fight.

Bobbie sighed. "He feels like you've given up on yourself. He feels like you've given up on him."

"You felt the tension between us the last few months before my fall. Even if I'd never broken my leg, I'd have been looking for a new coach. I'd already made some calls."

Bobbie sucked in a breath. "You don't need to tell your dad about that."

"I'm not, trust me." Jill flung herself back on her neatly made bed. "I need some time to sort this out, Mom. I have a degree I've never used, a long shot chance at being a midrate distance runner, and not much else. If I go back to training, I want it to be because I've decided that's the path I want to take. It has to be my choice. I can't make that choice when he's dictating my life."

"Jill, he's not dictating anything. He's trying to help. I wish you could see that. I wish you understood how much he's hurting right now. He thinks he's failed you."

"He hasn't, Mom. If anything, I've failed him. And I'm sorry for it, but I'm not going to change my mind, at least not until I've thought things through."

"I know you well enough to know this has been weighing on you. I wish you'd told me. I wish you'd told your dad."

"I wanted to tell you, Mom, but I knew you'd tell Dad and he'd freak out."

"So springing it on him like this is so much better?"

"No, of course it wasn't, and I'm sorry."

"You don't owe me an apology, Jill. You owe one to your father."

"I doubt he's ready to hear one without trying to talk me out of this."

"You have to understand what your quitting has done. He cleared his schedule this summer to work with you. We could have used the money from him teaching another class, but he didn't want that to interfere with your training."

Okay, Jill thought. That was hitting below the belt. She had enough guilt on her shoulders without carrying the burden of her parents' finances. "I'm going to get a job, Mom, and then I'll take over my student loan payments. I'm not planning on sitting around doing nothing."

Her mother sighed. "That's not what I meant. I just mean he's under a lot of stress right now."

"I'm sorry for adding to his stress, but, Mom, I know if we'd continued down this path, it would have been worse for our family in the long run."

"How can you say that?" her mother asked.

"I don't expect you to understand my decision, but I'd like to ask for some consideration. I'm an adult. I'm trying to do the adult thing and get out from underneath you two."

"Oh, Jill. You're not a burden."

I feel like one, she wanted to say.

"Will you be at dinner on Sunday?"

Oh, Lord. Sunday seemed like a universe away. "Of course, if you'll have me."

"Don't be silly. Whatever you decide to do with training doesn't affect the family. Your father would be hurt if you didn't show up. *I'd* be hurt."

"I'll be there."

***

Tommy Golden sat at his desk with a steaming cup of coffee perched on a coaster from The Tap and so much work in front of him that he wasn't sure where to begin. The guy he'd hired to work the office this summer quit last week when he reunited with his girlfriend and, in a concession to her job as a massage therapist, moved back to Colorado Springs. He left Tommy short on workers and long on work.

Summers were crazy. All four of his businesses were open, operating, and generating enough income to warrant his full attention. Even with help, he felt pressed to be everything to everyone and work 24/7. He knew he needed to hire an office manager, but he loathed giving up control to anyone. He'd built each business, except the restaurant, from the ground up, and he didn't want to have anyone to blame if they didn't succeed. For Tommy, like the flight crew of Apollo 13, failure was not an option.

He stifled a groan when his little sister knocked on his

door, delaying his work. He loved Olivia, but whenever she sought him out, she wanted something, and he wasn't feeling very charitable at the moment.

"Hey," she said as she poked her head around the door. "You got a minute?"

"Not really."

"Jill's here. She wants to talk to you about a job."

Tommy watched Jill's brows draw together as she approached the now open door. "Olivia," she warned. "I told you I'd ask him."

"I know, I'm just saying hello to my brother."

Tommy didn't have time for Olivia's antics. "Did you need me, Jill?"

She cleared her throat, eased past Olivia, and shut the door in her roommate's face. "I need a job."

"You've got a job, remember?"

"I'd like an office job. Olivia thought you could use some help."

He glanced at the mountain of files on his desk, the list of people he needed to call, and the wall clock just behind Jill's head. "You could say that, but...are you qualified?"

"I got my accounting degree from Colorado State two years ago February. I haven't exactly used it, but I'm hoping to change that."

She lifted her shoulders and let them fall when he just stared, uncertainty warring with common sense. He couldn't do it all, and yet he wasn't sure Jill was the answer to his prayers.

"I can work mornings and evenings after my shift at The Tap doing whatever you need," she said. "Managing payroll, accounts payable and receivable, profit and loss statements, tax deposits..."

"You never used your degree?"

"After graduation, I started training full time. I needed a flexible schedule and waitressing was the best fit."

"What about the training? I thought you were back at it."

"I am, or I was. I'm taking the summer off." She grabbed

her earlobe and pulled, her eyes narrowing on his face. "Look, I overheard the guy at the desk tell Olivia your summer help quit. I wouldn't ask if I didn't think I was up to the job. I know what your standards are, Tommy. From the looks of things here, you could use some help as soon as possible." She shoved her hands on her narrow hips and wound her fingers into the belt loops of her low-slung jeans. "If you want some time to think about it, fine. I'll be at The Tap."

However flighty Olivia was, she'd somehow managed to befriend someone as driven and straightforward as Jill. He knew better than to look a gift horse in the mouth. "When can you start?"

Her cocky smile was the only answer he needed. "Today after my shift soon enough?"

"You're hired." He extended his hand and they shook. He felt a weight lift off his shoulders. "I'll need to spend a few days getting you up to speed."

"I've got nothing but time." She eyed the stacks of files on his desk warily. Surely after living with his messy sister, she could handle this.

"I'll have this office organized by this afternoon." He took a sip of his cooling coffee. "You've given me a place to start."

"Feeling's mutual. Thanks, Tommy. I won't let you down."

"Counting on it."

CHAPTER 14

Ty began the morning with a half-day beginning wading trip with a father and son in town from Texas. The Petermans, fifty-year-old Bill and thirteen-year-old Hunter, were friendly, listened carefully, and were persistent in perfecting their cast. Much to Bill's chagrin, Hunter mastered the cast quite naturally while he continued to struggle.

Ty enjoyed the beginners' trips, which was why Tommy had booked him for the morning run before letting him float the river that afternoon with two experienced fishermen and businessmen from Arkansas. The beginning trips reminded him of his time growing up on the river with his dad and Bryce, both teaching him the love of the sport and the appreciation of time spent angling.

The businessmen, Ty knew, were in pursuit of the perfect brown and the biggest rainbow to capture on film and impress the boys back home. Whatever their reason, Ty was grateful to spend the day with a pole in his hand and the water at his feet.

He snuck into The Tap for lunch before heading out for his afternoon float. He spotted Jill passing out drinks to a table of four as he slipped behind the bar counter and gazed at the menu. Except for a few new sides, it hadn't changed much since last year, and he tucked the menu back into the slot by the unmanned hostess desk.

"What'll ya have today?" the waitress asked. Ty recognized her from last summer when she'd been about to pop with a baby. She looked thinner, of course, but she had dark circles under her eyes that makeup couldn't hide. "I'll have the hot ham and cheese sandwich with fries, please, and a tea."

She pulled a container of assorted sugar packets from under the bar and set it before him. "Anything else?"

"Nope."

"Be right back with your drink." He noticed her nametag said Meredith. She tucked his order into the rack and immediately began filling a cup with ice. She spun on her heels and shot past him after delivering his tea with a half smile. Ty stirred a sugar substitute into his drink and eyed the crowd as he took his first sip.

The place was packed for a Tuesday. The father and son he'd just led were recounting their morning over burgers and fries at a table near the back. They'd met up with a woman who looked half Bill's age with an adorable six or seven year old girl. Considering the hefty tip in his pocket, Ty wasn't totally surprised by the young wife.

"Well, well, well," Eddie said as he slapped Ty on the back and took the seat next to him. Ty hadn't seen him coming since he'd been looking around the restaurant. "How's the bet?"

He gritted his teeth and leveled Eddie with a narrow eyed stare. "Shut up about the bet. There is no bet."

"Ouch. Not going well, huh?"

"I don't want it getting back to Jill that there's a bet when we never made one."

"You chicken out already?" Eddie asked as he waved the young mother over to fetch his Coke and cheeseburger.

"You smell like the backside of a cow." Ty noted Eddie's dirt covered clothes and his stained hands. "You going to wash those hands before you eat?"

"I already did."

"Well, move down a seat so you don't ruin my appetite.

You stink."

Eddie gave a barking laugh. "You recreation guys haven't figured out that real men who do real work tend to smell by midday. It's a sign of success."

"I spent the morning in the river with fish in my hands and I don't smell like scales."

"That's because you didn't break a sweat doing it," Eddie said. "Meredith," he called to the waitress. "Can I get that to go? I've got to stop by the feed store before heading back to the ranch," he explained to Ty.

Meredith brought Ty's sandwich and refilled his drink while Eddie asked about her baby.

"She's good." Meredith's whole face lit up when she spoke of her daughter. "She's teething right now, so she's not sleeping great, but otherwise fine."

Jill snuck behind the bar and Eddie punched Ty in the leg, almost making him spit out his first bite. "Hey there, Jilly," Eddie said. "How's it going?"

"Just fine," she said and spared a quick glance at Ty. No way was he going to attempt to talk to her when that idiot was around. "You?" she asked.

"Oh, ya know. We're cutting hay all day praying the rain holds off for awhile."

"Looked clear on my morning run, but it's the afternoon you've got to worry about."

"How's your leg feeling?" Ty managed to interject.

Her chin shot up and she lifted one shoulder before turning around to fill two cups with ice. He shouldn't have let his gaze wander to her backside with Eddie right next to him, but he couldn't help himself. He'd never seen a woman look better in a pair of jeans. "Running's good," she answered when she turned around. "I'm slower than I'd like to be, but that'll come back with time."

"Hey, Jilly," Eddie said. "Pretty boy here thinks I stink. Why don't you give the two of us a sniff test and tell me who smells like he works for a living?"

Jill wrinkled her nose. "I can smell you from here, Eddie,

and I can only hope that scent comes from work."

"Oh, it does, sweetheart. Long, hard, back breaking work."
He jerked his thumb at Ty. "What about him?"

Ty watched Jill's head cock to the side as she gave Ty a
teasing look out of narrowed brown eyes. His pulse ratcheted
up a beat or two. She moved slowly, bracing her hands on the
bar and leaning over his plate, too far to feel her breath on his
skin, but so close he could see her pupils enlarge. "He smells
like the best hot ham and cheese this side of the Rio Grande."

Perhaps that was because Ty's mouth had popped open
when she'd come in for a sniff.

Eddie giggled in a way that Ty would have teased him for if
his brain had been firing on all synapses.

She held Ty with a penetrating gaze before turning toward
the door to the kitchen.

Ty grabbed her arm as she spun and, with a light touch,
brought her wrist to his face. "You smell like a field of
wildflowers on a cool spring day, the kind of day when you
want to take off your shoes, lie back in the grass, and turn your
face up to the sun." Her hand fell limp in his grasp, her eyes
widened, and her mouth went slack. He dropped her arm, but
not before rubbing his nose along the inside of her wrist one
more time.

She walked backwards toward the kitchen door, her eyes on
his until she disappeared.

"Holy cow!" Eddie snickered. "No bet my ass. This game is
on."

Ty rubbed his aching belly. That, he thought, just might be
true.

***

Jill sat in Tommy's office staring at the mountain of files that
looked the same as when she'd left him that morning. He'd
come into The Tap as she was taking off her apron and asked
if she was ready to get started. Any job where she could sit was
a welcome reprieve after the busy lunch hour.

Tommy explained his filing system, which basically

consisted of different filing cabinets for each business entity, told her how he'd managed the payroll and taxes thus far, and left her to feel her way around.

"Don't touch anything you don't understand," he'd warned before leaving for the front of the raft shop. "If I'm not here, make a list of questions and ask me later, but please don't do anything without checking with me first."

She discovered that Tommy had a very organized way of keeping his books, but hadn't made any updates in the ledger in a few days. "I've been swamped," he explained after popping his head into the office to see how she was doing. "This effort to save the ski pass is eating away at my time and I've let things slip thinking my summer help was on his way. When he didn't show..." he motioned to the mess on his desk, "things got a little crazy. I'm not usually this disorganized."

"I wouldn't call you disorganized, Tommy, I'd call you insanely busy. I'll get you up to speed, and between the two of us, it should be all systems go."

"I'd love you forever," he said and headed back out to man the desk.

He didn't need to love her forever, she thought. Only let her figure out her life for the next few months. It felt good to use her brain again, to have a task, or several, to complete. She liked her life organized and everything seemed to move forward when the path was laid out clearly in front of her.

She felt her face heat at the memory of her behavior at lunch. What had possessed her to lean over Tyler's plate and tell him he smelled like hot sandwich? Momentary insanity caused by her life being in total upheaval and her hormones waking up from a long season of hibernation was the only plausible explanation. That, and the fact that she'd heard him and Eddie talking about the bet.

Then he'd turned the tables and made her feet leave the ground with his sweetness. It was all a ploy, and a very well-crafted ploy, because, really, what girl could resist a man describing her smell as a field of wildflowers, especially in the middle of her shift in a bar? Not her, and certainly not after his eyes had held hers captive with his piercing stare. But she wasn't going to let her guard down for a second. He'd probably felt her pulse flutter in her wrist as he brought it against his lips and thought he won the bet already.

She mockingly knocked her head on the desk once, twice before giving it a shake and getting back to work. Tommy needed her to concentrate and make some headway before the end of the day. She wasn't going to do that with thoughts of Ty's lips on her mind.

She locked up the office at five thirty and walked around the back of the building where her coup sat waiting. The sound of a muffled curse had her twisting around to the shed Tommy kept in the back. She stifled a gasp at the sight of Ty, wearing an army green pair of convertible quick dry pants and a flannel shirt over a gray t-shirt. She cursed her body for its reaction to him. He seemed to be struggling with the lock on the shed.

"Can I help you with that?" she asked. She'd considered tiptoeing to her car, but thought better of it now that she was somewhat responsible for the property.

Ty swung around in surprise. He took off his ball cap, wiped his brow, and replaced it on his head, backwards. "I can't remember the combination. Tommy gave it to me, I opened it up this morning, and now I can't remember. I think four hours on the river has wiped my mind clean."

And formed a nice v of sweat on his chest where her eyes could focus. "I think I saw it written down somewhere in one of the files. Give me a second and I'll see if I can find it."

"I don't see his car." Ty's eyes scanned the parking lot. "I doubt you can even get in the office right now." He pulled his phone from his back pocket. "I'll just give him a quick call."

"He's at a meeting. I've got the keys."

"You do?" Ty's long stride matched her gait.

"I'm helping him in the office this summer."

"Is that why you're still here?"

"Yep." He followed her into the small hallway off the main check-in desk. She'd hoped he'd stay outside and let her root through the files without worrying about the fireworks going off in her stomach.

She turned her back to him and began rooting through the top drawer of a three-drawer filing cabinet. She nearly gasped when she felt him step behind her and peek over her shoulder. It wasn't hard for him to do considering he had her by four inches. He didn't smell like hot ham and cheese now, she mused. He smelled like a man, ripe with the scent of work and sweat. She struggled not to drool and lean back into his chest.

"Here we go," she said and pulled the file from the drawer. To her surprise, he didn't step back when she turned around and they bumped chest to chest. When he reached out and put his hands on her hips to steady her, the fireworks in her belly ignited to a full-fledged inferno. She swallowed hard and inched over to set the file on the now empty desk.

The back of her jeans brushed against the front of his pants when she leaned over to find the numbers. "The storage unit lock combination is 34-25-16." Her voice sounded funny, but that wasn't unusual considering the ball of lust in her belly.

He wrapped his hand around her ponytail and let her hair slide through his fingers. "So soft," he murmured.

That was it! She whipped around as he plugged the combination into his phone. When she straightened, she felt like a cornered rat. She absolutely wouldn't be the butt of someone's joke, no matter how attractive he was. "Just what kind of game are you playing?" she demanded.

"Excuse me?" he asked.

"I may be at a low point in my life right now, but that's not a good enough reason for you to use me to win some stupid bet with Eddie. Just because you don't have a girlfriend doesn't mean I'm going to be your summer fill in."

He stepped back, his hands falling to his sides. He opened his mouth, closed it, opened it again, and then slammed his lips together before muttering, "What?"

"I know how you summer guides think. You come into town, hook up with any and all willing partners, and then go back home with a bedpost full of notches and a dozen stories to tell of the women who fell at your feet." She poked him in the chest. "I will not be a notch in your bedpost, Tyler Bloodworth, no matter how pretty you talk or how much money is on the line."

"There is no bet!" Ty threw his hands in the air. "And I don't treat the women I'm with as notches in my bedpost. You don't like me, fine. But don't like me because of me, not because of some stupid bet that never existed."

"Then how come you said what you said about the way I smell? And how come you're always staring at me?"

"Because I like the way you look, Jill. I like everything about you, including your prickly attitude."

"I don't have a prickly attitude!"

His brows shot to the brim of his hat and his eyes widened almost comically. "Oh, really?"

"Quit twisting my words around."

She tried to turn away when he caught her chin in his hand. "What do you mean you're at a low point in your life?" he asked. "I thought your leg was better."

Damn him. For some stupid reason, she'd rather argue with him than endure the concern on his face. "It is."

"So what's wrong?"

All her bluster disappeared and in its place was an overwhelming sense of sadness. How could he take her from aroused, to pissed off, to close to tears in a matter of seconds? "I quit training. I gave up everything I've ever wanted because I thought I didn't want it anymore. I felt good about my decision for about six hours and now I'm having a bit of a panic attack."

"So start training again."

"It's not that simple. I fired my trainer. I've got a job now. I feel like I can make a difference here, at least for a little while. Training was starting to feel like chasing my tail."

"So spend the summer making a difference and figuring out what you want to do for the rest of your life." He brushed his thumb along her cheek, sending a shiver through her body.

She huffed out a breath, exhausted from getting everything off her chest, and asked the question that had kept her up at night. "What are you doing back here, Ty? Why didn't you go to Wyoming?"

He ran a hand down her arm, but let go before their fingers could meet. "I've got things to do here, Jill. Something to finish. Something to prove."

His cryptic answer had her shaking her head. "How's that working out so far?"

He pursed his lips and a ghost of a smile lit his face. "Not too well, but I'm pretty persistent." He stepped back, giving her a chance to take her first, full breath since they'd entered the office. He lifted his phone. "Thanks for the combination."

"You're welcome," she said as he turned his back and left. Crap. She'd just yelled at the only guy who'd piqued her interest in years. And now that she'd been up close and personal with him not once, but twice today, she wanted him more than ever.

CHAPTER 15

Ty stuck the nozzle of the gas pump into his truck, forced to grip the lever by hand when he realized the automatic holder was broken. He slid his sunglasses from around his neck onto his nose, leaned against the body of the truck, and glanced around the town of Hailey.

He knew the town was the agricultural center of the valley, with its acres of potato farms and cattle ranches. Ty loved the summertime hay-cutting season when the air held the sweetly bitter smell of cut grass, so different from the Kentucky bluegrass smells of home. Tractors worked the land from morning until night. He often thought about the appeal of farming. Working the land with your hands, outside from sunup until sundown, where hard work and the luck of the weather could make or break a year.

He stood up straight when he spotted Lyle Woodward coming out of the gas station's food mart with a large drink in his hand and a cocky smile on his face. Ty had him by a few inches in height, but Lyle held the ace of spades: he had a long standing relationship with Jill that Ty was willing to bet included a romantic past.

"Hey," Lyle called out as he approached the SUV opposite Ty's truck. "You're Jill's friend, right?"

"Something like that," Ty muttered and stuck his free hand out to shake. "Tyler Bloodworth."

"Lyle Woodward. Good to meet you."

The lever on the gas tank clicked shut and Ty eased the nozzle into the slot on the pump.

"What brings you out to Hailey?" Lyle asked as he sipped his drink.

Ty wiped his hands on his jeans. "Headed to Westmoreland for supplies."

"I figured a guy like you would be on the water on a day like today."

"I will be this afternoon, but I've got to make a quick run into town."

"You here to catch a wave or catch some fish?"

"Fish," Ty answered. "I'm working with Tommy this summer."

"Pretty much everyone in the Lower Fork works for Tommy this time of year." Lyle scratched at his scruffy chin. "Where you from?"

"North Carolina."

"What part?" Lyle asked.

"Sequoyah Falls, about three hours north of Atlanta."

"I used to live in Atlanta," Lyle said. "What brings you out this way?"

"The fish," Ty said. He couldn't tell if Lyle was making conversation or interrogating him on Jill's behalf.

Lyle took another sip and eyed Ty over the lid. "We've got over two miles of the Rio Grande on our property. You're welcome to fish it anytime as long as you give me a heads up before you come out."

Ty dipped his chin. An invitation to fish private water wasn't an offer he'd expected from Lyle. It was an offer he couldn't refuse. "You serious?"

"Sure. As long as you don't mess with the cows, my stepdad won't care."

"I appreciate the offer and I'll take you up on it the next time I'm free." Ty dug his phone out of his back pocket. "Can

I get your number?"

Lyle lifted up the corner of his mouth in a grin. "Jill's got it. I gotta run." He bolted for the SUV and pulled out of the lot before Ty could respond.

"Huh," Ty muttered. "What the hell was that all about?"

***

Jill had just gone over her ledger updates with Tommy and he'd left her to continue when Ty poked his head in the office. "Hey, Jill. Do you have a minute?"

She swallowed and fought the urge to run her hand over her ponytail. She'd bothered with more makeup than usual this morning, but by now she'd chewed off her lip gloss and probably smeared her mascara. Ty had been in the back of her mind since their office encounter and she'd kept an eye out for him since arriving at the shop. "Sure." She held out her hand toward the seat in the corner.

He ignored her invitation to sit and leaned both arms on the desk, his face closer than she was comfortable. She laced her fingers and looked up into his beautiful eyes. "Can I get Lyle's phone number from you?"

"Oh." That was so not what she thought he'd say. She reached for her purse, but dropped her hand when she remembered her mistake. "I, um, accidentally left my phone in the charger at home. I don't know his number off the top of my head."

He pursed his lips at her and then stood up to his full height, pulling his phone from his back pocket. "What's your number?" he asked.

She shouldn't have felt like a swooning teenager who'd been asked that question by the high school quarterback, but she did. She gave him her number and he programmed it into his phone. "There," he said. "I just texted you my number. When you get home, would you mind texting me his?"

"No, of course not." She looked down at the paper in her hands. She shouldn't ask. It wasn't any of her business, but... "Why?"

Ty flashed her a quick grin that had her toes curling in her shoes. He really was too good looking. "He offered to let me fish his stretch of the river. I want to set something up before he forgets."

"Lyle won't forget. His mind's like a steel trap." But she did wonder what had possessed him to invite a stranger to fish on Dodge's land.

"Where is his place, exactly?" Ty asked.

"About seven miles north of the Dairy Barn, right along the highway the locals call the Rifle Range."

"What's the property like?"

"It's beautiful. Over a thousand acres right at the base of the canyons. The river is spectacular, although I'm not sure about the fishing. I don't think Lyle or his stepdad are big fishermen."

"It was a generous offer." He eyed the desk. "Everything going okay in here?"

She glanced at the orderly surface. "So far so good. I'm organizing the office. Tommy seems to appreciate my help."

"He doesn't suffer fools, so if you're still here, you're helping."

"I hope so."

"Any more panic attacks?" he asked.

She felt her cheeks heat. Couldn't he do what she'd decided to do and forget that embarrassing little incident the other day? "Not so far. I'm trying to take it one day at a time."

"Sounds like a good strategy." He stuffed his phone back in his pocket, but made no attempt to leave. "You know, I was thinking about your issue with what to do after this summer."

"You were?"

"Yeah." He leaned one hand on the desk and crossed his ankles. "Whenever I have a problem that seems too big to handle, I go fishing. Not with a client, not with anyone, just by myself. I find I breathe easier when I'm doing what I love. I think you should keep running. I've seen you run and you get this look on your face that's like you're in another zone. The kind of zone that makes the rest of us want to cut off our arms to get there."

How did he know that? How could he understand so perfectly that when running felt best, she was lost in the joy of it, her mind comfortably blank, each and every sense alive? "I do?"

"You do. So whatever you do this summer, don't lose that love."

"I'm trying to find it again," she confessed. "I miss it."

"I know you do. It's still there, Jill."

She nodded at him, perilously close to tears. "I hope so."

He studied her, his eyes so full of compassion. Just when she thought she'd drown in the cool depths, the corner of his mouth lifted into a cocky grin. "If you can't find that zone, let me know and I'll take you fishing. Something tells me you just might like it."

An afternoon on the river with the best looking, most genuine guy she'd ever met sounded like the path to finding a whole different kind of zone. She cocked an eyebrow and smirked. "Fishing? Me? I wouldn't know where to begin."

"I'm a pretty good guide. You could start with me."

Oh, she'd like to start with him. Maybe his lips, that fascinating scar over his eyebrow, the scruffy chin, the broad shoulders, narrow waist, and long, blunt ended fingers. She'd start and never stop. She shook her head and tried to calm her racing heart. "I'll give it some thought."

As if she needed an excuse to think of him.

He still didn't make any attempt to leave, but held her captive with his eyes. Her heart raced, her breath came out in short bursts, and she felt her insides turn to liquid. "Ty?" she breathed, her voice a shaky whisper.

"Jill?" he mimicked.

She stood up on legs she willed to stop trembling, her fingers splayed on the desktop for purchase in case her legs gave out under his stare. "I'm not exactly schooled in this whole thing," she waved her hand between them, "but I get the feeling you're hitting on me."

He grinned and she wouldn't have been surprised if a

canary yellow feather popped out of his mouth. "You're pretty perceptive."

"Okay...why?"

"Excuse me?"

"I mean, you could have anyone here. Anyone anywhere. I saw your girlfriend. She was petite and blonde and gorgeous. Pretty much the exact opposite of me. I know you know Olivia. She'd run naked through the streets to get your attention, not that she'd need to do that to get a man's attention, but..." She lifted her shoulders and let them drop as he flashed a mischievous grin.

"Do you own a mirror?" he asked.

"Yes," she stated unequivocally. "I do, which is why I'm asking, quite poorly, why me?"

He stepped around the desk. She turned, afraid to break contact with his stare, and the back of her legs ended up pushed against the desk. "For the very reason you're asking and about a hundred more."

He lifted a hand and ran the backs of his fingers down her cheek. The zing it produced felt like lightning coursing through her blood. She felt the electric zap as it whipped through her body, setting fire to every single nerve ending. It was a wonder she didn't burst into flames with just that one touch.

He lightly gripped her chin, lifting her lips to angle perfectly over his. He touched his lips ever so gently to the corner of her mouth. Her hands found their way to his t-shirt and she had just enough firing synapses to register the wall of solid muscle beneath her touch. Then it all went dark as he breezed those lips over hers again and again, whisper soft, never quite making full contact. He cradled her head in his hands until she was practically panting with want. His teasing brushes were the most tantalizing torture she'd ever experienced.

"Jill, I forgot—"

Jill spun around and stared in horror at Tommy's stony expression. He sighed heavily once and slumped against the doorframe. "Seriously?"

CHAPTER 16

"My fault," Ty said. He placed a hand on Jill's shoulder, felt her muscles tense at his touch, and squeezed. "She was working and I interrupted."

"Hell of an interruption," Tommy muttered. He rubbed the back of his neck with a hand and swung his gaze between Ty and Jill. "I didn't realize I'd need to reiterate my no fraternization policy."

"I think we're both familiar with the rule," Ty said. "I hope it's not a deal breaker. If that's a problem for you, I understand and I'll have my stuff out of here by the end of the day."

Jill whipped her head around and stared at him, her eyes wide. "Ty, what are you doing?"

He shrugged at Tommy and met Jill's stare with his own. "Making myself clear, to both of you."

Tommy rubbed his face with both hands. "I so don't need this right now." He dropped his hands and crossed his arms over his chest. "Are you saying you'd quit if I asked you two not to see each other?"

"We're both adults, Tommy, and neither one of us works for you in the same capacity. If this is a terminable offense, then terminate me, but I'm not going to stop seeing her."

"Look, what you two do on your own time is your business. I don't want to see this kind of thing," he waved his hand between the two of them, "on the job ever again. Are we clear?"

"Yes," Jill said. "Crystal clear, and I'm sorry."

Tommy looked at Ty. "The policy stands and I mean to enforce it. If everyone sees the two of you making kissy faces at each other all day long, it's going to turn into one big love fest around here and I can't afford to have my employees distracted by their hormones. Distracted employees are dangerous on the water. If I look the other way here, I'm going to need a promise from you that you'll keep this under wraps."

"Absolutely," Jill said.

"Not a problem," Ty concurred. "No one will know."

Tommy looked at Jill. "You'd better tell Olivia to keep her big mouth shut, or she's going to ruin it for everyone."

"I will. She won't say a word."

"I'll believe that when I see it." He let out a big breath. "Listen, I've got a delivery coming in this afternoon for the restaurant and I'm not going to be back in time. Can you stay and double-check the invoice when the delivery comes? Last time they shorted us on chicken."

"No problem," she said.

Tommy looked at his watch and up at Ty. "You've got a wade in ten."

"I'm ready. They'll have the time of their life."

"They'd better," Tommy murmured. He looked between the two of them again, shook his head, and turned on his heel to leave. He left the door ajar on purpose.

Ty turned Jill to face him and noted the pink hue that crawled up her neck. "Are you okay?"

She nodded. "What the heck were you thinking? He could have fired you."

"He could have fired us both. I wanted him to know it didn't matter, at least not to me."

"How can you afford to be so flippant about your job?"

"It's just a job. I could go fifteen miles up the road and get another one this afternoon."

"You'd do that? Just to prove a point?"

"I'd do that, Jill, because I'm not walking away from you." He snaked his hand up her neck and let his thumb rub behind her ear. Her lids became heavy under his stare. "Not for Tommy, or this job, or anything else."

"Ty..."

He leaned in and kissed her forehead, drugging himself on her scent before pulling back. "You've got my number. Use it."

***

Tommy pulled into the parking lot and saw Tyler's truck backed up to the storage building where he was obviously storing his boat after his afternoon float trip. He'd had some time to sit with what he saw the other morning and hoped he could get back to his friendship with Ty without feeling like he'd been manipulated.

"Hey, Ty," Tommy called. "You got a minute?"

Ty stuck his head out of the shed and held up a finger. "Almost done here," he said and disappeared inside. Tommy snagged a Coke from Ty's cooler in the bed of his truck and savored the ice-cold taste after a long day of meetings with the valley's most vocal opponents to the ski village development.

Ty closed and locked the shed before grabbing a drink of his own. They both plopped onto the back of Ty's truck bed and let their feet dangle from the tailgate, sipping from their cans of soda. "So," Tommy began. "You and Jill?" Ty turned his head and met Tommy's stare head on. "She's a great girl," Tommy admitted. "Smart as a whip, easy on the eyes, and anyone who can put up with my sister is a damn saint."

"You don't have a problem with us being together?" Ty asked.

"No," Tommy said. "Other than the fact that you both work for me."

"Details," Ty shrugged.

"Were you really going to quit?"

"Were you going to make me?"

"Shit, man. When the hell did this happen, because I didn't see this coming."

"Last year."

Tommy's brows shot to his hairline. "*Last* year. You were with Dana last year. Are you telling me you were with both of them?"

Ty's gaze narrowed and Tommy had his answer. "I don't play that way."

"Yeah," Tommy said. "I didn't think you did." He took a long swallow and watched a couple of campers go into the restaurant. "So, I'm guessing Jill's the reason you're back?"

Ty nodded. "Mostly. Well…she's the whole reason, but I like you, so it wasn't exactly a hardship."

Tommy laughed. "Did you hide it really well or am I just so busy I can't see what's in front of my face?"

"A little bit of both." Tommy watched Ty nervously pick at the button of his fishing shirt. "She's skittish. I think if she knew she's the reason I'm back, she'd freak, so I'm not telling her yet. I'm taking it one day at a time. You just happened to walk in on my first real move."

It took only a second for Tommy to realize the feeling in his gut was envy. Not for Jill, but for the prospect of having someone to care for. "Looked like a good one."

"It was." Ty slapped Tommy on the back. "I appreciate you looking the other way about this."

Tommy hopped off the tailgate and tossed his empty can back into the cooler. "I've been thinking about that and I believe I've come up with a solution."

"You firing me after all?" Ty asked.

Tommy jerked his head toward The Tap. "I'm going to see if Jill wants to run the restaurant this summer. Take over everything. She's done wonders for the office in just a couple of days. She's freakishly organized and extremely detail oriented. If I could pass that off on her, it'd free up a lot of my time."

"And this solves things how?"

"If she's only running the restaurant, she won't be

overseeing the fly and raft shop, thereby eliminating the conflict of interest."

"You'd do that for us?"

"No, I'd do that for me. I've never really enjoyed the restaurant."

"Then why'd you buy it?"

"It's a good business. It makes money. I just don't like running the day to day."

"Sounds like you've got it all figured out," Ty said. "Leave it to you to turn things around in your favor."

"Hey, I'm that good. Plus, I didn't want to fire you."

When Ty laughed, Tommy felt some of the weight slip off his shoulders.

"I'd have just gotten a job at your competitor," Ty deadpanned.

"Don't I know it." Tommy flipped his keys around his finger as he and Ty walked toward the raft shop. "Do me a favor? Let me talk to Jill about this and get her okay before you do any more PDA."

"Sure," Ty said. "It's kinda fun sneaking around like we're a couple of teenagers."

Tommy looked at Ty and shook his head. The kid was twenty-four and spending the summer as a fly guide chasing after a girl. For all intents and purposes, he was a teenager. "Enjoy your youth while it lasts, my friend. Sometimes being a grownup really sucks."

CHAPTER 17

Jill sank onto the couch in her apartment and blew a lock of hair out of her face. She couldn't believe how tired she was after a full day at work. She'd started at the office, done her regular lunch shift, and finished back in the office adding to Tommy's job performance standards requirements for her new position as restaurant manager.

She hadn't been this tired after training twice and working in between, but she knew the exhaustion came from using her brain all day. She'd missed feeling useful and was very excited about the challenge Tommy had presented to her the day before. Not only did he trust her with a huge part of his business, but he also gave her and Ty a path around his fraternization policy.

A path they'd yet to explore.

When her phone beeped, signaling a text, she fished it out of her purse and smiled. She hadn't seen much of Ty for the past few days, except for a few steamy glances at The Tap, but that hadn't stopped him from texting her. The man was seriously sexy with the phone.

I think Tommy is punishing me by keeping me on the river morning until night so I can't see you. Don't be shocked if when we meet, I've grown scales.

Jill couldn't wipe the grin off her face. *You'd make scales look good. Are you still on the water?*

She let her head drift back into the cushion while awaiting his reply. Olivia bound into the room and dropped her bulging book bag onto the coffee table, knocking the TV remote control to the floor. "I'm so over school! Why did I sign up for classes this summer?"

"So you can graduate and get out of school," Jill answered.

Olivia threw herself onto the floor and lay face up, spread eagle on the carpet. "My brain hurts."

"I know the feeling."

Olivia popped her head up and gave Jill a questioning stare. "Your brain hurts? Since when?"

"Since your brother made me manager of The Tap."

Olivia sat up on her elbows. "Seriously?"

"Seriously. I start tomorrow."

"Wow. I never thought he'd relinquish control of any part of the business." She wiggled her eyebrows. "You must have totally impressed him with your giant brain."

"I don't know about that," Jill muttered as her phone beeped.

Heading home now, Ty texted. *You want to come up?*

Did she ever, but she promised herself she'd run every day. *I've got to run. Raincheck?*

"Who are you texting?"

Jill's head whipped up and she tried to make her face as normal as possible. "No one."

"No one, huh? I don't think that's actually possible, not with that stupid grin on your face."

She shot to her feet and made a grab for the phone. Jill held it over her head while Olivia attacked. "Can I have just a little bit of privacy, please?" Jill begged.

"No," Olivia said. "Not when you're acting like a doofus right in front of my face. Who is it?"

Jill kneed Olivia and bounced off the couch, the phone safely gripped in her palm. "It's Ty."

"Oh, really? And what does he want?"

Me, she wanted to say, but thought better of crowing to Olivia. "He wants me to come over."

"Wait a minute." Olivia got slowly to her feet and planted her hands on her hips. "We seemed to have skipped a few steps. What haven't you told me?"

Jill dropped her gaze and walked into the kitchen for a glass of water. Olivia followed closely on her heels. "He's interested."

"So we'd already concluded. What happened, Jill? Don't make me string this out of you."

"He came into the office a couple of days ago and one thing led to another and he kissed me."

"A couple of days ago?" Olivia drew one sharp breath through her nose. "Why didn't you tell me?"

"Tommy caught us and asked us not to say anything to anyone. He thought it might encourage his other employees to consider workplace romance a good idea."

"So you didn't tell *me*?"

"I wanted to, but I knew you'd have a hard time keeping it to yourself and I didn't want to put you in a bad spot with your brother."

"How very considerate." Olivia ripped open the refrigerator and pulled out a soda. "I can't believe you didn't tell me."

"I'm telling you now," she offered.

Olivia stuck her chin in the air and looked away. "I really want to be pissed at you right now, but I'm too curious. How was it?"

"It?"

"The kiss!"

"It was..." she closed her eyes and the memory of his lips on hers ignited a small fire in her chest, "fantastic. He's incredibly skilled."

"I'll just bet," Olivia smirked. "So what are you still doing here? Go, make out with the fantastic kisser. One of us should get lucky."

"I can't. I've got to run."

Jill's phone beeped.

Want some company? he asked.

Hummm. She knew he was in shape, but she couldn't imagine running with him beside her. She really wanted to see him, and yet she wanted to say no. But saying no might make him stop asking, so—

"Are you going to stand there all day scowling at your phone or are you going to answer him?" Olivia asked.

"He wants to run with me."

"Is that code for something illicit?"

Jill wrinkled her nose at Olivia. "No, gutterbrain. Run means run."

"So what's the big deal? I bet he looks great in a pair of running shorts. Maybe he'll run shirtless."

"I've never run with anyone I'm attracted to." An image of Lyle in college running a few steps ahead of her flashed through her mind. He'd motivated her to increase her pace, lengthen her stride, and nearly pull a hamstring. "It seems like a bad idea."

"Why? You insist on running every day, God knows why, and Ty wants to spend time with you. So go run, get all sweaty, and then maybe share a shower after?"

"This is why I didn't tell you."

Olivia laughed. "You know I'm just kidding." She nodded with her head at the phone in Jill's hand. "What are you going to do?"

"I guess it wouldn't hurt to try."

Olivia swung an arm around Jill's shoulder. "That's my girl."

***

Ty pulled over at the small grocery store in the heart of the Lower Fork, stalling. He could use some more cereal, but he didn't want to get too far up the mountain if Jill took him up on his offer of a run.

He reached for his phone as he put the truck into park.

I'm game if you are, she texted. *Meet me here in 20?*

Bingo. He rifled through the clothes he kept in the back

seat, found a pair of basketball shorts and his running shoes, and figured changing in the grocery's restroom was the best plan. He'd just reached for the door handle when his phone rang.

"How's operation fishbait going?" Jesse asked.

"Operation fishbait? What are you, Dad, twelve?"

Jesse laughed. "Uh-oh. Somebody doesn't have a sense of humor."

"I've got a great sense of humor, just not about this. What do you want?"

"I want to know how it's going. Has she succumbed to the Bloodworth charm?"

Ty sighed. Why now, of all times, did his dad turn into a cheeseball? "The plan is not to bed her as fast as possible. Besides, I think she'd deck me if she thought that was all I wanted."

"Is it?"

"No." He thought of Jill, sitting at her desk as the sun turned her hair to ebony. "She's funny, and smart, and she has no idea how beautiful she is. Coming back was the right thing. I just need to be patient."

"God knows you didn't get that from me. How's everything else?"

"Good. People are nice out here. The fishing's good." Ty eyed the time and tapped his fingers on the steering wheel. "What's going on at home?"

"Nothing much," Jesse said. "Your mom and Bryce are cooking up some kind of plan with the vacant space across the river from The Pizza Den. I'm not sure, but Angelita seems to think they want to open another restaurant."

"Really? That's...weird."

"I think so, too, but no one asked me. Season's shaping up to be a good one. I'm looking forward to seeing your ugly mug when we come out there in a few weeks."

"I called and got your reservations all set. The kids are going to love it."

"They miss you, Ty. We all do."

"I miss y'all, too. Listen," Ty straightened in the seat and pulled the keys from the ignition, "I've got to run. Call you in a couple of days?"

"Sure, sure. Don't be too patient. If I'd waited on Angelita to make the first move, I'd probably still be waiting."

"Thanks, Dad, but I think I've got this."

He changed in the grocery's small restroom and pulled into Jill's apartment complex ten minutes later. Hers was the far top unit. He took a deep breath and prayed he wouldn't embarrass himself by running with a professional.

When she answered his knock on the door, his mouth went dry. She wore a fitted racer back tank and black shorts. Her hair swung from a high pony in the back and she offered him a shy smile. "Hi," she said.

"Hi." He couldn't stop his hand from reaching for his belly. She looked so much as she had last year when he'd scooped her off the ground in pain. He snuck a glance at the three-inch scar on her right leg. "You ready?" he asked.

"Yes." She pointed behind her with a thumb. "Do you need a water or anything?"

"No. I'm good."

"You kids have fun," Olivia called from the couch where she sat with a book cradled in her lap. All he could offer was a lift of his chin in acknowledgment.

They jogged down the steps. "Olivia reads?" he joked.

She knocked the back of her hand against his stomach. "Very funny. She's studying."

"What? That mommy porn everybody's reading now?"

"It's a textbook. She's studying to be a teacher."

Ty stopped at the base of the stairs and stared. "You're kidding, right?"

"No. She's actually pretty smart."

"I thought you two were the same age. What's taken her so long?"

"She took a few semesters off here and there when she felt overwhelmed. I think she regrets it now." She grabbed hold of the handrail with her left hand and pulled her right foot with the other to begin stretching her quad muscles. Ty mimicked her position on the other side of the staircase.

They switched legs, did a few lunges on the stairs, and then Jill stood up straight, clicked a button on her watch, and glanced at Ty. "You ready?"

He ignored the flutter of nerves in his stomach and tried to concentrate on her shapely legs. "Whenever you are."

She began at a slow jog. "How far do you want to go?" she asked.

"How far do you normally go?"

"I usually warm up for about a mile and then run five or six more."

He did his best not to gulp. "Uh, that sounds like a challenge."

"Do you run on a regular basis?" she asked.

"It's been a while," he confessed. Over a month, he figured as he matched his stride to hers. If she ran this fast in warm up, there was no way he'd make it more than three miles. "I ran a couple days a week when I was at school."

They passed the grocery store and she led them down a side road that fed into an upscale neighborhood. He looked around and tried to get his breathing under control. "This looks like a nice neighborhood."

"It's mostly vacation homes for the ski crowd. They get rented out a little in the summer months." She wasn't even breathing heavy. This was the worst idea in the history of bad ideas.

They continued on in silence, or what little he could hear over the in and out of his puffing breath. "Look," he said. "You go on ahead if I'm holding you back."

"No, I'm fine," she lied. She was talking to him as if they were sitting across a table from one another. She wasn't even out of breath.

"Jill. Go on. I'm going to slow my pace, enjoy the view, and I'll meet you back at your apartment."

She gave him an impish smile. "Are you sure?"

"Please, before I truly embarrass myself and pass out."

"Don't do that," she teased. "Just lengthen your stride and concentrate on breathing from your diaphragm. You're all chest right now."

Maybe that's why his chest felt like it was going to explode. "Good idea. Go on." He waved her off. "I want you far enough ahead so you don't realize when I turn around and head back."

"Listen to your body, Ty," she called over her shoulder. Now that he'd given her the green light, she took off like a gazelle. The sight of her flying in front of him, the slender yet powerful muscles of her legs pushing her forward, made his breath hitch for a whole new reason. She was magnificent.

He slowed his pace and ran another ten minutes with the sights and sounds of the quiet neighborhood for company before turning around and heading back to her place at the first hint of dusk.

He stretched against the same staircase, lumbered up the stairs, and knocked on the door. Olivia answered wearing short shorts and a hoodie sweatshirt. "Well, well, well," she purred. "Look what the cat dragged back in."

CHAPTER 18

"Water," Ty panted. "I need water."

Olivia chuckled, opened the door wide, and sauntered into the kitchen using her most feline walk. Much to her dismay, Ty was too busy wiping his brow with the end of his shirt to notice. Oh, well. At least she got another glance at his chiseled torso. "Back so soon?"

"It's been a while since I've run. I need a little practice before I offer to tag along with Jill again. I swear she's got jet fuel in her veins."

"Always has." She plucked a bottle of water from the refrigerator and tossed it at Ty where he leaned against the counter.

He unscrewed the cap and guzzled half the bottle before coming up for air. "Christ, that tastes good." He set the bottle on the counter and leaned back, taking huge sips of air. "I'd like to clean up before she gets back. Can I use your bathroom?"

"My bathroom?" No way was she letting him see all the things she used to make herself beautiful. "No. Jill's is down the hall, second door on the left."

"Thanks," he called.

"Don't even think about stealing her underwear."

His answering grunt made her laugh out loud. She huffed out a breath as he disappeared inside Jill's room. Tyler Bloodworth was totally hot and totally uninterested in anything but Jill. She couldn't work up much of a pout considering her friend needed a hot distraction even more than she did.

As much as she hated to admit it, Olivia was quickly becoming bored with the men in the valley. She'd always loved the different factions of men. The guides, both fishing and rafting, shared her love of the outdoors and the laid back lifestyle. If she wanted a more mature, thinking type, there was Westmoreland and the college. Farmers and ranchers abounded in Hailey and Del Noches, providing a hard working distraction.

The sound of Ty clearing his throat brought her back to reality. He smelled like Jill's soap and held a towel in his hand. "I was going to splash some water on my face, but decided a shower was necessary. Where do you want me to put this towel?"

"You can toss it in the laundry room, thanks." She pointed past the kitchen to the small closet that housed their stacked machines. When he came back to the den, he walked straight through instead of stopping to chat. "Where are you going?"

"I'm going to wait for Jill outside." His eyes flicked to the clock on the wall. "She should be back soon."

"I won't bite, you know."

He hesitated and then turned back. "I'd like to watch her come back." He leaned toward the window to scan the horizon. "She's so beautiful when she runs."

Olivia couldn't keep the grin from her face. "You're really into her, aren't you?"

"You think I shouldn't be?" He glared at her, his eyes narrowed.

"No, that's not what I meant. I just…I guess I'm not used to being around a guy so willing to admit he's interested."

"I don't play games. If I like someone, I'll be the first to admit it." He shrugged. "I really like Jill."

"She's lucky, Ty, that it's you. She's special. I don't think she could handle any games right now."

His teeth flashed as he looked out the window. "She's coming. Do you mind if I grab another water for her?"

"They're her waters."

He jogged to the kitchen and was gone before she had time to reach for her book and settle it in her lap. "Lucky Jill."

***

Jill's stomach clenched when she saw Ty leaning against his truck tossing a bottle of water between his hands. Despite his wet hair, he looked like he'd just stepped out of the shower instead of run a few miles. She probably smelled like a locker room.

She slowed her pace to a jog, then to a walk, and clicked off her stopwatch. Not bad, she thought, considering her slow start. Her leg felt stronger and her endurance was improving daily.

She pulled the hem of her shirt up to wipe the sweat from her face before realizing she'd just flashed her stomach at him. He rubbed the center of his shirt as she approached. "How'd you do?" she asked.

"Let's just say I had time to hydrate and shower before your return."

"I knew you didn't look or smell as bad as I do. No fair." She took the bottle he offered and sipped.

"You don't look or smell bad, Jill. Strangely enough, you're not even breathing hard."

She shrugged. Years of training had her recovery rate, especially on an easy run, down to nothing. "I wasn't exactly killing myself."

"I'd hate to try and keep up with you when you were. I couldn't run that fast if someone was chasing me with a gun."

She evaded his stare and stretched her quads. "You're not used to the altitude. And I'm not that fast. Trust me, I'm mediocre at best."

"Hello? You just broke your leg."

"Nine months ago. I can't really use that as an excuse."

"An excuse for what? You're amazing."

She couldn't have stopped the blush if she wanted to. She only hoped her overheated face hid her embarrassment. "I appreciate your compliment, but I'm not that good. If I was, I wouldn't be considering giving up the dream."

He shrugged. "So you're a little burnt out. Happens to everyone. Doesn't mean you're done forever."

"I wonder sometimes," she muttered before sipping from the water again. "It's always been about the competition. I don't know if I can love it without that aspect."

"Always?" He bumped her arm with his elbow. "Even back when you first started?"

"You mean when I was ten?" She leaned against the truck facing him. "No, I guess not. I just knew I was faster than everyone else and it made me feel good. Powerful, I guess. I knew who I was when I was running."

"My mom's a runner," Ty said after tucking a lock of her hair behind her ear. "She's a bear when she doesn't run. It's a part of her, a part of who she is, and she's never competed, other than a fun run or two."

"My mom says the same about me when I haven't run. *Get outta here and go run around the block*, she used to yell at me when I'd get under her skin. She was right. I'd run off some steam and everything just kinda leveled out."

He reached his arm around her neck and softly pulled her ponytail. "You hungry?"

As if on cue, her stomach grumbled. "Starving."

"Why don't you go take a quick shower and I'll buy you dinner?"

"You can come up and I'll attempt to make us something."

"I could, but Olivia's up there and I'd rather spend time with just you."

A handful of butterflies took flight in her stomach. She held out her hand and felt that same powerful feeling she'd just described when he linked their fingers. "Come up while I shower?" she asked.

"Lead the way."

***

Ty took her to Del Noches to a hole in the wall place with the best Mexican food he'd ever tasted. Or maybe everything was better when Jill was near. Ty couldn't be sure.

The cab of his truck had never smelled better than when she'd slid in beside him, her minty soap mixing with whatever alluring fragrance he'd hinted in her bathroom. It had taken every ounce of restraint not to dig through her personal things and discover more of the woman who'd entranced him with her quiet beauty. The need to discover the places she held deep inside was overpowering, but he wanted her to open up and show him herself.

They shared a love of hot food, each devouring the meals on their plates. He watched as she shoveled in bites of her enchiladas like she'd never eaten before, and then sit for long stretches and let her food go untouched while listening to him tell a story.

"You're not the typical summer guide," Jill said after shoving her empty plate away. She sat back in her chair and twirled a piece of hair around her finger. She'd left it to air dry and he marveled at the loose curls that popped into place as if by magic. "There aren't many guides with a master's in economics and a teaching job waiting on their return."

He shrugged. "Would you prefer if I lived in a tent and spent the summer yearning for the ski season?"

"No," she said emphatically. "If those were the kinds of guys I found attractive, I'd have probably been married and divorced three times over by now."

"I doubt those guys would have married you. Just had their way and moved on."

"How right you are." She folded her arms on the edge of the table and leaned toward him. He could see the lights from the take out counter sparkling in her eyes. "So with all the things you could be doing over the summer, why come here? Why spend another summer fishing in nowhere Colorado?"

He didn't want to lie to Jill, but everything in his gut screamed telling her the truth would send her running. "I like to fish and I really like working for Tommy. My dad and I are opening up a fly shop in the fall to go with his rafting operation."

"Are you going to guide and teach at the same time?"

"I want to do both. Between the two of us, my dad thinks we can handle it. I have to trust him, trust that as a successful businessman, he wouldn't put his family at risk on a whim."

"You're his family."

Ty smiled. "I'm a very small part of his family."

She frowned and Ty had to fight the urge to run his finger along the ridge between her brows. "What do you mean?"

"My parents are divorced. Have been for a long time. They're both remarried and have young kids. My dad has three daughters under eight and my mom has six-year-old twin boys."

"Wow. That must be...weird. My brother is only five years younger than me and I feel like we have nothing in common."

"They're all great. I can come by, play around with them for awhile, and then leave before they get on my nerves."

"So where do you live back home?"

"When I was at school, I lived on campus. When I came home, I'd switch off between my mom and dad's houses. When I go back for good, I'm going to stay at one of the rental cabins on my grandfather's property. He's getting older and it'll ease everyone's mind knowing he won't be alone all the time."

"You're very close to your family," she said, staring down at her hands where she twiddled her thumbs. Something about the way she said it made him think she had trouble at home.

"Yes. They're coming in a couple of weeks to visit. The whole lot of them, except my granddad."

"That's great." The corner of her mouth lifted in a halfhearted attempt at a smile. He reached across the table and put his hand over hers.

"What is it?" he asked. "Is everything okay with your family?"

She lifted her shoulders and shook her head. "Not really. I told you I fired my coach. My dad was my coach. I kind of blindsided him with the news and I haven't heard from him since. My mom's laying on the guilt trip. He could have taken on another class this summer, blah, blah, blah." She pulled her hands back and shoved them under the table. "We'll get past it, but I'm feeling especially guilty right now."

"You had to do what was best for you. Sometimes we hurt the ones who love us the most by spreading our wings." She stared at him with her sad eyes, but didn't say anything more. "My dad didn't understand why I wanted to come back here this summer. I didn't tell him until right before I left."

"Why would he care? Did he want you to stay home and work with him?"

"No, he wanted me to go to Wyoming." He wasn't sure if he could explain his dad's need for him to live life in the now, but with Jill, he wanted to try. "My parents had me young. High school young. My dad missed out on a lot of stuff he wanted to do, so he's always drilled in my head that I shouldn't put things off. I've always wanted to fish the Platte and he thought I was throwing away an opportunity that might not come again."

"I guess that makes sense," she said with an appealing tilt to her head that made her dark hair shine in the light. She narrowed her eyes at him. "So why didn't you go?"

He wished she could see herself, sitting across from him, her hair spilling around her shoulders, the graceful flow of her neck. If she could, he knew he wouldn't have to answer her question with another evasion. "Every time I thought about where I'd be this summer, I kept coming back to this place. To the people here," he hedged. "I listened to my gut."

"Any regrets?" she asked.

He looked her dead in the eye, held her stare as her chest rose and fell once, twice. "Not one." His gaze drifted to her mouth where she sank her teeth into her lush bottom lip and grinned. "You ready to go?" he asked.

"Yeah, I'm ready."

CHAPTER 19

Jill was glad for the challenge of work. She went over her notes with Tommy, set up an ordering and delivery schedule with a list of vendors, and nervously stood by his side as he announced to the team that Jill would be in charge of the restaurant in addition to serving on the lunch crew. Her coworkers seemed surprised at the changing of the guard and she knew the easy camaraderie she'd established with them would change.

So much change. Too much in a short period of time. Her life no longer existed around training; she was responsible for more than just herself for the first time ever, and her budding relationship with Ty had awakened a womanly desire long dormant.

Blocking out the searing kiss they'd shared the night before became impossible when he sauntered into The Tap for lunch. The measly shaft of light at his back caught in the golden blond of his hair. His easy gait reminded her of the way he'd angled himself against her at the door. The strong fingers that only hours ago had burrowed into her hair and held her captive while he drew moans of pleasure from her lips. And his mouth, the knowing smile that touched his lips shared the secret of longings passed between them as they'd made out like teenagers against her apartment door.

Her face heated at the memory. If he knew that he'd only to crook a finger and she'd drop everything to feel that mouth on hers again... The heavy lidded look he spared her said he knew all too well. He was too cocky, too aware of his effect on Jill, and too gorgeous for his own good. She couldn't figure out how a guy like him, who could have any woman at the snap of his fingers, would seem so hell bent on being with her.

"What can I get you?" she asked him, purposely avoiding his eyes for fear everyone in the restaurant would know what they'd done and the mountain of things they'd yet to explore.

"I'll have the tuna salad sandwich with fruit," he said.

Her eyes flung to his. "Fruit?"

His dimple flashed. "I figure I'd better start eating better if I'm ever going to have a chance to keep up with you."

She would have given anything to stop her cheeks from heating. She knew he meant running and not the way she'd arched against him last night, her body begging for what her mouth would never admit. "Okay, then. Fruit it is."

The season was in full swing and The Tap was packed by the time he'd finished his lunch and paid the bill she'd slipped in front of him on her way to refill a drink. She pocketed his tip with the others she'd gathered that day, and only later, counting her money to share with the teenager she'd hired to bus the tables and clean the dishes, did she discover the note he left.

I'm working with Tommy tonight at the fly shop. I'll stop by the office later to see if you're still there.

She lifted her eyes to the clock on the computer. Just after three. He'd be on the river until at least six. Now that she was manager, she'd planned to adjust her schedule so she could come by at lockup and get used to those procedures. Her new responsibilities would put a serious crimp in her burgeoning relationship.

She sat up straight at the thought. Relationship? How could she think of their time together as anything other than a summer-long diversion? He'd said he came back for a reason;

he had something to prove. Jill couldn't think of herself and the time they spent together as anything other than a byproduct of his time here and his need to fill that void in his life for a little while. A man like Ty, she felt sure, wasn't used to being alone.

What would he think of her when the summer was over, she wondered? What would she think of herself?

A summer of changes, indeed.

She needed to remember what this summer was to both of them. She sought to find her place in life or at least a balance she could live with. Tyler sought to prove something to himself or perhaps his father. No matter what his quest, he'd be gone at the end of the summer. She'd do well to remember that before jumping in with both feet and ending up with a broken heart.

***

Ty loaded up his gear early Sunday morning and drove down the mountain at the first hint of dawn. As he meandered down the steep slope and around the bending turns, his mind went to Jill. She was probably asleep right now, tucked sweetly between the covers of her double bed. Ever since his one foray into her room, he pictured her there, lying beneath the heavy denim cover, her hair spilling atop her pretty white lace pillows.

She could just as easily be up and running along the quiet streets, the cool morning air puffing out in misty bursts. He could see her in his mind's eye, the long elegant gait, the strength of her stride. No matter what, he promised himself, he'd make the time to see her before the day was over.

Between her work schedule and him taking the slack when Shane fell off a raft and injured his shoulder, they'd barely seen one another except in passing. He was becoming desperate to touch her again, feel her breath on his face, taste her earthy flavor on his tongue.

He shook off his melancholy mood when he passed through the Lower Fork and didn't see her and focused instead on his destination. Lyle had suggested an early morning fish along his stretch of the Rio Grande. When Ty had asked Tommy about the property, his boss seemed surprised at Lyle's offer, confirming what Ty had suspected all along: the generous invitation was probably an interrogation.

He'd already concluded Lyle's interest in Jill was more than friendship. The two had a bond and Ty felt an inkling of unease that he'd either be warned to steer clear or deemed unacceptable by her close friend. He intended to stake his claim on Jill Jennings, Lyle Woodward be damned.

He followed the directions Lyle had provided, left at the Dairy Barn and seven miles north along a road as straight and flat as his own mountain drive was curvy and steep. Ty entered the property by a well-tended caretaker's house and followed the gravel road that ran between two barns, a corral, and numerous fenced pastures. A gaggle of black and white cows feasted on hearty green plumes of grass, chewing and staring as his truck kicked up a tornado of dust in his wake.

The house sat directly along the river, an impressive wood and stone cabin with covered decks and flowers in containers flanking the driveway. He parked his truck near a bordering fence so as not to block the drive and walked around the back to get a better view of the river.

He heard it first, the whistling water rolling over rocks and boulders. In the distance, he saw two mule deer crossing the river at a calm and shallow juncture. The air smelled of hay and something he couldn't name, a freshness that felt like a filter through his lungs.

He startled when Lyle walked up behind him.

"Beautiful, huh?"

"It's breathtaking. I've not seen the river this far down. So much character," he said as his eyes roamed the landscape.

"I never tire of looking out the window," Lyle said. "I guess you found it okay?"

"Right where you said it would be." Ty shoved his hands in his pockets and met Lyle stare for stare. He wouldn't have been surprised if Lyle had unzipped his pants to mark his territory.

"I'm not much of a fisherman, but I think the best place to cast your line is upriver. We'll take the four wheelers and you can pick the spot."

"Sounds good. I'll get my stuff from the truck."

Lyle strapped Ty's gear to a mud-caked four-wheeler and directed Ty to follow in a smaller version. "Won't we wake your family starting these things up so close to the house?" Ty asked.

"My stepdad's already up and working. My mom was making coffee when I saw your truck."

"Lead the way," Ty said.

They followed a deeply rutted path along the riverbank, around huge cottonwood trees and fingers of overflow slews. Ty spotted a large carp float to the surface of one of the larger bodies of water. Dove's dispersed with a rustle as they rounded a sharp bend in the river and two ducks took flight when Lyle cut the engine of his ATV and Ty followed suit.

"How does this look?" Lyle asked over his shoulder before dismounting.

Ty gazed around at the wide stretch of river. The water bubbled over a curving line of boulders in the river where the current emptied into a slow moving pool. "Let's start right there," he pointed to the spot where the fast moving river narrowed and lipped over into a slower pool of water, "and watch the head of the pool. If we don't see any signs, we can fish the tongue or go back and hit the tail."

"What kind of signs?" Lyle asked.

Ty stopped Lyle just as the water licked their boots, thankful that the sun's position left their shadow in the rocky bank and not on the water. "Different things. Splashes, rings, wakes, tailing, or bulges."

"Okay..."

"Signs there are fish in the pool. Watch the surface and see if you notice any movement."

Ty pulled on his polarized sunglasses from around his neck and Lyle squinted at the water under the brim of his ball cap. "I don't see anything."

"Patience is the name of the game. There." Ty pointed to a spot just beyond the lip. "Did you see that bulge in the water?"

"Ahhhh…"

"Like a swell on the surface. That means a fish is feeding just below the water. I think it's safe to start here considering the water flow and a bulge." He knew Lyle understood next to nothing about fishing and that watching for too many signs would bore him to death. For all intents and purposes, he was giving a beginning lesson.

Ty strapped on his vest, showed Lyle how to use one of his poles that he'd already attached a wet fly to, and demonstrated the best way to cast. "That's it," Ty said as Lyle's line flew back and forth in a delicate arch. "Now mend the line just a bit."

"Do what?" Lyle asked.

"You want your fly line to drift at the same rate as the fly," Ty said. "You see how your line is ahead of the fly?" He pointed to where the line lay atop the surface of the slow moving water. "Just flip the line back with your wrist in the other direction and that'll adjust the line into proper position."

Lyle accomplished the feat in a couple of flicks. "I never realized there was so much to fly fishing," he said. "My brother and I always used spinning rods when we'd fish."

"Nothing wrong with that," Ty commented as he cast his line at the tongue of the pool.

They fished companionably, staying between ten and twenty yards apart. They kept their voices hushed when speaking about a cast or whenever Lyle had a question about what Ty was doing. When Ty caught an eighteen-inch rainbow, he walked Lyle through helping him with the net to bring it in and take a picture before releasing the fish back into the water.

A good while later, as the sun rose high in the sky, Lyle suggested a break and unhooked a small cooler from the ATV. He walked to the trunk of a cottonwood tree where it had fallen like a gift in the shade of its neighbors. Ty felt the refreshing breeze kiss his sweaty shirt as he unzipped his vest and draped it over the four-wheeler.

"This sure is a beautiful piece of land," Ty said as he took the seat next to Lyle and accepted a soft drink. "How long have you owned it?"

"My family's owned the land for fifteen and we've lived here for ten."

"Has it always been a ranch?"

"It sat vacant until we moved here, my mom, brother, and me. My stepdad's ranched it since then; of course, he wasn't my stepdad then."

"Is your dad back in Atlanta?" Ty asked.

"He died in a plane crash twelve years ago. We moved out here not long after."

"Sorry about your dad," Ty said after swallowing a bite of roast beef sandwich.

Lyle passed him a bag of chips. "Thanks." He kicked at a rock with the toe of his shoe. "It was a long time ago."

"Your stepdad's well respected in the area, so it seems like you got lucky in that department."

Lyle snorted in agreement. "Yes, we did. Didn't like him at first, of course I'm not sure I would have liked any man who came sniffing around my mom, but he's a good man. He works hard, doesn't play games or pull punches. And he loves my mom and my brother and me with everything he's got. We're lucky to have him."

"I've got one of those," Ty admitted. When Lyle glanced at him out of the corner of his eye, Ty explained, "A stepdad. A good one. He helped raise me. He's the best thing that ever happened to my mom, and he's blessed us all with a set of wild eyed twin boys I'm proud to call my brothers."

"Wow. I always thought I was lucky I didn't have to compete with another set of kids."

"No, they're great. My dad's remarried and he's got three girls. I know it sounds crazy, but the kids are a blessing. They're all a lot younger, so maybe that's why I don't feel like I'm in competition with them. I guess I've just got more people to love."

Lyle finished off his sandwich and balled the foil wrapper in his fist before tossing it back in the cooler. "Is that what you're doing out here?" he asked. "With Jill? You fishing for more people to love? Or maybe someone to love you?"

CHAPTER 20

J ill faced her father over the steam from the pot roast and potatoes. Sunday dinner, which was technically Sunday lunch at the Jennings' house, had never been fraught with so much tension. Even Josh, Jill's eighteen-year-old brother, was uncharacteristically quiet.

The silence broke when Bobbie asked Jill to pass the salt. It was a ruse, Jill knew, as her mother was committed to her low sodium diet. "Did I tell you I saw Mrs. Bitner at the grocery store this morning and she said Mandy got hired on by a firm in Denver? A big time firm," her mother said with wide eyes. "Oh, I wish I could remember the name, but I get all those initials confused."

Jill figured it was only a matter of time before Mandy Bitner made her splash in the big city. Her mom bringing up her high school classmate's success wasn't exactly the segue Jill was hoping for when announcing her new job. "I got a new job, too." Her eyes bore a hole into her mother's practical white plates. "I'm managing The Tap this summer."

Jill could have heard a pin drop in the silence that followed. She snuck a look at her father, his brow furrowed and his mouth drawn in a tight line.

"Is that why you quit training?" he asked. "To pursue your

lifelong dream of bar management?"

She wouldn't do herself any favors by losing her cool. She met him glare for glare and said as calmly as possible, "Tommy needed some help; I had the time. I'm actually enjoying the work. I *do* have an accounting degree."

"Ah, yes. The bachelor of bartending." He looked at Bobbie. "Our money well spent."

Josh had the nerve to snort in laughter.

"I think that's great, honey," her mother injected. "Tommy's lucky to have you."

"At least you're not wasting your life as a waitress," her father said as he placed a bite of roast in his mouth.

"I'm still waitressing at lunch," she admitted. "It helps me to work both sides of the business."

"Well, let's raise our glasses to our daughter's new career as a barkeep."

He was the only one who lifted his glass of water until Josh decided he wanted in on the fun. Jill knew Josh was reveling in her being the black sheep for once.

"Oh, I'm sorry," her father said. "Is that in poor taste?"

"Gary!" her mother admonished in a harsh whisper. "That's enough."

"Oh, I don't know, Bobbie. I think it's just the beginning. The beginning of the end."

Jill stood up and fought the urge to fling her plate in her father's face. The man knew how to push every one of her buttons. "I've lost my appetite, Mom, but thanks for a lovely meal. I just remembered there's somewhere I have to be." She picked up her plate and carried it to the kitchen with shaking hands.

Her mother followed closely behind and grasped her by the shoulders as she swiped the food into the trash. "He doesn't mean what he says, Jill. He's just hurt."

"Well, I guess now we're even." She stacked the plate in the sink and turned around to face her mom. "I'm not coming back until he can be civil."

"He will be."

"Really? When? Because it's been two weeks, Mom, and that was no where near civil."

"He just needs some more time. You've moved on with your life and I'm proud of you for your job. I really am, if that's what you want—"

"I don't know what I want," Jill said.

"Neither does he, and he's got nothing to do for big chunks of the day but sit around and be mad at you."

"And that's my fault?"

"That's just the way it is."

"Can't he work with the runners at the college this summer?" Jill asked. "He did found the summer running program."

"They hired extra help when he said he wanted to work only with you," Bobbie explained with a pitiful look of appeal.

Jill pulsed around the small kitchen, from one end of the counter to the back door to the refrigerator, over and over again. "I thought I'd be training with him. I didn't have any idea I'd need a break."

"I know that, and underneath all that anger, he does too. He'll find someone else to work with. He's already put some feelers out."

"Oh." Jill stopped mid-stride and faced her mother. "He's going to train someone else?"

"Well, that would be the most logical solution. Honey," Bobbie stepped in front of her and rubbed Jill's arms, "you didn't think he'd stop training, did you?"

"I guess I hadn't thought that far ahead." About anything, she admitted to herself as a seed of jealousy slid under her skin. She didn't like the feeling, not one little bit.

"Why don't you come back in? I've made an apple pie for dessert and you know that's your favorite. Neither one of you can be mad over pie."

"I can't, Mom." She truly couldn't wait another second to get out of her family home and get back to her apartment. She'd lace up her shoes and run off the anxiety that was clogging her chest. "Next time. I promise."

***

Ty's easy smile turned hard and brittle. Lyle had to admire the guy's control and the short leash he kept around the temper that flared in his eyes. "Did Jill say something to you about me?"

"No," Lyle said. "Jill's face said something to me about you. I know her face."

"It's a beautiful face," Ty said. He wrapped his half eaten sandwich in the foil and set it on the log. He wiped his hands along the front of his pants as if flexing his fingers in preparation for a fight.

Lyle considered the warning and decided to tread carefully. "A very appealing face, and right now, very vulnerable."

"You think I'm going to hurt her?" Ty angled his body toward Lyle.

Ty had him by a couple of inches in every direction and, despite his affable persona, Lyle didn't think he'd be afraid to use whatever means necessary to his advantage. "No. You've been out here all morning patiently teaching me to fish. You love the land, you love the outdoors, you love your family. I don't think you're shallow enough to want to hurt Jill intentionally. But just because I don't think you'd mean to hurt her, doesn't mean you won't."

"You think I will? If I start something up with her, you think she'd end up getting hurt?"

"You're only here for the summer. You've got a job and a family waiting for you back home."

"I do." Ty nodded. "I don't intend to start something with Jill I'm not prepared to see through. All the way through."

Lyle wanted to like Ty. He did like Ty. But he liked Jill more, and he felt the need to protect her from heartbreak, especially now, when she was so unsure of her path. "So where do you see this going?" he asked.

Ty lifted his brows and sucked in a breath. "Pardon me for sounding like an ungrateful jackass after fishing your land and eating your food, but what business is it of yours?"

"Jill's my friend."

"That's it? All you want from her is friendship?"

Lyle raised his hands in the air. "I'm not interested in anything more than friendship with Jill. A few years ago," he lifted one shoulder, "we gave it some thought. It felt wrong, so we brushed it aside and now we're friends. Just friends. I care about her and I don't want to see her hurt."

"Neither do I."

"Good. Then we're both on the same side."

"I'm not on any side." Ty stood up.

Lyle decided to stay seated on the log. Body language, at a time when he'd insulted a man and laid claim on the woman he was interested in, would convey more than words.

"I like Jill," Ty said. "I want to get to know her. There's something about her." He swung around and faced the river. "I wasn't free to pursue anything last year, but now I am and I'm not going to let you or anyone else stop me."

Lyle got to his feet. "What about Jill? Have you thought about what she's going to do at the end of the summer when you've stirred her up and then leave? She holds herself back from most people. If she lets you in and you walk away, you're going to hurt her no matter what your intentions."

Ty let out an audible breath. "I'm not going to discuss this with you when I haven't even discussed it with her, but suffice it to say I don't have an end date in mind."

"Whether or not you have an end date in your head is beside the point. You're leaving at the end of August. She lives here."

Ty turned around, a sneer on his face, his hands on his hips. "Thank you for stating the obvious."

"Look, you can be mad at me all you want. And you can indulge yourself and take Jill for a spin while you're here. Hell, I'll be the first to admit she needs a little excitement in her life. But whatever you do, don't let her fall in love with you. She doesn't have much experience with men and she needs to feel in control. She'll act in control, but underneath, if she falls, she'll fall hard. And you and I both know you won't be here to pick up the pieces when she does."

The nerve pulsing at Ty's jaw should have made Lyle uneasy, but the way his mouth twitched and when he drew breath in and out and back again without ever speaking told him he'd done the right thing by warning Ty off. Jill would be furious if she knew, but he'd rather her be mad than brokenhearted. "You want to fish or talk?" Ty asked.

"I've said what I came to say and I've got some work to do back at the house. Stay and fish as long as you want and drop the ATV at the garage when you're done."

"Appreciate it," Ty said and held out his hand.

His grip was firm and the look in his eye steady. Lyle knew Jill was a goner. Oh, well. He'd said his piece. The rest was up to them.

CHAPTER 21

Jill was too furious to do anything other than change her clothes, lace up her shoes, and hit the pavement. As she stretched in the parking lot, she knew the ball of anger in her gut wouldn't ease by running her normal easy route along the street and through the neighborhood. She craved a challenge: steep hills, twisting turns, and savage drops.

Before she could question her motives, she sprinted back up the stairs, grabbed her keys, and headed for the mountains.

She parked at the base of her favorite trail in the gravel lot just off the main highway, locking her car and palming her key. Her chest filled, her stomach fluttered, and her limbs felt loose and tingly. She hadn't run in the mountains since the day she went down and everything in her life took a turn for the worse.

Jill shoved her doubts aside and took a deep breath of mountain air. Only five miles from her apartment and the elevation soared to over ten thousand feet. She felt the rise in her shallow breaths as she began her warm-up run up the gently sloping trail.

It took longer for her to find her rhythm and for her lungs to handle the thinning air. She tried not to obsess over her father's outrageous rudeness at dinner, her brother's snotty attitude, and her mother's appeals. She needed to watch the road for obstacles, carefully order her breathing, and maneuver the increasingly arduous ascent.

Her mind wouldn't disengage. She'd expected the meal to be difficult, but never did she expect to be at the receiving end of her father's biting tongue. She didn't like the way it felt to be the bad kid at the dinner table and her brother relishing the moment felt like a slap to her already bruised ego.

The road began its winding swath through stands of aspens and pines. The sharp scent of the woods filled her head and took her out of her misery as she loped along and eyed the flaking bark of the pines infected by mountain pine beetles. As she ogled the dying trees throughout the forest, she felt her worries begin to lift off her shoulders. Even the trees had problems.

A rustling around the next turn had Jill coming to a dead stop. Standing not twenty feet in front of her was an elk. His massive antlers were dusted with velvet and his nose snuffed at the air. She stood stock-still. In the distance, she heard the bugling sound of his pack over her huffs of breath. He took off just as a truck rounded the bend and screeched to a stop at her back.

Jill bolted around and pushed off the hood of Ty's truck where it came to a stop just inches from where she stood. She recognized his furious face through the windshield a moment before he slammed the truck into park and opened the door. "What the hell are you doing standing in the middle of the road? I almost ran you over."

"Did you see it?" she asked, still enthralled with her close up encounter with the giant creature.

"See what?"

She pointed into the downslope of the forest. "The elk. He was just standing there. Right there in the road."

"The only thing I saw in the road was your gorgeous backside. You almost became my hood ornament."

"I can't believe how close I was to a wild animal."

Ty glanced behind him before skirting the hood and taking her by the shoulders. "Do you run with mace?"

"What?"

"Mace, Jill. What would you have done if he'd charged you?"

She jerked her shoulders free. "He wasn't going to charge me."

"He could have. And what about mountain lion?"

"What about them?"

"You don't think a mountain lion would charge? Actually, a lion would stalk you first and then pounce when he had an opportunity."

The last thing she needed after her family lunch was another lecture on how irresponsible she was. "I used to run up here all the time. Before today, I've never seen anything other than a deer or two."

"They're here. Every species of wild animal. I can hear the coyotes howling at night and I'm pretty sure I saw a wolf early one morning."

"Bully for you."

"Your smart tongue and quick legs aren't going to save you from everything in the world."

"Oh, that's rich, coming from you. What do you use to protect yourself? Your charm and good looks?"

He walked around to the passenger side door and opened the glove compartment. He pulled out a can of mace that fit snugly in his palm. He swung it in her face. "This, plus I've got a hunting rifle at the cabin."

"Well aren't you smart. I guess I should run with a gun and just hope it doesn't go off while I'm running."

He shoved the can of mace in her hand. "Here. This is yours now. I don't want to see you running up here without it."

Jill could feel the steam building in her veins, chugging up through her thudding heart, billowing along her neck, seeking escape. "How dare you! How dare you treat me like a child!"

"Do you really want to fight about this?"

"It's a little too late for that question."

"There're dangers all around here, Jill. I don't want you

running up here without some form of protection."

"I've never felt afraid or threatened."

"Just because you don't recognize the danger doesn't mean it's not there."

She poked him in the chest with his can of mace. "You know what you can do with your protection?"

To her utter amazement and fury, he began to laugh. "God almighty, you're a piece of work. I can't figure out what it is about you that gets my blood boiling."

"Don't laugh at me," she said through gritted teeth.

He unsettled her by running his fingers along her jaw. "I'm not laughing at you. I'm laughing at us. Get in the truck."

"I'm running," she managed to squeak out. The light touch of his fingers had left her racing pulse weak and thready.

"So run to my place. With the mace," he added with an annoyingly sinful lift of his brows. "I want to see you."

"You're seeing me now."

He ducked his head and brushed his lips along the side of her neck. "Don't make me beg."

"Okay," she said in a throaty whisper. "But only because I want to and not because you told me to."

"Understood." He shot her a cocky grin and went back around the truck to slide behind the wheel. "Be careful," he called through the half open window.

"I always am." Except now, she wanted to say as his truck moved slowly past her and disappeared around the next bend. Now she wanted to throw caution to the wind and explore just how wild she could get.

***

Ty picked up his clothes from around his room and tossed them in the laundry machine, setting the load to clean. He looked around the cabin trying to see what he could improve in the next few minutes before Jill stopped by. If she stopped by.

He started in the bathroom after taking a quick shower. He wasn't a pig. Both his mother and father had never let him get away with leaving his towels on the floor or going for too long before cleaning the fixtures. A quick clean up wouldn't hurt when trying to impress the girl who'd just ripped him a new one and then melted in front of his eyes.

How was he supposed to resist her intoxicating combination of fire and ice? He'd been in one hell of a bad mood before he almost ran her down, a bad mood that even an afternoon spent on a beautiful stretch of private river couldn't cure. In his young life, he'd found a day spent fishing cured pretty much everything that ailed him. But not this time. Not when the outing had been a ruse for warning him away from the one thing he wanted most.

He'd let Lyle's words sink in all afternoon. Jill was vulnerable. He knew that. Anyone with a set of eyes could tell she couldn't see two steps in front of her now and that it made a driven woman like her uneasy. He didn't want to complicate her life, but he'd be damned if he was going to walk away from her based on one person's assessment that he'd only add to her troubles. It seemed to him that having a person genuinely care made everything better, not worse.

If Ty could make her feel just an inkling of what she made him feel, then he knew walking away wasn't in anyone's best interest.

He finished with the bathroom, washed his hands in the kitchen sink, and popped the top on a bottle of beer when he heard a knock on the door. He set his beer on the crate that served as a coffee table, rubbed his hands over his face, and opened the door. He eased his shoulder against the frame when she stood on the small stoop stretching her calves on the low stair.

"I'm only here to return your mace." She held out the can.

He watched as that fascinating line of irritation formed between her brows. "It's yours to keep."

"I managed to run five miles and didn't see anything larger than a squirrel."

"This time," he said, rubbing his stomach where it began to ache as it always did when he looked at her.

She reached out to grab his hand, probably intending to pass off the mace, but Ty managed to circle her wrist before she could make the exchange. "Do you want me to use this on you?" she asked.

"I'd hope you'd use it on anyone you found threatening. Am I threatening you, Jill?"

"You're threatening my patience," she admitted. "Does that count?"

"It might, if I thought you had any to begin with."

She huffed out a breath and tried to pull her hand free. "Is this a seduction technique, Ty? Because, really, manhandling went out with the Dark Ages."

He dropped her wrist and stood back, inviting her in with the wave of his hand. "I haven't even begun to seduce you yet."

She rolled her eyes, marched inside, and slammed the can of mace on the coffee table next to his forgotten beer. When he noticed the slight hesitation in her gait, he put a gentle hand on her shoulder. "Your leg hurts?"

"It's just a little sore. I'll ice it when I get home."

He walked past her to the freezer and pulled out an ice bag. "Here," he tossed the bag at her face, "ice it now. You don't want to wait."

She sighed and sat down on the couch and lifted her leg, gently placing the bag on her calf where a three-inch scar marred what was an otherwise flawless stretch of golden skin.

"Do you want a towel to go under that?"

"No, it's fine."

He joined her in the den, picking up his beer before taking a seat at the other end of the couch. "Beer?" he offered.

"No, thanks, but I'd love a water."

"Coming right up."

He filled a glass, delivered it to her, and watched her look around the cabin as he resumed his perch on the couch. "So what do you think?"

She pursed her lips. "Not bad. Relatively clean for a bachelor."

He chuckled when she ran a finger along the end table to check for dust. Finding nothing to comment about, she leveled those caramel eyes on him. They stared at one another as dust motes danced in the shaft of sunlight from the window.

"You really need to quit showering every time I take a run. It's annoying when you smell better than I do."

"Who said you smell bad?"

She shook her head and readjusted the bag on her leg.

He scooched closer, lifted her legs, and placed them on his thighs, holding the ice bag to her incision site. He nodded toward her calf. "Does it bother you often?"

"Not usually. I think the hills may have aggravated it a bit."

"Too much too soon?" he asked.

That line between her brows was back, along with a scathing glance in his direction. "I can handle a mountain run."

As if she were a wild animal that needed taming, he began to rub her knee with his free hand. "Never said otherwise."

She sat staring at the glass in her hand. The way her shoulders slouched and the corners of her mouth tilted down in a sexy pout, she seemed as if she were carrying a heavy load. "Sometimes it feels like I'll never compete again."

"Yes, you will." At her pointed stare, he said, "Maybe not professionally, but for pleasure."

"It's hard to accept it'll only be for pleasure when it's all I've ever wanted. All I've ever dreamed of." She looked up at him, her owlish eyes full of pain. "Do you have any idea what it's like to lose the one thing you've always wanted?"

"No." He needed to tread lightly because she wasn't anywhere near ready to hear what he had to say. "You have to have known this day would come, the day you couldn't or wouldn't compete anymore."

"Of course I did, but I thought it would be after I'd won something, not before I even got the chance to try."

"Fair enough." He continued to rub her knee. "What did you see yourself doing when it was all over?"

"I don't know," she said in the toneless voice of a petulant three year old. Her arms hung from her slumped shoulders like unmanned oars on a drifting boat. "Coaching?"

"You think you've got the patience to coach?"

"You don't?"

"No."

"Well, thanks for the pep talk, Ty. You've really worked your magic." When she tried to get up, he held her legs firm.

"Why? Because I won't let you feel sorry for yourself? You're young, you're healthy, you're—"

"I don't think a bum leg counts as healthy."

"A bum leg is nothing in the scheme of things. Ask any war vet what he thinks about your bum leg."

She huffed out an irritated breath and he gentled his hold.

"You've got your whole life ahead of you," Ty said. "You've had amazing experiences, worked like a dog, and now you're moving on. So the after part comes a little sooner than planned. As an athlete, it's a risk you've always known was there."

"I never thought it would happen to me."

"That's what made you so good. When you think you're invincible, you're unbeatable."

"I've never felt invincible, but I always knew I could hang with the best. I miss feeling that way."

"I didn't really know you back then, but I imagine I like you better this way. I'd bet you were hell on wheels with an ego to match."

"I was never hell on wheels, but I was good. A part of me wants to be again."

"You can be. If that's what you want. Your dad believed you could compete at an elite level again."

"I don't know what I want." She shrugged her shoulders and gave him a sidelong glance. "You're an awfully good listener. You must have spent the morning on the river."

"I did. Met your friend Lyle and fished his ranch." He watched her as he took a sip. Her face gave nothing away.

"How was it?"

After pulling his eyes from where her shapely legs rested upon his lap, he said, "Very enlightening."

"Enlightening? I thought fishing was about fish. I didn't realize you were searching for the meaning of life."

"It can be about both. Isn't running more than exercise? Doesn't it clear your head?"

"Yes," she said quickly. "It does. When I let it."

"When you let it?"

She leaned back against the cushions, lifting her chest in the process. He willed his eyes to stay on her face.

"Sometimes I can't shut my mind off and I get careless."

"Is that what happened when you broke your leg?"

She lifted her brows suggestively. "I got distracted when I broke my leg."

"Yeah? So did I. I've been distracted for almost a year now."

She swallowed audibly and averted her eyes. Not ready to hear that, he noted when she shifted again and changed the subject. "We're having a big party at The Tap on Wednesday night to celebrate Olivia's birthday."

"I heard."

"Are you coming?"

"Am I invited?"

She lifted a shoulder and peeked at him from under her lashes. "I wouldn't bring it up if you weren't."

"Then I'll be there." He reached for her hand where it rested against her flat stomach and began playing with her fingers. They were so soft, the nails clipped short, and his thumb rubbed the callous on her writing hand. "But not because it's Olivia's birthday and not because it's a party. I'll be there to see you." He linked their fingers as she stared at him, all bluster gone, and in its place, he sensed an innocent pining. How had she gone so long without someone, anyone making her feel special?

"You'd better not tell that to the birthday girl. She's determined to be the center of attention."

"She never is when you're around."

"Ha! That's where you're wrong or delusional."

Ty leaned closer, bringing his arms to rest by her hips,

encapsulating her in the corner of the couch. "I think it's called enchanted."

When her eyes dropped to his mouth, he didn't hesitate. He could barely think through the need to taste her. He'd lied when he said she didn't smell. She smelled like wildflowers and the soil where they flourished. She smelled like freedom, and when she arched to meet him, he tasted victory.

He brushed his lips against hers and pulled back, triumphant when her eyes remained dark and heavy with pleasure. Their gazes locked as he tasted her chin, the delicate skin under her ear, and as he sunk his teeth into her bottom lip. She moaned and linked her fingers behind his head, pulling him closer and probing his mouth with her tongue.

If she knew what a thin hold Ty had on his tether, she wouldn't have opened for him, wouldn't have let a purr escape her lips as he ran his hands up her sides and brushed the edges of her breasts. She wouldn't have let her head fall back when he bit her nipple through the thin material of her shirt, still damp with sweat. Because she didn't know, because she couldn't possibly know how much he wanted to strip them both of their clothes and show her, he buried his lips in her neck and tasted the salty sweetness of her skin.

She wedged her palms up his chest and pushed him back. "I can't do this. I can't do this when I'm so sweaty and gross."

"Jill." Ty pleaded. "You can't know what you do to me."

She grabbed his face in her hands and brought his mouth back for one scorching kiss before pushing him away and gasping for breath. "Not like this, Ty. You flatter me more than I can say, but not like this."

Leaning back from her felt like fighting the pull of a magnet when everything in him wanted to bury himself inside her. "It won't ever happen until you say so, Jill."

"No, that's not what I mean. God, I can't think when you touch me." She kicked her legs free and stood up to pace the room. "I don't think they come much better than you, Tyler Bloodworth. But I'm not going to...we're not going to..."

"Take things to the next level?"

She nodded. "When I'm sweaty and gross and pissed off at my parents."

"Why are you pissed off at your parents?"

She let out a frustrated sigh and prowled around the small space like a caged tiger. Her just-under-the-surface energy didn't help his body to cool down from their encounter. He'd just experienced a taste of her wildness and hungered for more. "A number of reasons, but mostly because they can't understand my decision to quit training and they don't approve of my job."

"Do you think you did the right thing?" he asked.

"Yes. At least for now, I'd have to say yes."

"Do you like your job?"

"Yes. No one's more surprised than me at how much I like it. And I'm good at it, too." She stopped pacing to explain. "I don't mean to sound like I'm bragging, but I know when I'm good at something or not, and I'm good at this. The employees respect me, the vendors know I'm not going to take any crap, and the patrons continue to enjoy the food and beverages."

"I know Tommy's happy with the job you've been doing."

"I know. He's told me. He's a really great boss."

Ty stood up and moved to where Jill had turned to the window. He wrapped his arms around her and felt a piece of his heart click into place when she relaxed against his chest. "I'm sorry you were made to feel like less than what you are. Your dad can't separate his dreams from yours. Our parents don't always realize how hurtful their words can be."

"Oh, I don't know, Ty. I think he took aim today at the bull's-eye on my chest."

He kissed the side of her neck and had to force himself not to hold her tighter. "You're still standing."

"I think I'm technically leaning."

"Lean as long as you want."

CHAPTER 22

Olivia stared at her reflection in the mirror and swished her puckered lips from side to side. She'd tried on and rejected a mountain of outfits and still wasn't convinced the mini skirt and off the shoulder blouse was the best choice. She was turning twenty-three and she wanted to look more mature, if only for one night.

The men in the valley thought of her one way and one way only: Olivia Golden, Tommy's too sexy for her own good younger sister. Tonight she wanted to be sophisticated Olivia. Almost-teacher Olivia. And yes, sexy Olivia.

Jill came in wearing her bathrobe and carrying a pearl gray sundress. "How about this dress?" she asked. "It's strapless, the faux wrap creates a nice peek-a-boo effect with your legs, and the color would look great on you."

"Where'd you get this?" Olivia asked, snatching the dress from her roommate and holding it in front of her by the mirror.

"I wore it to my brother's graduation. It's classy and sexy. Isn't that the look you were going for?"

"Exactly what I was looking for." Olivia started stripping out of the skirt and top and had the dress on in less than thirty seconds. "I love it, Jill." She turned around to admire how her tanned and muscular back and arms looked from the rear view. "It wows from the front and the back. Do you mind?"

"Of course not. You look amazing."

Olivia squeezed Jill and gave her the up-down. "What are you going to wear?"

"Good question. I know I'm not officially working tonight, but my managing the restaurant adds an element that has my brain all fuddled."

"Oh, please. The only thing fuddling your brain is Tyler Bloodworth."

Jill rolled her eyes.

"Why can't you admit you're totally into him? You spend every waking moment either with him or thinking about him. More importantly, he's totally into you and everybody knows it."

"He's so...I'm just..." She flopped onto the only corner of Olivia's bed that wasn't covered in clothes. "I keep waiting for the other shoe to drop."

"What other shoe?"

"Come on, Olivia. He's so out of my league. I feel like the minute I let on that I'm into him, which, of course I completely am because, hello, who wouldn't be, he's going to realize what a dork I am and dump me. I'll end up looking like a fool."

Olivia pulled her up by the arms so they stood toe to toe. "I've never seen a guy as attracted as Ty is to you. When you went running together, he stood at the window so he could watch for you. He *told* me he really likes you. No guy would tell a girl's roommate he likes her if he was going to dump her when she responded. As a matter of fact, I wouldn't be at all surprised if he came back to the Lower Fork for the sole purpose of starting something up with you."

When Jill bit her lower lip and slanted her eyes away, Olivia grabbed her shoulders. "What?" she asked.

"Nothing."

"That look was not nothing. What is it? Did he tell you he came back because of you?"

"No. Don't be silly."

"But?" Olivia prodded.

"But he did say something that made me wonder."

"Tell me! If I have to pull this out of you piece by piece, we're going to miss my party."

"I told him I got distracted when I broke my leg, because I'd looked over at him when I stepped on the rock and fell, and he said he'd been distracted for almost a year now."

Olivia cocked her head and watched Jill watching her reaction. "I'd say that's as good as an admission. Holy shit, Jill, the guy's got it bad. You are so freaking lucky."

"I know, I mean, that's crazy, right? We never did anything other than exchange a few looks last summer."

"You never told me about any looks."

"If I'd told you the hottest guy I'd ever seen, a guy with a girlfriend that flew out here from the east coast to see him, was giving me looks, you'd have told me I was crazy."

"Depends on the looks. Were they hot and smoldering?"

Jill slapped her arm and headed for her room. "You forgot about the drooling."

Olivia eyed her pile of clothes and began rifling through her discards. "That'll be tonight," she promised.

***

"I can't believe you talked me into wearing this," Jill said as she tugged at the hem of Olivia's short shorts. "I feel like an idiot."

"You look hot," Olivia said. "I can't wait to see the look on Ty's face when he gets a load of you."

"He'll probably ask me what the hell I was thinking." She tried to catch her reflection in some of the metal appliances of The Tap's kitchen, but all she could see was her top half. That was bad enough. How she'd let Olivia bully her into wearing short shorts and a form fitting flannel shirt rolled up her arms, cinch tied above her waist, and unbuttoned down to her bra, she'd never know. At least she'd talked Olivia into her red cowboy boots and not the three-inch kitten heels Olivia wanted her to wear.

When she tried to button her top higher, Olivia slapped her hands away. "Stop it. Stop fidgeting and relax. He's going to swallow his tongue."

"We already established that he likes me the way I am. Why do we have to play these stupid games?"

"Because they're fun. Here." Olivia handed her another shot of tequila and lifted her own tiny glass filled to the brim. "To the men who want us and the women who want to be us."

Jill downed the shot and made a face as the tequila warmed her empty and nervous stomach. "I feel kinda floaty."

"Perfect. Time for your entrance." She pushed Jill toward the kitchen door, but stopped and shoved Jill behind her. "Let me go first because I want to see Ty's face when you come in."

"Are you sure he's still here?"

"Yes, I'm sure. If you don't quit hiding back here in the kitchen, he's going to commandeer the microphone and start paging you." She fluffed her hair and struck a pose. "How do I look?"

"You look amazing, but I think you'd look better if we switched outfits."

"Not a chance. I'd just look like myself if I wore that. In this dress, I look sophisticated. And sexy."

Jill grabbed Olivia's arm before she could push through the door. "Did you happen to notice him doing something with his hands when he saw you?"

"What do you mean, something with his hands?"

Jill tried to mimic the move she'd seen Ty perform almost every time he first glanced at her. "He does this kind of…tummy rub when he sees me. I want to know if he did it when he saw you."

"No. He gave me a friendly hug, told me happy birthday, and asked where you were."

"Will you just watch and see if he does it?"

"A tummy rub?"

"Just trust me and pay attention."

"Whatever." Olivia flipped her hair. "Wait a couple of minutes before you come out so I have time to get in position."

"Okay."

Jill heard more calls and birthday wishes as she stretched her neck and shook her hands. She felt as though she were about to audition for a singing show in front of a live audience. When the clock passed the two-minute mark, she eased the door open, said a small prayer, and tried to walk as casually as possible with the feel of air dusting the bottom of her butt cheeks.

The bar was crowded with people sipping drinks and munching on appetizers. Tommy spotted her first and let out a low whistle through his teeth. "Kind of a different look for you, Jill. Has Ty seen you yet?"

She could feel her cheeks heating as her eyes scanned the room. "No." She didn't see Ty anywhere, so she sidled up next to Tommy and started taking drink orders.

"Oh, no, you don't," he said as he drew a draft beer from the tap. "You're not on tonight and I'm not paying you overtime."

"I'm just helping out."

He delivered the beer, turned and grabbed her shoulders, and pushed her out from behind the bar. "Go. Olivia's orders. Just for today, she gets her way."

"But…"

"No buts, but I've gotta say yours is looking very nice in those shorts."

Olivia appeared from out of nowhere and grabbed Jill's hand. "Loverboy's at a table by the stage," she whispered in Jill's ear. "No belly rub for me, and I can't wait until he sees you." She waved her hand in the air at her brother. "Two tequila shots for the birthday girl and her best friend."

She handed Jill a shot. "To the men who want us and the women who want to be us," Olivia shouted before knocking back her shot to the hoots of the crowd. "Drink up, girlfriend."

Jill obliged, figuring they didn't call it a shot of courage for nothing. When Olivia pulled the empty glass from her hand, dragged Jill through the crowd, and brought her to a stop in front of Ty's table, Jill had to work hard at not wobbling.

Ty was laughing at something Eddie said, his chair tipped back, the beer in his hand on the way to his mouth. When he turned his head and spotted her, the front legs of the chair hit the ground, the beer slopped over the lip of the mug, and his hand settled just under his rib cage. "Jill?" he choked as his eyes made quick work of her outfit.

"Hi," was all she could manage.

Eddie slapped his beer on the table and comically scanned her up and down. "Holy shit, Jilly. You want to dance?" His eyes never made it to her face.

The laughter died from Jill's tongue when she stole a look at Ty's stunned expression. "Ahh, no, thanks."

Olivia knocked Jill with her elbow when Ty started rubbing his hand over his abdomen. "I've been looking for you," he said.

"Now you found me." The stupefied look on his face that only moments ago had her ready to flee suddenly felt like a giant rocket blast to her ego. It didn't hurt that Eddie hadn't taken his eyes off her legs. She leaned forward, giving him a bird's eye view of her cleavage, took a sip from Ty's mug, licked her lips, and resumed her position in front of the table. One of the trio of musicians Tommy had hired whistled at her backside while tuning his guitar.

Ty shot to his feet at the same time the lead singer spoke into the microphone directing everyone to sing 'Happy Birthday' to Olivia as she joined him on stage and basked in the attention. Ty moved to stand at Jill's side, slipping his hand around her waist. "Are you trying to kill me?" he asked. "Or get me killed?"

"Excuse me?" He only scowled at her when she batted her eyelashes.

"Are you drunk?"

She swiveled around and tucked her hands into his back pockets, pulling them chest-to-chest. Of course she was drunk. She'd never have the nerve to grab him in public otherwise.

"Not really."

"Not really? Christ," he said through gritted teeth when he grabbed her hips. She felt his fingers graze the skin of her backside. "I don't even want to see what these shorts aren't covering from behind."

She wiggled her butt and he groaned, pulling her tighter. Olivia pulled Jill's hand from his pocket just as she reached up to nip at his pouting lip. "It's ladies dance."

Ty loosened his grip, but didn't let go. "Why don't you sit this one out?"

Jill felt torn between her loyalty to Olivia and her desire to be with Ty.

Olivia made the decision for her, pulling on her arm. "No way, party pooper," Olivia said. "She was mine first. You just have a seat and you can have her when I'm done."

CHAPTER 23

Ty sucked in a breath as Olivia whipped Jill around and he got a look at her flipside. He could only stand and stare as Olivia pulled Jill into the center of the dance floor and they began a complicated two step that made Jill's mile long legs flex and jiggle in the muted light. Ty didn't have to glance around to know that every set of male eyes watched her gorgeous ass slide and bump along to the tune.

If he got out of the bar without getting into a fistfight, it would be a freaking miracle. As if to test the theory, Lyle came to a stop next to Ty.

"Well, I see Olivia's birthday wish came true," he said.

Ty wanted to glare at Lyle, but he couldn't drag his eyes away from Jill. "What do you mean?"

"Jill. Last year Olivia talked her into skinny-dipping at the hot springs in Grover. I guess this year they're playing dress up?"

"I think Jill's drunk."

Lyle laughed. "She'd have to be to wear those shorts." He took a sip from his long neck beer. "Damn, I don't envy you tonight."

"How so?" Ty asked.

"Jill doesn't drink much. When she does...let's just say

139

you're going to have your hands full."

"As long as they're my hands."

When the song changed and a young red head slipped his palms onto Jill's hips to lead her around the floor, Ty shoved his beer at Lyle and pushed through the crowd.

Olivia blocked his way by placing two hands on his chest. "Lighten up, Indiana Jones. She's having fun."

"She can have fun with me. How much has she had to drink?"

"What are you, her keeper?"

"I'm the guy who plans to keep her upright, so I'd like to know how much she's consumed."

"A shot or two or four."

"Of what?"

"Tequila."

Lyle chuckled next to them. "Olivia, you just love stirring the pot."

"Shut up, Lyle. You always think you know best."

"It'd be hard not to know better than you."

"What are you two talking about?" Ty asked.

"Jill gets a little crazy on tequila," Lyle said with a slap to his back. "You'll enjoy it at first, until she's puking her guts up all night."

Ty had heard enough and he'd seen enough of the red head's wandering hands to know he needed to rescue Jill and fast. He cut in without asking and considered himself the better man for not shoving his fist into the kid's face when he grumbled and then stalked off.

"Ummm, you're back," Jill purred and crawled her fingertips up his chest and linked her hands behind his neck. "I was hoping you hadn't left."

Uh oh. She was drunker than he'd first suspected and getting looser by the minute. Her heavy lidded eyes and dilated pupils had him hoping he could get her home before she started puking. "I'm not leaving without you."

"I'm not ready to leave yet." And to prove it, she flipped around in his arms, slithered her backside down his legs and up again before lifting her arms up and doing it once more.

"Jill." He snagged her wrists, crossed her arms over her chest, and held her backside snug against his crotch. "Baby, you gotta stop."

"Why?" She giggled and flipped around in his arms when he loosened his grip. "Don't you like it?"

Ty gritted his teeth. "Too much. But you're drunk and we're not alone."

"I wish we were alone," she said in a throaty whisper. "You do things to me, Tyler, without even trying." She nipped at his chin and he felt his knees go weak. "You make me forget who I am, what I am, what I want to be. All I want to be when you're around is yours."

It was everything he wanted to hear and nothing she would remember saying. Before he could even muster a reply, the song changed. She squealed in his ear and started bopping around the dance floor, her hair a riot around her face as she swung her head to and fro with the beat. Olivia appeared from out of nowhere and the two of them took over the small space in a swirl of motion.

Ty made a beeline for the bar. It only took a minute for Tommy to work his way down to where Ty stood with his eyes glued to Jill.

"What can I get you, man?" Tommy asked.

"A large glass of water."

"Water?" Tommy's brows shot up. "You done already?"

"Jill's wasted. I need to get something in her to stem the bleeding."

Tommy shook his head and filled a plastic glass with ice. "That's Olivia. She gets her drunk every year. I should have warned you."

Ty accepted the drink. "Yes, you should have."

He waited by the edge of the dance floor until the song changed to something slow. Olivia was spun around by one of her fellow rafting guides and Jill stumbled into Ty's arms. He handed her the water and ordered her to drink. She gulped it greedily.

She spotted Lyle standing in a group and called his name. They each took a step toward one another and embraced. Ty choked back a growl when Lyle's hand grazed the skin between the top of Jill's shorts and the bottom of her shirt. Lyle caught his warning glare and stepped back.

"You're not driving tonight, right?" Lyle asked.

"Nope. Ty's taking me home." She reached out and snaked her arm around his waist while resting her head on his shoulder. She closed her eyes for a few seconds and then looked up at Ty. "Is it just me, or is the room spinning?"

"That's it." Ty swung her up into his arms and made his way through the crowd toward the door. "I'm taking you home."

"Now?"

"Now." While the only one he needed to fight was her.

***

Jill peeled her eyes open one at a time. It wasn't hard to do considering one was smashed to the edge of the mattress and the other felt like it was keeping her pulse. She tried to jerk her head upright when she realized the sun shining through the window was much brighter than it should have been at her usual waking time of six thirty, but her head protested and she groaned into her pillow.

She felt a hand on her waist and slowly rolled over. Ty lay on his side, tucked neatly under her covers, his chiseled chest bare, his eyes on hers. "How you feeling?" he asked, his voice froggy from sleep.

"Is there a word that means both road kill and completely mortified?"

Ty lifted the corner of his mouth. "Shitty?"

"That pretty much covers it." She placed a hand to her head and closed her eyes. God only knew what she looked like. He probably wanted to get out of there as quickly as possible. "What happened?"

"Well, you managed to attract every guy in a fifty mile radius with your outfit and your dance moves before throwing up multiple times in the bathroom when I got you home."

She shoved the pillow over her head. "Tell me you didn't see that."

He pulled the pillow away. "Say again?"

"Please tell me I excused myself and hurled into the toilet without any assistance."

"I could, but then I'd be lying."

"Oh, God. I'm so sorry."

"Don't be. You're a cute drunk."

"No, I'm not. I'm a completely helpless dimwit who ends the night puking. What's cute about that?"

Ty rubbed his hand over her stomach where, thankfully, she wore a tank top and sleeping shorts. She couldn't tear her eyes away from the way his pectoral muscles bunched when he moved his arm.

"You're very dainty when you throw up and you apologized a lot."

"A dainty vomiter? That's a new one."

He brushed the hair away from her face and twirled a lock of her hair around his finger. "And you say the most interesting things."

She slammed her hands over her face. "Don't tell me. Please, let me believe I become witty and charming when I'm drunk."

"Oh, you were charming, all right. Let's just say you were very complimentary on the ride home."

She peeked at him from behind her fingers. "I don't even remember the ride home. I'm never drinking again."

"Says the woman who manages a bar."

"Oh no. I've got to get to work." She glanced at the clock on her bedside table. "My shift starts in an hour."

"I called Tommy. He got Meredith to fill in, but he said there's a delivery truck coming in between three and five he'd like you to cover."

"Thank God." She turned on her side and reached out for his hand. "Thank you, Tyler. What a bust last night was for you. I'm sorry I ruined it."

"Jill. I wanted to spend the night with you and I did." His grin had her queasy stomach doing backflips. "I got a vertical lap dance and a visual that's burned on my brain, thank you very much. I got to help a woman I care about, a woman so stubborn she has to be falling down drunk to let me help her, and I got to wake up with you."

The cheerleader in Jill's belly crashed against her raw stomach lining. "Did we…"

Ty laughed out loud. "No, we didn't. I'd kinda for like you to remember when we make love."

When. It didn't escape her foggy brain that he said *when.* The cheerleader began doing cartwheels. "I'm sure that'll be brand worthy. On the brain," she added when his brows shot together.

"I'm sure it will." He sat up and tossed back the cover. His boxers sported dancing fish. "I've got a float in an hour. Do you mind if I use your shower?"

"I'd say you earned it." She eased up on her elbow and looked her fill as he walked toward the bathroom. "Ty?"

"Yeah?"

"How'd I get in my pajamas?"

"Olivia was home by then. I had her help you."

Jill stared at him in awe. He talked about when they'd make love in almost the same breath he explained that he hadn't undressed her while she was drunk. "I'm not perfect, Jill. I wanted to, but I want you to remember that, too."

When the door shut behind him, she collapsed onto the pillow. "You are perfect, Ty. In every way that counts."

CHAPTER 24

Olivia sat on the couch cradling the mug of coffee in her hands after downing two aspirins and a half a bagel. It was a curse that she could drink herself silly and be unable to sleep. Today was no different. But if she had been able to sleep, she would have missed seeing Ty tiptoe out of Jill's room holding his shoes.

"You don't have to sneak out, you know."

He let out a startled gasp. "You scared the life out of me." He sat on the chair to put on his boots. "I thought you'd be out until at least noon."

"I wish." She took a sip of coffee and set the mug on the table. "How's she doing?"

"She's felt better. She's back asleep."

"Thanks for taking care of her last night."

Ty sat forward and rested his forearms on his thighs, his hands dangling between his knees. "I understand this is a yearly ritual for you. Getting Jill drunk on your birthday."

"Yes, it's a tradition of sorts. It didn't take much this year since apparently she hadn't eaten anything before we got started."

"Don't you think that's a little irresponsible? Who would have taken care of her when you were dancing the night away if I hadn't been there?"

"She's twenty-two years old. She can get drunk without a babysitter. Besides," she added as he continued to scowl at her, "Lyle would have been happy to help."

"I'm sure he would have," Ty mumbled. He rubbed his hands over his face. "What's the deal with that guy anyway?"

Olivia shrugged. "They're friends. They used to run together. He's a total know-it-all who thinks nobody's good enough for Jill." She lifted her mug and took a sip, eyeing him as she did. "He's probably in love with her."

"I knew it." Ty shot to his feet. "All that talk about breaking her heart."

"Excuse me?" Olivia asked. Now *this* was getting interesting.

"Nothing." He grabbed his keys from the counter and opened the door. "Do me a favor, would you?"

"Sure."

"Jill's got to be at the bar by three. Make sure she's up?"

"By three?" Olivia looked at the clock on the wall and stretched out her legs. His eyes didn't even move from her face. Damn it, she was losing her touch. "She won't be late."

At ten-thirty, when Olivia was well into a Little House on the Prairie marathon, Jill stumbled out of her room, her hair wet, her face scrubbed clean of makeup. Olivia sat up and patted the couch in invitation for Jill to join her.

"Sorry I ruined your birthday," Jill said after plopping down and burrowing her legs under the cover Olivia had pulled from her bed.

"Who said you ruined my birthday?"

"I hardly remember anything past dancing with you. God only knows what I said or did after."

"I'm guessing you didn't do the deed with Mr. Hottie because I'm betting you wouldn't forget."

Jill slammed her hands over her face. "I had to ask him if we did. How pathetic is that?"

"Apparently he didn't think so. I swear, Jill, that boy is

whipped."

Jill pulled the cover up and tucked her feet under Olivia's outstretched legs. "Did you help me into my PJs last night?"

Olivia chuckled at the memory. Neither one of them could stand on their own, so they'd used each other for balance. "Above and beyond. You owe me."

"How bad was it?"

"What do you mean?"

"Was there vomit everywhere? Was Ty pissed?"

"No, either you puked in the toilet or Ty had it cleaned up by the time I got home. And no, your boyfriend has an endless well of patience for all things Jill."

"He's...I think I dreamed him. He's so perfect he can't be real."

"He's real enough to be jealous."

Jill sat up. "What do you mean?"

"He said something about Lyle warning him off."

Jill's eyes got so big, Olivia thought she'd march straight to Lyle's house and read him the riot act. She was feeling just bad enough to keep her seat. "Tell me you're kidding."

"I know you love Lyle, but he's worse than a woman, butting his nose in where it doesn't belong."

"Why would he do that?" Jill asked. "I know he's not jealous. We tried the whole romance thing and it didn't feel right."

"Right for you or right for him?"

"Right for either of us." She scrunched down into the cushions and pulled the blanket up to her chin. "I so don't need this right now."

"Yeah, it must be hell having two men fight over you."

"Speaking of jealous..."

Olivia bit back a denial. She *was* jealous and it stung. "Sue me. I woke up alone this morning. But I did dance with Del."

"Who's Del?" Jill asked.

"He's the new raft guide. He's a little young and way green on the water, but he's totally cute."

"What did Tommy say?"

"What he always says. He warned Del to stay away from his sister or he'd lose his job."

"So he's now more of a challenge?" Jill guessed.

"Absolutely. Besides," Olivia said, "if you and Ty can work and play together, why can't Del and I?"

***

Lyle popped his head through the crack in Jill's office door. Her feisty nature seemed a little dim as she sat typing on the laptop. Her skin seemed especially pale against her dark hair and black t-shirt. He knocked and offered a sympathetic smile. "How ya feeling?"

"Oh, God." Jill dropped her head in her hands. "I forgot I saw you, too."

"I saw a lot more of you then you saw of me." Lyle came in and stretched out as he sat in the metal chair facing Jill's desk. "What was up with the outfit?"

"I'll give you one guess," Jill said.

"Olivia?"

"Bingo. You know she gets her way on her birthday."

"I don't know why you let her manipulate you like that."

Jill sat up straighter behind her desk. He knew a little poke to her sensitive spot would put some color back in her cheeks. "I don't let her manipulate me. She's my friend. She enjoys herself on her birthday and I play along for her sake. If I'd put my foot down, she would have backed off."

"So you wanted to flash your ass in front of everyone?"

"No." Jill's eyes flared. "I got caught up in her enthusiasm after drinking a couple of shots. It was stupid," she admitted. "But I never said I was perfect." She stood up and paced to the window. "How bad was it?"

"A little fuzzy on the details?" he asked.

The back of her head bobbed as she nodded. "You earned the undying respect and admiration of every guide south of the Rio Grande. But don't worry," he added with a lift of his hand, "your boyfriend made sure everyone knew you were taken."

She spun around. He could tell by her pinched expression

he'd hit a nerve. "In other words, I made a fool of myself."

Lyle stood up and faced her across the desk. "Jill, you were drunk at a bar. Big deal. It's not a front page story."

"I work here. I'm trying to earn the respect of my boss and my employees."

"Didn't you hear me? You did earn their respect."

She picked up a notepad and threw it at his head. He ducked as it sailed over his shoulder. "Why are you here?" she asked.

"Mom asked me to check on the tile she ordered at Barton's design store. Figured I'd make sure you were still among the living and kill two birds with one stone."

"You'd better hurry if you want to catch her. Tommy's holding a community meeting about the proposed development and I know Tracy Barton's in favor of the project. She thinks it'll bring a lot of business to her store."

"This whole development is really stirring people up. It's all anyone's talking about these days. You'd think, with the rodeo next week, they'd have better things to talk about."

Jill settled behind her desk and laid her hands on the keyboard. "As long as they're not talking about my ass, I don't care what they're talking about."

Lyle chuckled as he walked out of her office and out into the bright afternoon sun. He skirted the hood of his SUV, shifting his sunglasses into place when a sporty red convertible pulled into the lot. He stopped in the act of opening the door and turned to greet Jill's mom. "Bobbie Jennings. What are you doing out here on this fine day?"

She eased out of the car and dragged him into a full body hug. How the woman with the infectious laugh and contagious smile had given birth to her grumpy daughter, Lyle would never know. She stood back and gazed at him as if he'd presented her with a gleaming diamond.

"Lyle! I didn't expect to see you all the way out here in the Lower Fork. How are you?"

"I'm good, Bobbie. Just stopped in to say hi to Jill on my way to get Mom's tile at Barton's."

"Ooohhh, is she redoing her kitchen again?"

"No, they're fixing up the bathroom in the caretaker's house."

"How is Miguel?" Bobbie asked. "I heard his back's been bothering him again."

"Good as new, thank God. Dodge wasn't fun to be around when Miguel was laid up in bed for a week."

Lyle scowled when he glanced across the lot to the fly shop and Ty walked out with a couple of older men in tow. Bobbie followed his stare.

"Do you know that young man?" Bobbie asked.

"He's a fishing guide from North Carolina." Lyle searched Bobbie's eyes when he detected a note of curiosity in her voice. "Why do you ask?"

"I went by Jill's apartment yesterday to drop off Olivia's present." She lifted the gift bag from the back seat of the car. "I saw him coming out as I pulled in the parking lot. I didn't want to make the poor girl feel awkward by showing up right after her man had left."

Lyle lifted his brows in surprise. He knew Bobbie was open-minded, but watching a man leave her daughter's apartment early in the morning had to have been uncomfortable. God knew his mother would have blown her lid if she'd caught a girl sneaking out of his room.

"Have you seen Olivia?" she asked.

"No. You could check the raft shop."

"I will. If she's not around, I could leave it with Jill."

Lyle couldn't let this opportunity to slip through his fingers. "So what do you think about him?" Lyle asked.

"Who?"

"Tyler." When Bobbie stared at him blankly, Lyle nodded with his head in Ty's direction. "Jill's boyfriend."

In an almost comical jaw drop, Bobbie muttered, "*Jill's* boyfriend?"

Oh no. He'd done it again. "I gotta go, Mrs. Jennings." He patted her on the arm, hopped into his SUV, and got the hell out of there as fast as he could.

CHAPTER 25

Ty jogged back from the dock to the fly shop when he realized he'd left his dry bag on the counter before his afternoon float. When he spotted the same woman standing in the parking lot he'd seen moments before wearing a trendy outfit and a befuddled expression, he walked over to offer her assistance.

"You look a little lost," he said. "Can I help you find something?"

Her whole body shook as if he'd woken her from a trance. "Oh, no. I'm fine, thank you."

"You sure?" he asked. She seemed more confused than ever, staring at him as if trying to read something on his face.

"Mom?"

Ty turned around to find Jill, in jeans and a black shirt, striding toward them. She'd left her hair down and it bounced around her face as she walked. As usual, the sight of her left him more than a little dazed himself.

"Jill," the woman said. "Do you feel okay? You look pale."

Jill snuck a glance at Ty before a patch of red flooded her cheeks. "I'm fine. What are you doing here?"

She lifted the bag in her hand. "I came by to drop off Olivia's birthday gift."

"Oh." Jill looked up at Ty. "Have you met Tyler?"

Her mom's mouth turned down in a near mimic of Jill's when she was upset. How had he managed to tick her mom off already?

"No, I haven't." She held out her hand. "Bobbie Jennings."

Ty shook her hand and painted on his most friendly smile. "Tyler Bloodworth. It's a pleasure to meet you, Mrs. Jennings. I can see why Jill's so beautiful."

He may as well have called the woman a leper. "Thank you," she said with an accusing stare at her daughter.

Okay... Ty snuck a glance behind him to where his two clients were examining the fly rods on the dock. "I've got to get going. It was nice to meet you, Mrs. Jennings."

She gave him a curt nod of her head that felt like an arrow to his chest. "I'll call you later," he said to Jill before making a quick escape.

She nodded and bit her bottom lip. It felt like they were both in trouble. Great. He wasn't sure how he'd managed to screw up meeting her mom for the first time, but it was obvious he had.

***

"Well, that was certainly rude," Jill said to her mother after Tyler strode off. "Why were you so short with him?"

"Oh, I'm sorry." Her mother clutched a hand to her chest. "Did I insult your boyfriend?"

Jill's heart rate started doing a two-step. "My what?"

"Your boyfriend. At least I hope he is since I saw him sneaking out of your apartment first thing yesterday morning."

"Mom..."

"Don't try to deny it. Lyle confirmed he's your boyfriend. To think I condemned poor Olivia for having a man stay over at her place when all along it was you."

"If you'll stop reading me the riot act, I can explain."

Bobbie shook her head violently. "I'd rather not hear the details." She turned her face to the sun and closed her eyes before leveling an accusing stare at Jill. "I know I told you to do something wild, but really, Jill, who is this guy?"

"It's not what you think."

"It's not? He wasn't sneaking out of your apartment after spending the night with you?"

"Technically, yes, but nothing happened."

"Oh please," Bobbie said in a shrill voice. "Do you think I'm a fool? He's attractive, you're attractive, and you're both over the age of consent. I don't know why I'm so upset except for the fact that you have a boyfriend I knew nothing about."

"It happened kind of fast," Jill tried to defend herself.

"I'll say."

"Look, the last couple of times we talked, I was too busy defending myself to mention anything about Tyler."

Bobbie puckered her lips as if she'd tasted something sour.

"Come inside," Jill said. "Let's sit down and discuss this like adults instead of hurling insults at each other in the parking lot."

"I can't stay. Your brother's car is in the shop and I told him I'd pick him up from work."

"So you don't want to talk about Ty?"

"I do. But I don't have time right now. Bring him to lunch on Sunday."

"After the way you just treated him?" She raised her voice a full octave. "I don't think so."

Bobbie placed her hands on her hips and tucked her chin to her chest. "Jill Jennings. Are you ashamed of your family?"

Oh, brother. Her mother could lay it on thick. "Of course I'm not ashamed of my family."

"Good. I expect to see you and your boyfriend on Sunday."

Great. Just great.

CHAPTER 26

Jill was waiting on the dock when Ty came back from the float. He spotted her as his raft edged past the last bend, her legs dangling, her hair radiant in the dusky light. She stood up as he approached and stepped back as the two fishermen disembarked.

"I need to talk to you," she said and shoved her hands into her back pockets.

"Okay. I need to wrap this up first. Can you wait a few minutes?"

"No problem."

He watched her pace around his truck from inside the fly shop, picking at her nails and kicking dirt as the men settled their bill and left Ty a very nice tip. Jill was like a lit fuse when he finally approached her, her eyes a little bit wild and her hair scooped back into a messy ponytail.

"You spent four hours with them on the river." She shoved her hands into her front pockets. "Was it really necessary to recount every ripple of the water?"

"Part of the experience," he said and reached out a hand to steady her jittery movements. "You seem upset," Ty said, mimicking his dad's head tilt. "What's wrong?"

"I'm not upset. Well," she amended, "maybe a little. Okay,

I'm upset."

Ty laughed. "And people think you're moody, but clearly that's not true."

"What people?"

"Everyone. I thin—"

"Who's everyone? And why would they say that? I'm not moody."

Ty wanted to point out that her defensive stance and the line between her brows told a different story, but he knew better than to overstep. "I know you're not. It's your mouth."

"My mouth?" She let out one loud, skeptical snort. "What?"

"Your lips. They turn down at the edges, kinda like a pout. It's sexy."

"Sexy?" Another snort. "No one's ever called me sexy."

"That's because of your pouty mouth. And because you intimidate people."

"Do I intimidate you?"

"No."

"Why not?" she asked, the line back between those artful brows.

Ty shrugged. "I enjoy a complicated woman."

"Complicated?" She swung those caramel eyes in his direction. "You mean 'high maintenance.'"

"No, I mean multi-faceted, driven, unpredictable, and sexy as hell."

"Well," she said after a long pause. "You southern boys are certainly schooled in charm. When did you learn those lines? On the elementary school playground?"

"You see? Most women would take what I said as a compliment, but not a complicated woman like you." He brushed a finger to the end of her nose and considered himself lucky when she didn't try to bite his hand.

"My mother wants you to come over for Sunday lunch," Jill blurted out.

Ty felt like he'd been swooped up by a giant bird and placed on a tight wire between two mountains. No matter which direction he fell, there was hell to pay. "Oh."

"Oh? All you have to say is 'oh'?"

"What would you like me to say?" he asked. He took a step back when her cheeks turned pink and her hands fisted at her sides.

"She saw you leaving my apartment. She called you my boyfriend."

He couldn't stop the corners of his mouth from lifting at the way she said the word 'boyfriend' as if it tasted like lemons on her tongue. "Well, aren't I?"

"I guess...I don't know. We've never called this—" she waved her arm between them, "anything."

He took a tentative step forward. "Does that scare you?"

"What? Labeling this?" She shrugged and dropped her eyes to her hands where she'd clasped them in a white-knuckle grasp. "I don't know. If someone asked you who I was, what would you say?"

"As a matter of fact, the two men I took out this afternoon asked me that very question."

Her skeptical eyes shot to his face. "What did you say?"

He stepped closer, so close that he could see the flecks of gold in her eyes. "I told them you were my girl."

When she lifted her chin and placed a hand at the base of her throat, he trapped her between his body and the side of the truck. "You did?"

"I did. So, I suppose that makes me your boyfriend."

"I suppose it does." She moved her hand to rest it upon his chest. He wondered if she could feel his heart tripping against her palm. She lifted her hands to his head, winding her fingers through his hair and pulling his mouth down to hers.

Greedy. She assaulted his mouth with a hunger that had him leaning into her, aligning their bodies, begging for more than the kiss could provide. He dragged his mouth from hers as she scraped her nails down his shirt. "God, Jill, I want you. I want you so much I can hardly see straight."

"I know," she gasped. "I know." She arched against him and nipped at his neck before pulling back and looking up at him with a pitiful expression. "I have to run."

"Run? As in run, run? Now?" When he was ready to take her against the truck, propriety be damned?

"I'm too keyed up. I know myself and I have to get this out."

"Might I suggest another method of letting off steam?"

She laughed, throwing her head back and exposing a thin column of white skin he longed to mar with his teeth. "Go home," she said. "Let me run and then I'll come to you."

"Jill..." He gave it one last try, capturing her head in his hands and suckling her lips like wine until she was purring and boneless in his arms.

"I promise, Ty. Give me an hour, two tops. I'll be there. I want to be with you."

"Come home with me now."

"Wait for me?" she countered.

How could he not, when the need for her pulsed through him like poison. "Hurry."

***

The sky was alight with stars when Jill's car made its way up the steep incline toward Ty's cabin. The sound of the woods echoed through her open windows, beckoning her forward, urging her to speed when safety called for a steady hand and a cautious pace.

She felt nothing of caution tonight. Tonight she felt wild and reckless and free. Tonight she felt like a woman, more than she ever had in her life, racing along the gravel road to the spot where her lover waited.

Her lover.

She and Ty would be lovers tonight. She could hardly breathe through the impatience and fear. Her body felt swelled and ready, like a grape at the peak of ripeness just waiting to be plucked. Only Ty knew how to ease the ache that had burned deep within her for weeks. Months, really, when she thought back to last summer when he'd watch her from his porch.

His door opened as she pulled into the drive. He stood in

the doorway wearing a fresh t-shirt and jeans. His feet were bare. Somehow that one intimate flash of skin had her breath coming out in a shaky wave and her stomach smoldering with need. He didn't move from his perch, but watched her as she approached, his hand on his abdomen.

"I was worried you'd talk yourself out of coming during your run," he said when she stopped in front of him.

"I was trying to calm myself down." How did her voice sound so composed when she was fraught with anxiety?

He took her in from her flip-flops to where her jeans sat low on her hips and up to the thin blouse that covered her chest. His expression darkened as her nipples puckered under his stare. When his eyes met hers, she saw the hunger she felt reflected in his pupils. "Why are you scared?"

"I feel like I do before a race," she admitted.

His eyes flew to her chest before mocking her with a lifted brow. "How so?"

"Every time I stand on the starting line, I feel a little nervous and a whole lot excited. I'm not..." she bit her lip, "very experienced."

He reached out and clasped a lock of her hair, twisting it between his fingers. "Do you think that makes me want you any less? This isn't a performance, Jill. This is just you and me." He let his hand drop. "Do you know how many times I've dreamt of having you here? In my house? In my bed?"

He smelled like soap and the woods where he lived. "Take me to your bed, Tyler. I don't want to wait a second longer."

He crushed her to him, dragging her inside, slamming the screen closed with his foot. Lips locked, they bumped into a chair and the side table before he threw her over his shoulder and stalked down the hall to his bedroom, her laughter ringing through the halls. The only thing she registered was the wood paneling and a brown cover before Ty was all she could see, all she could hear, all she focus her attention upon.

She tasted the minty freshness of his toothpaste on her tongue, smelled the soap on his skin, and watched his jaw tighten as he lifted the shirt from her back.

"You're so beautiful," he said. "Your skin," he kissed a spot below her shoulder, "is so soft, so perfect." He drew his lips up her neck and back to her mouth. "This mouth. I can't get enough of this mouth."

She gathered his shirt in her hands, lifting slowly. It was so hard to concentrate when he was stealing her breath with his lips and her mind with the words he mumbled along her skin.

He sat up and finished the job, yanking off his shirt. Jill felt stunned by the sight of him before her. His wide shoulders lorded over a perfectly formed torso that narrowed to his waist. The dusting of golden hair felt furry beneath her fingers and formed a path that led her wandering fingers to the band of his jeans. She struggled with the button.

"Not so fast." His voice shook when he shooed her hands away. "I don't want it to be over so soon."

My God, she thought. He's as moved as I am. The knowledge that she could do to him what he'd done to her made something click inside of her. Or click off. She didn't think, she didn't analyze, she didn't measure. She simply let herself feel.

She felt the bunching of his muscles wherever she touched. She felt his breath hitch when she set her teeth on his shoulder and bit. She felt the length of him against her bare stomach and rocked her hips until he groaned.

She reached for his pants at the same time he unhooked her bra and tugged it off her arms. He nuzzled her breasts against his cheeks, past his lips, and finally, finally his tongue. She arched and let out a startled cry. The pulsing within her grew frantic.

She lowered the zipper on his pants and reached for him. "Jill," he said with gratitude or frustration, she couldn't tell. All she knew was that she needed him, all of him, around her, on top of her, inside her. She'd have given anything he asked to have him.

He hauled her jeans down and away, staring down at her like a man possessed. He reached his hand out and touched the lace panties she'd put on before coming to him. He swallowed once and licked his lips. When his fingers grazed her core, she closed her eyes and moaned.

"Baby," he said as he parted her. "You're so wet." He made quick work of her panties and kissed his way up her legs. She wanted to feel embarrassed; she'd never been so thoroughly examined and pampered. With Darren, there was no excitement, no foreplay. She'd always wondered why everyone made such a fuss.

She didn't have to wonder any longer. Everything inside of her was glowing, ignited by his touch, consumed by his fire. She'd never felt so free and yet so helpless, so completely out of control. She cried out as he brought her over a dark and dangerous edge. She opened her eyes when the heat from his skin was replaced by a cool blast of air.

He flipped onto his back, wrenched his jeans off, and reached for a condom on his nightstand. He positioned himself over her and rolled it over his length. "I can't wait any longer."

"I need you, Ty. I need you."

With one stroke, they were joined. He held himself still, buried inside of her, the muscles of his arms shaking with restraint. She arched against him, urging him to move, begging him to ease the throbbing inside. He started off leisurely, measuring himself within her again and again and again, watching her until she couldn't hold her eyes open any longer and she felt the rolling tide begin to swell.

The sound of skin slapping skin echoed in the room, inciting her passion. Grunts and groans escaped his lips. She peeked through her lashes and marveled at the look on his face. She'd never seen affable, unflappable Ty look so fierce, so completely focused. Only on her. Jill wrapped her legs around him and let herself go.

He collapsed on top of her, his breath escaping in short, choppy bursts. Their hearts pounding, their scents mingling, their limbs intertwined.

After nuzzling her neck with his lips, he raised his head and stared at her warily. "Are you okay?" he asked.

Was okay enough to describe feeling as if she'd been given

the secret handshake to enter the most exclusive club in the world? "You could say that."

His eyes narrowed on her face. "Did I hurt you?"

"No." She laced her fingers through his hair, steadying his gaze. "I've never felt so incredible. And that's such a feeble word for what I'm feeling."

His cocky grin shot straight to where they remained joined. "Better than winning a race?"

She let her hands wander down his back and come to rest on his most excellent butt. "Better than winning gold in the decathlon."

He chuckled and eased himself off of Jill, flipping onto his side and draping an arm over her stomach. His lips grazed her shoulder. "Make room on the podium, babe."

CHAPTER 27

Jill clutched the sheet to her chest, staring at the beams on the ceiling when Ty walked back from the bathroom. Still naked, he eased onto the bed and pulled her hand free so he could link their fingers. He could almost see the wheels in her head spinning.

"Is it always like that?" she asked.

He propped his head onto his elbow and thought again of how fragile she was. The woman who'd come alive at his touch, met him stroke for stroke, thrust for thrust, had a soft and vulnerable core. "No. It's never been like that because it's never been you."

She let out an impatient huff.

"Jill." He turned her head with his hand on her cheek. Her eyes were dark and fathomless. "You can't know how it feels to be with you. How long I've wanted you."

"No one's ever wanted me like this. No one's ever made me feel the way you do."

The thought, just the flash of her with another man made his chest drum with adrenaline. His fingers flexed on her face before he deliberately relaxed his grip and drew his hand down to cup her breast beneath the sheet. Her nipple peaked at his touch. "I feel you when you're around. Last year, when you'd run up here, I knew every time you were on your way. Something always pulled me to the door and there you were."

She arched into his palm and he felt a fresh wave of need for her.

"I wanted you then," she said on a sigh. "I knew it was wrong. I knew you were taken, but I wanted you. I tried to ignore it, but it kept tugging me toward you. My father warned me not to run up here."

To hide his grin, he drew the sheet down and lowered his head to her breast to kiss the delicate underside. For so long, he'd wondered if he was the only one who felt the connection. "Why did you try to ignore it?"

"Because you belonged to someone else."

He looked in her eyes, held her skeptical gaze. "I didn't. How could I have been hers when I ached for you?"

"Why did you stay with her all summer? You had to have known how I felt."

He let out a chuckle. "You're not that easy to read, Jill. Trust me."

"I know you're not a coward."

The arrow went right where she'd intended, a direct hit to the pride. He flipped onto his back and mimicked her position. She needed to hear his reasons. He needed to explain. "I couldn't bring myself to break up with her over the phone. When she was here, I couldn't do it because she'd just flown across the country to see me. I went to her as soon as I got back and told her it was over."

"She asked me if you were cheating on her."

He whipped his head around. "What? When?"

"At The Tap one afternoon."

Damn. He'd hurt Dana. He should have told her. He should have been honest no matter how much money she'd spent on the ticket. "It was you. It wasn't the same after you. I'd already let her go by the time she got here. I was so full of you by then." He inched closer so their bodies touched, torso to torso. "I've never gotten you out of my system. I don't think I want to."

"I don't think I want you to, either."

Slowly, with infinite patience, he tugged the sheet lower, gliding his hands over the muscles of her stomach. "Stay."

She answered with her body, rolling on top of him, giving him permission to look his fill at her implausible physique. She was so strong on the outside, pale skin over sleek muscle, and yet so delicate inside. The combination made him weak and needy.

Later, when they fell into an exhausted sleep, he curled around her and dreamt of the future.

***

"He's not coming?" Bobbie asked when Jill entered the house alone.

She set her purse on the entry table and walked past her mother into the kitchen. "He's working. He'll be here for dessert."

"Good thing I made dessert."

Jill spun around, surprised and a little hurt by her mother's sarcastic tone. Bobbie Jennings possessed many qualities, but a biting humor wasn't one of them. Especially where Jill was concerned. "Why don't you like him? You don't even know him."

"How could I know him when you didn't tell me he existed?"

The hurt, Jill now knew, was on both sides. "I'm sorry, Mom. I just…it seemed too good to be true for a while. I thought if I told you, told anyone, I'd burst the bubble and he'd be gone."

"Olivia knew," Bobbie said as she scooped wild rice into a serving dish.

"I live with Olivia. It's hard to hide things from her."

Bobbie carefully set the spoon on the counter and turned to face her daughter. Jill recognized the look on her mother's face. She'd seen it whenever her mom needed to calm down and gather her patience. "So tell me now. Is it serious?"

Jill's favorite chicken dish had never smelled less appetizing.

She chewed her lip. "Serious enough."

Bobbie's shoulders slumped. "What does that mean?"

"It means he's perfect and I'm trying not to get so caught up that I lose my footing. He's smart and easy going and so incredibly good looking. He gets me, Mom. He thinks my quirks are endearing instead of weird. He treats me like I'm beautiful."

"Oh, Jill." Bobbie stepped closer and rubbed Jill's shoulder. "You are beautiful."

"You're my mother."

"Yes. You're my daughter and I think you're beautiful because you're mine. But I'm also a woman who sees that her little girl has grown into a striking woman. I'm not surprised your young man is so attracted. I only wonder what took the men around here so long."

"I intimidate most of them."

Bobbie let out a sigh. "I always thought it would be Lyle."

"I did, too," Jill admitted. "For a while. It would never have worked. He just thinks I'm quirky."

"Are you happy?"

Jill couldn't suppress her smile. "Yes. But I also feel sick inside."

"Why?"

"He seems so sure about me and about us. And he's leaving at the end of the summer."

"Where does he live?"

"North Carolina."

"Oh."

"Yeah," Jill agreed. She began pacing the kitchen in her normal route, past the dishwasher, to the pantry, and around again. "No matter how great things are now, it's going to end in a couple of months."

"Oh, sweetheart. Don't go putting the cart before the horse. You may be ready for things to slow down by then. Remember how quickly things fizzled with Darren?"

Jill couldn't even begin to compare the two men. "This is different."

"Things are always rosy during the first few weeks. The shine will fade and get dull."

"And what if it doesn't?"

"Then you'll know it's real."

"I'm scared, Mom."

"I'd worry if you weren't scared. Falling in love is scary."

Jill grabbed her stomach. "I never said anything about love."

"You didn't have to. Come on," her mother said. "Grab the rice and let's eat."

***

Jill's mom answered Ty's knock. Her black hair was so dark and shiny it looked blue. Her bright smile was a contrast to the sneer she'd leveled at him the last time they met. "Mrs. Jennings. Thank you for having me. Sorry I couldn't join you for lunch."

"Come on in, hon, and please call me Bobbie. There's plenty of left overs if you didn't get a chance to eat."

"No, thank you, ma'am. I'm fine."

"Well, I hope you've got room for dessert because I baked an apple pie."

"Sounds delicious." Ty glanced around. What he could see of Jill's home had understated style. The living room served as an office for Jill's dad. He recognized Warlock State's green and gold on the wall and the big, bold desk seemed too manly for petite Bobbie Jennings.

She led him into the dining room where Gary Jennings sat at the head of the table, his elbows on the glossy surface, his fingers linked, his disapproving glare turned on Jill, who sat facing the heavily curtained window. She whipped her head around when Bobbie cleared her throat. "Look who I found."

Jill stood up and stepped next to Ty, running her arm from his shoulder to his wrist. He wasn't sure how touchy feely to behave in front of her parents, but when Gary stood and his expression didn't change. Ty figured the less physical contact the better. He held out his hand. "Mr. Jennings, Tyler

Bloodworth."

Gary narrowed his eyes at Ty as he shook his hand. "Do I know you?"

"We met at the hospital the day Jill broke her leg."

Jill's eyes flew to his. "You did?"

He nodded, but kept his eyes on Gary. Recognition dawned and didn't help to dim his suspicion.

"Ah, yes. I didn't realize you two knew each other then."

"We were friends," Ty said. No need to explain to Jill's dad that he'd watched and wanted her like a man obsessed. He had her now and this ritual, this passing of the guard, so to speak, was always an uncomfortable step. This time, he sensed Gary understood he might lose Jill forever.

"I take it you're more than friends now?"

What a pompous ass. No wonder Jill seemed so upset about this invitation. Ty wrapped his arm around Jill's waist. "Fortunately for me, yes."

Bobbie asked Jill to help her in the kitchen, and with a wary look in his direction, she disappeared through an adjacent door.

"Have a seat." Gary motioned toward the empty chair to his right. Ty skirted the table and sat down. "So what do you do?"

"I'm a fishing guide at The Golden Rule."

"You work with Tommy?" Gary asked. When Ty nodded, Gary said, "He's a good man."

"The best," Ty agreed.

"So you ski the slopes in the winter?"

"No, sir. I just finished my master's in economics. I'm starting a teaching position back home in the fall."

"High school?"

"A small college about the size of Warlock State."

Gary's brows shot under his dark hair. "And where's home?"

"Western North Carolina."

Jill's dad couldn't hide the smug smile. "Very nice," he said just as Jill and her mom joined them at the table.

"Tyler was just telling me about his teaching position back home," Gary said to Bobbie with an overly toothy smile.

Jill snuck a glance at Ty and lifted her brows in question. He shrugged and accepted a plate from Bobbie. "He's teaching economics."

"That's wonderful, Tyler. Does your family live near the college?"

"Yes, ma'am, they do."

"Ty has an interesting family," Jill said. "Tell them, Ty."

"My parents are divorced. They're both remarried and have young kids."

"They're all friends," Jill said as if the concept were foreign. "They get along and do stuff together."

"They're coming out next week," Ty explained. "Everyone but my grandfather. They're staying at the resort between Lower Fork and Del Noches. They're looking forward to the rodeo."

"I've heard that resort's very nice," Bobbie said. "I hope you get some time off to spend with them. Jill said you work quite a bit."

"I do, but Tommy knows they're coming."

"How'd you end up out here?" Gary asked. "Two summers in a row?"

"I wanted to fish out west. Tommy's a great boss and the fishing's good. I liked the people." He winked at Jill. "So I decided to spend my last free summer here."

"As a college teacher, this won't be your last free summer," Gary said in a condescending tone.

"I'm going into business with my dad. He owns a raft shop on the Powellachee. I'm opening my own fishing shop with him and I'll run that in the summer."

"So, you're going to be tied back east after this summer?" Gary asked. Ty knew all too well what he was getting at.

"I suppose you could say that." He noted the stricken look on Jill's face before she evened out her expression and averted her eyes. Tied back home meant their relationship would end when the summer was over. He should have felt gratified that the thought of him leaving left her upset, but he didn't. The thought of him leaving felt like the final blow to their relationship. It was too soon to talk about the future. He couldn't broach the subject when he was still reeling from their first night together. He'd have to start planting the seeds soon, before she started pulling away. If he understood anything about Jill, it was that she'd do just about anything to protect her fragile heart.

"Jill said you were a wonderful cook, Bobbie. This pie is delicious."

Her mother beamed under the praise. "Thank you, Tyler. I made an extra for Jill to take home. It's her favorite. You make sure she shares."

"Oh, I will," he said. He'd make sure of a lot of things.

CHAPTER 28

Olivia walked into Tap and stopped just inside the doorway. She glanced around until she spotted Jill serving burgers and sandwiches to a table of six by the window. Olivia walked behind the bar and waited for Jill to see her. When she did, she followed her to the kitchen where Stevie plated food and worked the grill like the seasoned line cook he was.

"What are you doing here?" Jill asked.

"Just making sure you're still alive. I've seen evidence of you at the apartment, but not much else."

"I've been staying with Ty." Jill loaded her tray with a salad and an especially appetizing plate of potato skins. "I'm sorry, I should have called."

"I'm not your mother, but when your mother does call, I need to know what to say."

"Oh, God." Jill stopped midstride with a horrified look on her face. "Did she call?"

"No, but if she did..."

"I'll be home tonight. Ty's going to help Tommy with something and his parents arrive tomorrow."

"Good," Olivia said. "You can fill me in on all the hot sex you've been having."

Jill's face burned and she snuck a glance at Stevie, whistling away over a griddle of burgers, his knowing smile a sure indication he'd heard Olivia's quip. "Would you keep your voice down, please?"

"Do you really think anyone in the three town radius doesn't know you're having sex with Ty?"

"They do now." Jill set the tray down. "Olivia, please. I know you're pissed, but please don't embarrass me."

"I'm not pissed. I'm lonely. I wish I was having hot sex instead of watching trashy TV alone."

"I'll be home tonight. We can watch trashy TV together."

"And talk about your hot sex?"

Jill sighed. "Maybe."

Olivia clapped. "Yeah. I've got a float in five. See you later."

Olivia smiled as she walked to the raft shop. Mission accomplished. Tommy almost ran into her when she entered the crowded registration area. "Where are you so hot to go?" she asked.

"I've got a meeting in Westmoreland and supplies to pick up along the way."

"Before your guys' night out?" she asked.

"What?"

"Jill said you were doing something with Tyler tonight."

"He's helping me repair some of the rafts." He nodded his head toward the crowd waiting to check in. "In case you haven't noticed, the season's in full swing and I need every boat we've got on the water."

"Sounds like fun."

"Sounds like business." He tried to squeeze past her and she stopped him with a grip on his arm. "Olivia, I'm going to be late."

"Do me a favor, would you?"

"I don't have time to pick up a bunch of stuff for you right now. Make a list and leave it on my desk and I'll try to grab whatever you need next time I'm in town."

"I'm in town all the time when I'm at school, remember?"

She huffed out an impatient breath. Would her brother ever stop treating her like a kid? "I want you to ask Ty about Jill."

"Ask him what?"

"About his plans. About where he sees this going."

"I'm not asking him that." He pushed past her and strode purposefully toward his truck.

"Tommy, wait," Olivia begged and stutter-stepped to catch up. "She's my best friend and he's leaving at the end of the summer. If she's in for a major heartbreak, I need to know."

"Then you ask him."

"You think he'll answer me?"

"Olivia, his relationship with Jill is none of my business. It's also none of yours."

"Protecting my best friend is very much my business."

"Then it's up to you butt your nose in. I'm steering clear of any personal questions. Besides, what if he tells me he's having fun for the summer and that's it? Are you going to tell Jill? Do you really think she's going to appreciate you butting into her relationship like that?"

"Yes, she would."

He opened the driver's side door and shook his head. "Just when I think you're growing up."

He got in and drove away without a backward glance. Screw him, Olivia thought. He had no idea how a female mind worked. Which was exactly the reason why he was alone.

***

Jill was looking forward to spending the night at the apartment. The back and forth, living out of a duffle bag and her car was exhausting. That, and the endless hours she spent wrapped around Tyler. She couldn't believe how wanton she'd become. He'd awakened something inside of her, a reckless sexual awareness that consumed her most of the day.

She tried to run off the tension not seeing him created and realized she'd shaved almost a minute off her time. Running every morning at Ty's in the high altitude had helped, she mused as she stretched in the parking lot and ascended the stairs to her apartment. She'd been feeling better and better about her life, working at The Tap, enjoying her runs more than she had in a very long time, coming home to him every night and sharing her life with a man for the first time ever. There was something so liberating about having someone to care for other than herself. She worried she cared too much.

Ty seemed excited for her to meet his family, but the thought of it had her stomach in knots. He mattered. Jill wasn't the type, would never be the type, to give herself to someone casually. As light as she'd tried to keep it, as much as she tried to remember he'd be gone at the end of the summer, she knew her feelings were deep and taking root.

Meeting his family would forge another connection. She didn't want to meet the people he would leave her to live with. She didn't want to imagine him at home in his life without her.

Olivia had come home while Jill was running and she'd left a trail of her things from the door to the kitchen. "I got pizza and beer," Olivia shouted. "Go take a quick shower and we'll get started with a TLC marathon."

"What's on?" Jill asked. Her stomach grumbled at the smell of the pizza.

"Who cares? Weddings, beauty contests, cupcakes, psychics. It's all good."

"Good point. I'll be right out."

With her hair still wet, Jill dressed in comfortable sweats and piled her plate with pizza. She settled on the couch next to Olivia, who'd already scarfed two pieces and was sipping a fresh beer. "So what's on tonight's menu?"

"It's a fiesta of weddings." She smirked at Jill. "Perhaps you'd like to take notes?"

Jill balled up her napkin and threw it at Olivia. "Very funny."

"Well, you're a hell of a lot closer to walking down the aisle than I am."

Jill suddenly realized why Olivia was being so snarky. "You really are jealous, aren't you?"

"What?"

"Not about Ty, but that I'm having regular and, let me just say, spectacular sex."

"Bitch. Of course I'm jealous." She set her beer down and crossed her arms over her chest. "Is it really spectacular?"

"He's a fly fisherman. He's patient and very, very good with his hands."

"Just his hands?" Olivia prodded.

"With every appendage."

"I hate you."

"No, you don't. You're just in a dry spell." She took a bite. "What happened to Del?"

"He's an idiot. Gorgeous makes up for a lot of things, but it can't hide stupid. Besides, he wasn't worth pissing off Tommy."

"Was he pissed?"

"He would have been if I'd let it get any farther." She shrugged and turned back to the television. "I need to graduate and get out of this hick town. The summers used to be exciting with all the new guides. Now they're all so immature."

"Either that or we're maturing."

"That's a depressing thought." She sighed. "I guess whatever motivates me to study is a good thing, right?"

"Right. When you graduate, you can get a job anywhere. I always thought you'd apply at a school in Westmoreland. Are you thinking of leaving the valley?"

"I don't know. I wasn't, but lately it seems so small. I see the same people everywhere I go. I'm bored with the same people."

"I like seeing the same people," Jill said. "It bothered me in college when I'd go places and didn't recognize a soul."

"You don't think the valley will hold less of an appeal when Tyler's gone?"

Jill took a sip of her beer and tried to ease the sting to her heart. "Probably."

"Is this getting serious, Jill? Are you falling for him?"

Jill examined the toppings on her pizza, afraid if she looked at Olivia, her friend would see the truth no matter what she said. "I care about him. I'm enjoying spending time with him. And the sex is, as mentioned, stupendous."

"And?"

"And I don't know. I've never felt about anyone the way I feel about him. I've never really had the opportunity."

"So how do you feel?"

She looked Olivia in the eye. She wouldn't lie to her friend. She could be honest and trust Olivia to understand her feelings. "I think about him all the time and not just in that obsessive way like when you've got a crush. We're different. He's so unflappable and easy going and I'm totally anal about everything. We shouldn't get along so well, but we do. We share the same values. We like the same music." She slapped a hand to her stomach. "Oh, God, Olivia. I'm falling in love with him. I'm totally screwed."

"Why?"

"He's going home at the end of the summer. I'm falling in love with a man I have absolutely no chance at having a future with. What is wrong with me?"

"Nothing, and I don't think you don't have a future."

"A long distance relationship? Across the country? When I can barely afford to pay my rent and car note? We'll never see each other." Jill got up to pace. "And do you really think he'll stay faithful surrounded by a bunch of beautiful college girls? I need to end this. I need to end this before I get any deeper involved."

"That's nuts, Jill. You don't know that he wants it to end. What if he asks you to go back with him?"

"To North Carolina? Leave my family and everything I've ever known?"

"You wouldn't be leaving everything, you'd be going toward something special. A future with the man you love."

Jill put her hands over her ears. "Stop, Olivia. Stop putting ideas in my head. He's never made any reference to me going with him when he leaves."

"What does he say?"

"He doesn't really talk about it. We don't really talk about it. When it comes up, he kind of brushes it off." She sighed and sat down. "I need to get my head in the right place. This is a summer fling. Nothing more, nothing less. I can't make it more because I'm stupid enough to have feelings for him."

"You don't think he has feelings for you?"

"I think he cares about me. I know he wants me. Right now, that has to be enough. It is enough."

"Okay." Olivia rubbed Jill's foot and lifted her beer in the air. "To stupendous sex."

Jill lifted her beer and took a tiny sip. Any more and she might not have been able to keep it down. "Can we watch something else?" she asked.

"Sure. These brides get on my nerves, anyway."

They settled on a reality adventure show and bundled up under blankets. Jill's eyelids grew heavy half way through and she never made it to the end. She fell asleep on the couch and woke up to the sensation of falling. She gasped and opened her eyes to find herself cradled in Tyler's arms. "Shhhh. I've got you."

"I thought you were helping Tommy."

"I was. I didn't want to sleep alone."

"How'd you get in?"

"Door was unlocked. You two need to be more careful."

She snuggled into his chest. "I'm glad you're here."

"Me, too. I missed you."

Jill held on tight. This was enough. It had to be enough. "I missed you, too."

CHAPTER 29

The Mountain Laurel Lodge sat on a sprawling hundred-acre estate at the foot of the San Juan Mountains. With rolling hills that bordered Bureau of Land Management land, it boasted hundreds of acres of horseback riding trails and access to fishing on the nearby Rio Grande.

Ty couldn't wait to see his family. He left every summer with nothing more than phone calls to bridge the gap, but something was different this summer. Falling in love had intensified his feelings about just about everything.

He needed to see his mom, smell her familiar scent. He needed to see his brothers and sisters roaming the hills and discovering the beauty of the west. He needed to see his dad, knowing that he'd left the shop during the busy season to visit and spend time with his family. Most of all, he needed to see Jill with his family and seal the last remaining piece of the puzzle. He needed to know they'd get along before he tried to move her beyond their casual dating and pushed for something more.

Ty sat inside the lobby, eating cookies and tying flies until his family arrived, talking to the owner's ten-year-old daughter, who explained in detail the encounter she'd had with a skunk the day before. She'd just gotten to the part where she'd tiptoed away when his stepdad walked through the front door and beamed at Ty. "It's good to see your ugly mug."

"Bryce." Ty stood up and greeted his stepdad with a hearty hug. "You finally made it."

"You try traveling with this crew and see if you get anywhere on time. I swear they all had to pee ten minutes apart."

His mother followed with the girls on her heels. "Tyler." She rushed into his arms and he picked her off her feet. There wasn't anyone steadier, more reliable than his mother. "Mom." She looked relaxed and happy, her blond hair loose from its usual ponytail. She wore shorts and a lightweight fleece jacket. "I've missed you."

"Oh, you have no idea," she said as she pulled back and stared up at his face. "I'm glad these summer trips are just about over."

"Not quite yet," he reminded her. As glad as he was to see them, pulling up stakes now wasn't an option. Not until he'd convinced Jill to come with him.

Before he could ask about the rest of the crew, Jesse and Lita entered arm in arm. They rushed to hug him together. "Look how tan you are," Lita said. "He looks happy, Kerri Ann. Don't you think he looks happy?"

His mother shrugged. "He looks like Ty."

"He looks like a happy Ty. So, where is she?" Lita asked.

"She's working," Ty explained. "I didn't think it would be a good idea to spring all of you on her at once."

"Why not?" his dad asked. "We're a package deal. She may as well figure that out now."

"She will, Dad. I promise."

"Come on, Lita," Bryce said. "Let's get checked in and let these two have some time with Tyler." They walked to the registration desk hand in hand. Anyone who didn't know any better would have thought they were the married couple. His family, Ty knew, was an unusual bunch.

"You look good," Jesse said. "River treating you well?"

"Always does. You guys find it okay?"

"Your directions were spot on. We had an hour stretch where everyone had to use the bathroom and there was no bathroom in sight. Happens every time. I swear it was easier to travel when the girls were in diapers and could just pee in their pants."

"How far is your place from the resort?" his mom asked.

"About twenty minutes. I'm up in the mountains, closer to the river."

"And Jill? Where is she?"

"She's about ten minutes from here at the base of the Lower Fork. She lives in an apartment with a girlfriend."

"Does she know we're coming?"

"Yes, she knows. I thought we could all have dinner at the restaurant where she works so you could see the town and the raft and fishing shop."

"Any meal I don't have to cook is fine with me," his mom said. "What's the dress code?"

"There isn't one, Mom. You could go just as you are to any place in town."

"Really? So it's not that different from home? At least not yet," she added under her breath. Ty wondered if she was talking about the new restaurant Bryce told him they wanted to open.

"Not too different unless you're talking about the trees and the weather."

Lita and Bryce returned with keys to two cabins. "We're next door to one anther so the kids can play," Lita said. "There's a fire pit between our cabins and they serve refreshments at happy hour."

"Perfect," Kerri Ann said. "I'm ready to unpack and unwind."

"I'll let you get settled in and come back and get you for dinner."

"You're leaving?" Brody asked. "Now?"

"I've got a private lesson in thirty minutes, but I'll be back. Be ready to go around six."

"I can't wait to meet your girlfriend," Lita said with a

beaming smile.

"If you act too excited, you're going to scare her away. Remember I told you she's skittish."

"I know. I'm just getting the excited out of my system now."

"You do that. I'll be back." After hugs and kisses, he was back on the road. He only hoped his family could keep their lips shut. If any of them let it slip that he'd come back for Jill, they could ruin everything.

***

Jill poked around the storeroom of The Tap, nervously checking inventory and taking stock of the list she kept taped to the door. If she hadn't been so organized and implemented a new system that kept the guesswork out of ordering supplies, she would have had enough to keep her mind occupied until Ty and his family arrived.

As it stood, she had nothing but time to worry. Brad, the night cook, had already shooed her out of the kitchen. She stood at the reception desk, arranging menus right side up when the door opened and a gaggle of folks paraded inside. Folks she'd never seen before.

Ty held the door for the kids, who came in first, pushing and shoving and talking all at once. There was a blonde woman, tall and lean, with Ty's chin and a nervous smile. His mother, the restaurant owner, Kerri Ann. The man behind her with the dark hair had to be his stepdad, Bryce. Jill recognized his father, Jesse, immediately as they could have been brothers, with their nearly identical eyes and broad shouldered build. The short, yet stunningly beautiful woman who bounced in after on sky high heels had to be his stepmother, the flamboyant Lita.

Ty brought up the rear and met her eyes with a look of nervous expectation. Jill came around the desk and clasped her shaking hands in front of her. "Hello. You must be Ty's family?"

A chorus of nods and yeses greeted her question. Ty

scooted around the group and wrapped his arm around Jill's shoulders. "Everyone, this is Jill Jennings. She's going to join us for dinner tonight."

One of the girls, a sweet, dark haired beauty, yanked on Ty's jeans. "Is she your girlfriend, Ty?" she asked with an adorable lisp.

"Yes," Ty said and looked Jill in the eye. "Jill's my girlfriend."

"She's pretty," the little girl said. Jill couldn't remember ever receiving a nicer compliment.

Ty mussed the girl's curls. "She sure is, Gabby."

Ty turned to Jill. "Do we have a table in the back?"

"Yes, right this way. I wasn't sure if we'd need any high chairs or boosters?"

"One booster," Lita said with a hand on the littlest girl's head. "Brooke can't quite reach the table yet."

"Ty, will you show them to the table and I'll get the booster?"

He nodded and the group prodded along behind. Oh, God. There were so many of them. She scooped up a booster seat and took a deep breath. She needed to get over her nerves. This was Ty's family. They were important to him. He'd entered the lion's den of her parents' house and her dad had been less than friendly. She owed it to him to prove he hadn't wasted his time out here with a dimwitted bubble brain.

She helped Brooke into the seat after placing the booster on her chair and took the empty seat next to Ty in the middle. Her stomach fluttered with pride when he draped his arm around the back of her chair.

"Everything's good," he announced. He turned his attention to the boys. With matching brown hair and blue eyes, Jill couldn't tell them apart. "The burgers here are great, guys."

"I'm getting a burger," one of them said. The other complied. "Me, too."

Jill assured Ella she could get buttered noodles instead of macaroni and cheese like her sisters and she rewarded her with a shy smile. They placed their order and Jill didn't worry about the service since she'd threatened Brad and the wait staff earlier to make sure everything ran smoothly.

She wanted to impress his family. While she didn't own this restaurant like Ty's mom owned hers, she was responsible for its management. She didn't want to seem incompetent in front of his parents.

The evening went off without a hitch. The food arrived quickly, the drinks were always filled, and to Jill's surprise, the children were well behaved. The conversation flowed seamlessly. Jill envied the easy way Ty interacted with his family, especially since things with hers had become so tense. There was a bond amongst the group. They were a family, the whole lot of them, and they'd missed Ty desperately. He belonged with them. She'd never seen him so at ease, and that was saying a lot since he always seemed very at home in his skin. Being around his family, being a part of their lives was not something he could live without.

As much as she enjoyed getting to know his parents, she felt the divide in their relationship become even wider.

CHAPTER 30

"I love her," Lita squealed in the lobby of the Mountain Laurel Lodge. "She's so natural and sweet. I just adore the way she looks at you, Ty."

"She's kind of quiet," Ty's mom offered.

Bryce knocked her with his hip. "Who could get a word in edgewise with this group?"

"I think she's great," Jesse announced. "If we haven't managed to totally scare her off, I think she'll fit right in with this clan."

Ty's head spun as the people he loved most in the world offered their unfettered opinions of the woman he knew he couldn't live without. Tonight, sitting in the restaurant with her by his side, he knew his feelings were real and permanent. He loved Jill and wanted her with him forever.

"She was nervous," Ty said. "It takes her a while to loosen up and relax. I know by the end of the week, you'll see why I love her."

His mother gasped. "You love her? I've never heard you use that word about a woman before. Are you saying you're in love with her?"

"Yes. I've never felt this sure about anyone. I know it seems fast," he explained in the face of his mother's stricken expression. "But I'm sure she's the one."

"Oh, Tyler!" Lita pulled him into a hug. "I'm so happy for you. She's such a lucky girl to have you."

"Does she love you back?" his sensible mother asked.

He shoved his hands into his pockets. "I haven't exactly told her about my feelings yet."

"Why the hell not?" his dad asked. "When it's right, it's right. What are you waiting for?"

"She's had a lot of changes in her life. I'm not sure she's ready to hear it yet."

"Don't wait forever." Bryce reached for his arm. "You know how long I waited to tell your mama about my feelings. I wasted a lot of years being miserable thinking the timing wasn't right."

"I know. I'm not going to wait years, believe me. I just need to ease her into it a little longer."

"You don't think she loves you?" his mother asked.

"I think so. I hope so. I know she has feelings for me and I know they scare her. I can't push too hard, too fast, or she'll shut down."

"I'm sure Ty knows what he's doing," Lita threw him a lifeline. "He knows her better than we do and he loves her. He'll know when the time is right."

Would he? he wondered on the drive back to the Lower Fork. He didn't know if Jill loved him. He hoped she did. Sometimes when they were together, he'd catch her looking at him with a deer in the headlights expression on her face, like she didn't know whether to hit the brake or the gas. And other times, when they made love and after, she would stare at him so intently he felt sure the words were on the tip of her tongue.

He drove to her apartment. He hadn't packed a bag and would have to return home early in the morning to change, but he needed to see her. He needed to be with her and see how she was feeling after the interrogation.

She answered the door wearing plaid pajama pants and a gray tank top. Her hair was piled high on her head in a messy pony. "What are you doing here? I thought you'd be with your family."

"They've had a long day." She shut the door behind him and stood with her back against the wood. "I wanted to make sure you were okay."

She sent him a sidelong glance. "Why wouldn't I be?"

"My family can be…overwhelming."

She moved past him and plopped on the couch. Some sitcom played at low volume on the television. "They're lovely. Your parents are so striking. I can't even picture them together."

"I can't really remember them as a couple," he admitted. "They're with who they're meant to be with now. They're happy."

"It's such an interesting group. The girls are adorable and your stepmom is a hoot."

"Lita's been a godsend. My grandfather had a crush on her when she first came to town."

"Really?" she asked.

Ty pulled Jill's bare feet in his lap and rubbed her arches. She scooched lower onto the couch and groaned in appreciation. "Oh, yeah. It was pretty funny."

"Your dad loves her so openly. The way he looked at her." She shook her head. "Ummmm, you're really good at that."

He brought her foot to his mouth and nipped at the tender skin on the top of her foot. "Even your feet turn me on."

"Is that so?"

"That is most assuredly so."

"Your mom doesn't like me."

Ty stopped pushing her pants up her calf and stared at her. "That's not true."

"It is. She seemed very unsure."

"She's more cautious. She's…we have a different kind of relationship. She was so young when she had me and then my dad took off for a couple of years. We've always been really close."

"I can tell. She's so proud of you, Ty. They all are."

"They're my family. Families tend to see only the best."

"Maybe yours does." She sat up and gripped a pillow to her chest, her mouth set into a deep frown. "My mom called a little while ago. My dad's found another runner to train."

"You knew he was looking."

"Yes. I'm happy he found someone else. I just wish they didn't feel the need to gloat."

"Are you sure that's not just your take on things?"

"She told me not to worry about Daddy being angry any more. Angry! As if I'm a petulant child who did this just to spite him."

"He seemed like a very proud man. I imagine you quitting hurt his pride."

"He's fine as long as you do what he wants you to do." She tossed the pillow aside and got up to pace around the room. She was more upset than she was willing to admit. At least to herself. "I was thinking of calling him and suggesting I do the race."

"What race?" he asked.

"The qualifier in Denver. He signed me up and I didn't think I'd be ready. My times have improved in the last few weeks. I think the mountain training has helped."

"From my place?"

"Yes. Between the steepness and the altitude, I'm able to really lengthen my stride down here on the flat road." She stopped in front of the TV and started picking at her nails. "I was thinking of having him take me and now I can't."

"I'll take you."

"What?"

"I'll take you to Denver. When's the race?"

"In two weeks. It's an Olympic qualifier. If I can run the course in less than an hour, fifteen, I'll make the trials. My times have been close to that cutoff. Closer than I thought I could get."

"You have to try, Jill. I can see it in your face. You want this."

"I don't know. I quit training because I didn't want it."

"I think you quit training with your dad because he was

driving you crazy. You never really quit training."

She sat next to him on the couch and sandwiched her hands between her legs. "I do want it, Ty. I'm afraid I'll feel like a quitter if I don't even try."

"Then let's do it."

"You'll come with me?"

"I wouldn't miss it for the world. I love watching you run. I love watching you do just about anything, but when you run, you set the world on fire. I've never seen anything as beautiful and graceful as you in motion."

She crawled into his lap and took his face in her palms. "How did I ever get lucky enough to find you?"

"I'm the lucky one," he said and took her lips like it was the first time and the last time and every time in between. She melted against him. He snaked his hands under her tank and brought them around to run his thumbs over her nipples. She was so sensitive there, so responsive wherever he touched her. All of her hesitations disappeared when they came together. He reveled in her trust. "Where's Olivia?"

She ran her tongue up his neck and bit his ear lobe. "She's on a date."

"Is she coming home?" he managed to say as she unbuttoned his shirt.

"Probably."

Ty grabbed her hips and hoisted her up as he stood. She wrapped her legs around him as he walked them to her room and dumped her on the bed. He stared down at her. "I want to make you scream. I want to make you forget about everything and anything but you and me."

"You always do," she said and reached for him.

He was helpless not to come. He couldn't say the words out loud, not yet. But here, in the dimly lit room, he could show her how he felt. He playfully yanked the pants from her legs and tossed them over his shoulder. She lay sprawled before him, naked from the waist down. Here she wasn't shy or unsure, but wild and powerful. She knew just how to move to tease him, to make him weak, to make him beg.

"Touch me, Ty."

She didn't have to ask twice. He shed his clothes quickly and then panicked. "Oh, crap."

"What?"

"The condoms are in the truck. Do you have any?"

"No." He reached for his pants. "Ty, wait. I'm on the pill."

He sat down on the bed, holding his jeans. "You are?"

Jill nodded. "It keeps my very irregular periods regular. I'm clean. There's only been one other and I've been tested."

"I'm clean, too, but I've never been with anyone without a condom."

"Really?" she asked.

"Yeah, it's kind of a tradition."

She sat up and slowly peeled the tank from her skin. "Don't leave me, Ty. Make love to me, skin to skin. Come inside of me."

Common sense warred with his emotions. He knew if he ever had sex without a condom, he'd never want to wear one again, not to mention that his parents would probably receive some kind of warning signal the moment he tried. But when he looked at Jill, naked, open, waiting, there was no choice. He'd die if he didn't touch her now.

He started at her feet, nibbling, lathing, working his way up over her calves. He suckled the skin behind her knee, drew his tongue up the inside of her thigh, and stopped to dabble where she liked it best. She bucked and moaned, gliding her hands through his hair. When she was close, just on the edge of release, he moved up to her breasts and let his hands take over. When he positioned himself at her entry, she was hot and wet and begging. Mission accomplished.

She cried out his name as he drove into her. The feel of her around him—him—made something inside of him go a little bit mad. He pushed her and himself to the brink and over the edge of sanity. When she propped herself on top of his chest and looked at him with a smug and satisfied smile, the words 'I love you' were bubbling up from his lungs over his voice box.

"Oh, Tyler," she said before he could speak. "Even during

dinner with your parents, all I could think about was being with you. Having you inside me. That's not normal."

"Yes, it is. I think about making love to you all the time. All day long."

"Does this fade? This need? This desire?"

"I've never felt this kind of need or desire before."

"I know I'm not your first."

"You're not as far away from my first as you think. But you're the first in other ways."

She sat up and stared down at him. "What ways?"

He wanted to say it; he wanted to confess with everything he had. "In all the ways that count."

CHAPTER 31

After her morning run, Jill joined Ty and his family for the rodeo parade. She helped Kerri Ann corral the twins while they raced after the candy thrown from the passing floats. They finally calmed down when assorted farm equipment and classic cars begain inching down the crowded street.

She enjoyed sitting on the curb of Hailey's main street with the chill of the morning still nipping at the day. When Ella hopped off Jill's lap to retrieve an American flag from a man on horseback, Ty pulled Jill to her feet and linked their fingers. "This is fun," he said. "I didn't bother to come last year."

"It is. I haven't been to one of these parades in years. I forgot how entertaining they are."

He pulled her in front of him and began rubbing her shoulders. "I wish you didn't have to work tonight."

"I know, but I'm the manager. Everyone wanted off. I was glad Stevie agreed to work the night shift so Brad could take his family to the rodeo." She moaned when he dug into the knot on her neck. "The kids will love it. Make sure they get to see the mutton busting."

"What's mutton busting?" Ty asked.

"Just trust me, Ty. Make sure you don't miss it."

190

He turned her around. "The only thing I'm going to miss tonight is you." He lowered his head and brushed his lips against hers in a quick, but intimate kiss. She should have been embarrassed, surrounded by people—his family—but she wanted nothing more than to sink in and let the kiss linger.

Instead, she buried her face into his chest and breathed deeply. His arms came around her and they stood linked together until Ella came back after showing everyone her prize, waving her flag in the air as if it were the most precious gift she'd ever received.

"Look, Jill. The cowboy gave me a flag."

Jill reached down and ran her hand over Ella's silky brown curls. "I know that cowboy. He'll be at the rodeo tonight."

Ella gasped. "You know him?"

Jill kneeled down so she was eye-to-eye with Ella. "He comes into the restaurant for lunch sometimes. He has a girl of his own, a little older than you. She has pretty curls in her hair like you."

"He's a cowboy and a daddy." She beamed and melted Jill's heart. Jill never thought about having kids, but the more she got to know Ty's brothers and sisters, the more she could see herself with children of her own. She reached out and pulled Ella into a hug when the thought of never seeing her again tugged at her heartstrings.

When she stood up, Ty wrapped his arm around her shoulders. "You okay?" he asked.

"Yeah." She closed her eyes and let him hold her before glancing at her watch. "I've got to go."

"So soon?"

"Unfortunately, yes. Have a great time today."

"I'll try to stop by either before the rodeo or after."

"No. Today is for you to spend with your family. I'll see you tomorrow."

"But—"

"No buts."

"I'll come by tonight on my way home."

"After working two shifts? I'll be exhausted. I'm serious,

Ty. Spend the day with your family. I'm sure they're tired of sharing you with me."

"Jill…"

"I'll see you tomorrow. And I'm locking my door tonight."

"Ouch." His smile faded and was replaced by a grimace. "I didn't realize you wanted some space."

"I don't, Ty. That's not what I meant. I heard the boys asking for a sleepover. Besides, they didn't come all this way to spend time with me. They came all this way to spend time with you. I have to work, you have the day off, so go and enjoy. I'll be right here tomorrow. Don't give me that look," she said when he scowled at her. "I'm giving you the day and the night to do whatever you want."

"I want to be with you."

"I want to be with you, too, but we can't always get what we want. And when I start quoting the Rolling Stones, it's time for me to go."

"I'll walk you to your car." When she tried to object, he said, "I'm walking you to the car, like it or not."

She reached up on her toes and kissed him before saying goodbye to his family. When they reached the gravel lot behind a restaurant that had long gone out of business, he pushed her back against the driver's side door, leaned his body in close, and angled his lips over hers. "I need to be with you, Jill. It's been two days."

"I know, I know," she said between kisses. "This is crazy."

"Why do they have to spend the night? I'll be with them all day long."

"They love you, Ty. And I'd imagine your mom and Bryce would appreciate a night alone. This is their vacation, too."

He ran his hands up her sides and brushed her breasts. "I hate it when you make sense."

"I'm nothing if not practical."

"You're beautiful, and tempting, and you smell really good." He touched his forehead to hers. "I miss you already."

"It's okay if you miss me. I'm going to miss you, too."

***

Ty stood in line with his mom for food at the rodeo's covered fairgrounds. He nodded his head at a rafting guide he recognized from the Golden Rule standing in line for beer.

"I can't believe they put kids on sheep," Kerri Ann said. "Who knew that's what mutton busting was?"

"I sure didn't, but Jill said we'd like it."

"It's too bad she had to work."

"I know, but she didn't think it was fair for the workers with families to miss the rodeo."

"She seems very dedicated to her job."

"She's not the type to half ass anything. If she's going to do something, it's going to be done right."

Kerri Ann inched forward in line. "You know, Bryce and I bought that old cottage along the river in Sequoyah Falls."

Ty stopped scanning the crowd and focused on his mother. "I heard. What for?"

"We've decided to open another restaurant. A fancy one." At Ty's lifted brows, Kerri Ann explained. "Why should folks have to go to Asheville every time they want a nice meal?"

Ty shrugged and let his mom continue. He knew better than to interrupt when she was trying to get something off her chest.

"So we bought that pretty little cottage. It's structurally sound, it's got three good sized rooms for intimate seating, and we thought we could have it open Thursdays through Sundays, when most folks want a nice evening out."

"How do you plan to work both places?" he asked. His mom was running herself ragged between running The Pizza Den and raising his brothers.

"I'm going to need some help. I figured I'd have to hire someone from Asheville, but then we came here and met Jill." She grabbed his arm and gave him a gentle squeeze. "I think your girlfriend would be the perfect candidate if you can talk her into coming back with you."

"Mom…"

"I know it seems like I'm paving the way for you, but Bryce and I need some help with the restaurant. Your girlfriend has experience and the smarts to be a real asset."

"I want her to come back to be with me, not because there's a job waiting."

"Tyler, a woman doesn't pick up and move across the country for a job, certainly not for this job. If she comes, it'll be for you, but this way she'll have something to do when she gets there."

"*If* I can get her there."

"You will."

Jesse walked up with Quinn on his shoulders. He plucked him off and plopped him on his feet by his mother. "What you been eating, boy?" Jesse asked. "Bricks?" He rubbed his lower back. "My back may never recover from hauling you around."

"What are you doing putting him on your shoulders like that anyway?" Kerri Ann asked.

"Bryce lifted Brody up to see the barrel racing and Quinn wanted up, too. Believe me, it wasn't my idea."

"Next shoulder ride'll be on mine," Ty told Quinn. "The old man is getting too frail to carry a loaded six-year-old."

"Mom, I wanna ride a bull when I get bigger."

"Oh, brother." Kerri Ann rolled her eyes. "I suppose you want a horse, too?"

"Can I?" His eyes lit up. "Can we get a horse?"

"Sure," Kerri Ann said. "You can get a horse just as soon as I get a maid. How about that?"

Quinn looked up at Tyler. "She's saying I can't get a horse?"

Tyler squatted down and rubbed his hand over Quinn's hair. "I think that's what she's saying."

"Can you bring us a horse home, Ty? There're lots of horses out here."

Ty looked up at his mom. "I'll try to bring something home. It won't be a horse, but something just as wonderful."

CHAPTER 32

Lyle entered The Tap at the end of the lunch rush and sauntered up to the bar. Jill was in a bad mood. She slammed dishes around in the bus bin with a scowl on her face.

"What's up with you?" he asked.

"What does it look like?" She scanned the nearly empty restaurant behind her. "Meredith's little girl is sick, so I was short a waitress and we were slammed. I'll be lucky to have these dishes done by the dinner hour."

"You doing dishes now?"

"No, but they can't get done until I get them to the back." She stopped piling plates into the bin and arched a brow at him. "Kitchen's closed. If you want to visit, grab a bin from behind the bar and make yourself useful."

"Nice to see you, too," he grumbled as he got up and did as she said.

"So, besides the lunch mess, how are you?" He joined her at the large table in the back. "I didn't see you at the rodeo."

"Somebody had to work while everyone else had fun."

"Why are you so cranky?"

"I'm not cranky." To prove the opposite, she slammed the bin onto the table and began tossing dishes so carelessly he thought they might break. "How are you?" she asked. "How's the book coming?"

"Slow. I keep having to stop and do research, which sends me off track. Plus, I'm in the running for a biography."

"I didn't think you wanted to write non-fiction?"

"Mom's editor passed my name along to one of her friends who's looking for a biographer for some young business phenom."

"That sounds boring," Jill admitted.

"It did to me at first, but here's the best part. He's –"

At the sound of a crash, Lyle followed Jill into the kitchen where Stevie stood staring at a potful of chili on the floor. "What happened?" Jill asked.

"I knocked it with my elbow and the whole damn thing spilled." He lifted his feet and shook. "Got all over my new boots."

Jill retrieved a mop from a storage closet and handed it to Stevie. "Good luck."

Lyle followed her out of the kitchen after nodding at Stevie.

"I read your mom's latest book," Jill said as they grabbed new bins and went back out to the restaurant. "It was really good."

"She's already half way through the next one. I just can't write that fast."

"You will once you've been doing it as long as she has."

"That's what she says."

"So," he cleared his throat. "How are things with Tyler?"

Jill brought her gaze to his, her face a mask of suspicion. "Why do you ask?"

"I haven't seen you around. Figured you've been busy with him."

"I have. His parents are in town and his brothers and sisters are taking turns having sleepovers."

"Hoping to make it into the rotation?"

"I'm not going to lie to you, Lyle. I'm ready to be the only one in the rotation."

"Is this serious, Jill?"

She averted her eyes and dumped a bowl of chili into the bin. "It feels serious."

"You know he goes home at the end of the summer."

"Of course I know that. But that's over a month from now." She hefted the full bin in her arms. "I might be ready for him to go by then."

"Jill." Lyle placed his hand on her arm. "Who are you trying to convince? You or me?"

"Why are we talking about this? Why do you keep pushing and prodding me about him? Are you jealous?"

"No, but I don't want to see you get hurt."

"You think he's using me."

"You don't?"

"No. He's not like that. What we have isn't like that. I've spent all week with him and his family. We watched movies with the boys and I gave the girls a pedicure."

"So what's the end game? Have you talked about it? Has he ever brought up what happens when he goes home?"

Jill swallowed. "No."

"Maybe you should," Lyle suggested. "Bring it up, see what he says."

"I don't know."

"You mean you don't want to know."

"Stop putting words in my mouth and stop putting pressure on me. I'm going to start nagging you about your book and see how you like it."

"Okay, okay. I'm done for today." He followed her into the kitchen, but when they came out, he didn't pick up a fresh bin. He knew when he'd pushed her enough. "How's the leg?"

"It's good. I've decided to run in the qualifier in Denver in a couple of weeks."

"I thought you were done?"

"I've been training on my own and I've shaved a couple of minutes off my time. I think I can do this, Lyle. I think I've got a shot."

"Are you serious?"

"Serious enough to want to try."

"Are you back with your dad?"

Her face fell and the scowl was back. "He's training someone new. Some girl from New Mexico. He's taking her to the qualifier."

"You want to show him up," Lyle guessed.

"I want to do my best. I've worked too hard for too long not to give it a shot."

"What if you qualify?"

"I'm not going to play the 'what if' game. One race at a time."

"You need a ride? I could do a little research in Denver."

Her face turned pink. "Ty's taking me."

"Of course he is." She was in way over her head and she refused to admit it. Trying to talk some sense into her wasn't working. "I'd better go," he said. "I've got work to do."

"Good luck with that."

***

Jill sat in her office staring at the spreadsheet she'd created for inventory. Despite the fiasco at lunch, things were under control. She got up and walked to the window. She was looking for Ty's truck, or Ty's boat, or anything of Ty's. Seeing him every night and not being with him made her edgy and needy and as close to annoying as she'd ever been.

How had he turned her into a sex addict? She whipped around at the knock on her door. Ty popped his head inside and frowned at her empty desk.

"Hey," she said.

His face lit up when he spotted her. He stepped inside and closed the door behind him. Without a word, he walked to her, turned her around, placed her against the desk, and ravished her mouth. She welcomed the invasion.

"Oh, God, Ty. I've missed this."

"Does your door lock?"

"Yes, but…"

He reached over and snapped the lock in place. "Ty…"

"Tommy's gone to Westmoreland. I just saw him pull out."

198

"I know, but—"

He cut off her objections by drawing her shirt over her head. "I've got twenty minutes."

"Ty, we can't." She pointed to the window. He reached behind and twisted the blinds closed.

"Yes, we can." He unzipped her pants and groaned when he found her wet and ready. Something about the idea of doing it in the office, in the middle of the day when people milled all around them had her shivering in anticipation. "Hold on to me," he said as he pushed her on top of the desk, freed himself, and plunged. He captured her cry with his mouth.

She gripped the edges of the desk and arched back, giving him access to her breasts. He used his teeth as he slapped against her again and again and again. She wasn't sure how she'd explain the noises coming from her office, the screech of the desk against the floor and the slapping of flesh against flesh, but she couldn't bring herself to care. Hadn't she just been brooding over not seeing him and lamenting her need when he'd burst into the office and met her demands as if he'd been summoned? He yanked her knees up and, with one final thrust, set them both free.

She sat up and tried to figure out if her legs would support her. She was still quaking and unsteady and a little embarrassed to be sprawled naked on her desk when he remained mostly dressed. Ty dropped his forehead to hers. "Jesus, Jill. I'm sorry. I couldn't wait another second."

"Don't apologize. I was fanaticizing about pulling you into the storage shed and having my way with you."

His eyes darkened and he gripped her head. "Don't let me stop you. I love my family, but they're killing me."

"When do they leave?"

"Tomorrow." He stepped back, tucked everything back into place, and gathered her clothes, but didn't hand them to her. "You have no idea how sexy you look right now."

She held out her hands for the clothes. "You've already had your way with me, Ty. You don't have to use flattery."

"You're beautiful, Jill. You make me weak with wanting

you."

"Stop."

"When they're gone, I'm going to make love to you in every room of my house. I've got a full-length mirror in my closet and I'm going to show you how beautiful you are. How you look when you come."

"Ty…"

"I know. I've gotta go."

He kissed her and helped her into her clothes, running his fingers through her hair and planting a kiss on her nose. "That *might* get me through."

"I'll be here if you need me."

With a grunt, he was gone.

Oh, boy. Jill gripped her chest and felt her heart beating a steady drum. If she couldn't go a week without him, how in the world would she survive when he was gone?"

***

Ty dragged the last of Lita's suitcases to the rental car. "Is this the last one?" Jesse asked. "Because if it's not, I'm going to have to strap her to the top of the car."

"She promised that was it, besides a small carry on bag."

"Small my ass," his dad mumbled as he hoisted her suitcase into the billowing SUV and held a hand to his back. "Son," he slapped Ty on the shoulder, "a word to the wise. Women don't pack light."

"Speak for your own woman," Bryce said as he wheeled out two medium sized suitcases and the boys followed with one each. "My woman is easier than yours."

"Yeah," Jesse agreed. "On just this one thing."

"I can hear you," Kerri Ann called from inside the foyer. "And we'd better get going if we're going to make our flight."

"Gather the troops," Jesse shouted. "It's time to get this show on the road."

"I hope y'all had fun," Ty said as they gathered around the cars.

"The boys haven't stopped talking about riding the horses

and the four wheelers," Kerri Ann said. "They can't wait to get home and tell their friends."

"I'll email those pictures I took of us fishing," Ty said.

"The girls miss you already." Lita gathered Ty in her arms. "They love Jill and want you to bring her home."

"I'm trying my best."

"He's set the bait," Jesse said. "All he has to do now is reel her in. Nice and slow."

"I've got a month to convince her she can't live without me."

"What if she won't come?" Kerri Ann asked. "What will you do?"

"I don't know," Ty admitted with a clutch in his gut. "I really don't."

"She loves you, Ty." Lita rubbed his arm. "I can tell by the way she looks at you."

"I just hope love is enough. She's got a lot going on. She's running a qualifying race next week. I'm taking her to Denver. If she qualifies for the Olympic trials, she could be off on a quest that doesn't include me."

"Or she could be off on a quest that fulfills one part of her," Jesse said. "Loving someone doesn't mean giving up everything you want to accomplish with your life. Lita made big adjustments to live with me and start our family."

"I've never regretted it." She linked her arm through her husband's.

"I'll be asking her to make all the changes," Ty said his greatest fear out loud. He'd be giving up nothing and getting the world if she moved across the country with him. "If she won't move, I'll have to consider my options."

"Are you willing to do that?" Bryce asked. "Move out here? Make your life here?"

"I don't know," he said. "I'd have to consider it or I couldn't ask her to do the same."

Kerri Ann hugged him hard. "Work your magic. Talk to her about the restaurant. I don't want you so far away."

CHAPTER 33

Jill lay sprawled on Ty's chest, her heart pounding, her body loose. "I loved your family, Ty, but I'm so glad they're gone."

"You and me both." He rubbed her bottom. "I'm starving."

She swatted his chest. "Is that all you think about? Sex and food?"

"I *am* a guy," he pointed out.

"I'm starving, too. What've you got in the kitchen?"

"Not much. We might have to venture out for sustenance."

"We could drive down to my place. Order a pizza, eat it in bed?"

Ty cleared his throat. "Where's your roommate?"

"Around. She had to work this afternoon." Jill rested her chin on her fist and stared into Ty's beautiful face. He hadn't shaved in a couple of days and, if possible, the unkempt look made him even more attractive. "She was a little snippy with me last week about being gone all the time. I think she might like some company."

"Seriously? I don't really want to share."

"You'd better be talking about me and not yourself."

He pinched her butt. "Listen to your dirty mouth." He

wagged his brows. "I like it."

"Why don't you like Olivia?" she asked.

He huffed out a breath before sitting up and moving some pillows behind his back. "I don't dislike Olivia; I just think she's annoying."

"Most men only see how pretty she is. I think it really bothers her that you don't find her attractive."

He shrugged. "I noticed her when I first came here. I'm not dead," he said to deflect Jill's anger. "But she's pretty insecure. She knows she's pretty and that's about it."

"She's smart. She does really well in school when she applies herself."

"So why doesn't she apply herself? Why hasn't she finished school?"

"She wasn't ready to grow up. Her dad was so hard on her and Tommy. Their dad's attitude pushed them in different directions. Tommy's driven and seems to always be proving himself, even though he's one of the most successful men in the valley. Olivia went in the opposite direction and does things on her own schedule. I think she regrets not finishing her degree."

"Is she close?"

"Another semester and she'll be student teaching, so less than a year."

"I get needing a break," he admitted. "This teaching job would pay more than double if I had my PhD. I need to be sure this is what I want to do before I devote that much more time to school."

"You don't think you'll like it?"

"I think I will. There aren't too many jobs that let me off in the summer to run the fly shop."

"True."

Jill got up and started collecting her clothes where Ty had ripped them off of her. Her stomach ached whenever he talked about his life apart from her.

"What do you think you'll do when the summer is over?" he asked.

She sat down on the bed and turned away from him. He wasn't asking anything more than she'd asked herself, but it seemed impossible to explain her indecision, especially after he'd spoken so negatively about Olivia. "I don't really know."

After a long pause, he said, "If you qualify for the trials, will you go?"

She shrugged and stared at the picture on the wall. The pretty autumn scene had become her favorite in the house. "It's expensive. I'd have to pay my way to Oregon."

"I could front you the money," he said.

She turned around and looked at him. "I can't ask you to do that."

"Why not? It's your dream, Jill. Nothing should stand in the way of your dream."

"I have to qualify first."

"You will. I've got a good feeling. Besides, I'll be waiting at the finish line."

"Then I'll run faster than I ever have." She threw his shirt at him. "Speaking of running, let's go eat. I need to run before it gets too dark."

"Don't forget our date with the mirror."

She gasped. "I thought you were kidding?"

He lifted one side of his mouth with a suggestive grin. "I never kid about sex."

***

Ty washed his hands and stared at his reflection in the mirror. "Coward." He shouldn't have asked her about her plans. What did he expect her to do, beg him to take her back with him? Jill had too much pride to even ask. He should have just told her how he felt, told her he wanted to start a life with her. Instead it sounded like he was pulling away.

He saw the look on her face when she'd turned around after she held her back so straight against him. He recognized the way she put up a wall, clutching her clothes to her chest, speaking in that damn toneless voice. He hurt her because he was too much of a coward to tell her the truth. The problem was he couldn't be sure of how she saw her future. Did she plan to train for the next four years? Did she want to work full time for Tommy? The restaurant was open year round.

"You'll never know until you ask her."

Tonight, he decided. He'd ask her tonight. *After* the mirror.

CHAPTER 34

J ill worked like a dog for a week, morning, noon, and night. In order for her to have the two days off she needed to get to and run the race, she had to pay it forward and make sure Tommy was covered in her absence.

Ty worked overtime too, taking all the jobs he could get, staying on the water 'til near dark and back again at the break of dawn. They'd collapse at the end of the day exhausted in one bed or another.

By mid-week, she felt the kind of focus come over her that always had in the past when preparing for a big run. She found herself going over the course in her head, running the hills, skirting around corners, finishing in less than an hour, fifteen. She learned a long time ago if she could envision it, if she could believe it possible, she could achieve her goal.

She wanted to qualify. Her dad would be there with Charla, his new runner. She hadn't told her dad she was going. She didn't want to create any more tension in her family when they'd finally gotten past the worst of her betrayal. This felt like another and she wasn't ready to confess just yet.

On the Thursday before the race, she'd just gotten home from a six mile run, content with her time. Fresh from the shower, she intended to dress and head back to the restaurant to check on the dinner hour when there was a knock at the door.

Ty stood on her small porch, clutching his cell phone, a look of sheer panic on his face. "What's wrong?" she asked.

He barreled past her into the den, rubbing his forehead. "Lita called. My dad threw his back out this morning."

"Oh, no. Has that happened before?"

"No. She said he'd been complaining of a strained muscle since they got back, but it totally went out pulling rafts this morning. The doctor gave him a shot and told him he's got to rest for two weeks."

"Two weeks?"

Ty sighed and paced behind the couch. She'd never seen him so antsy, so jerky in his movements, or so distressed.

"I know you're worried, but I'm sure he's going to be okay."

"I know he's going to be okay. It's the business. When they got back from their trip out here, the shop was in shambles. The guy he left to watch it while he was gone did a terrible job. My dad doesn't trust anyone at this point and he needs me to come home and cover for him until he's up on his feet."

"You're leaving?" Jill choked.

"I don't want to, Jill. But I have to. I can't leave him without someone to man the shop."

Jill nodded while she fought back the tears and the panic. Ty gone so soon? "When do you have to go?"

"I fly out of Colorado Springs tomorrow."

"Tomorrow?" She lowered onto the couch when she felt her legs give out. "What about your truck? And your boat?"

"I'll fly back out when he's better and drive them back."

"If you're gone for two weeks, you'll only have...what? A week or two before you go back for good?"

"If that much."

"Oh, Tyler."

He rushed to her side, clasping her hands in his. "I know. I wasn't expecting this."

"Of course you weren't." Her stomach felt as if she'd

swallowed a bucket of ice. "I know you have to go, I'm just disappointed."

"Jill," he grabbed her hands so tight her fingers ached, "there's so much I have to tell you. I should have talked to you weeks ago, but I wasn't sure it was the right time."

"What are you talking about?"

He closed his eyes tight, and when he opened them, her heart skipped a beat in anticipation. "I love you, Jill."

She sank into the cushion, her mouth open. "What?"

"I'm completely in love with you."

She tried to form words, she tried to make something come out of her dry and aching throat, but nothing but a shaky breath escaped.

"I want a life with you. I want us to be together."

"I..."

"I know this seems sudden, but it's been building all summer. I think I knew from the very first moment I saw you that you were the one."

"Tyler...how? We live on opposite sides of the country."

"We don't have to."

She shook her head. He couldn't be asking what she thought he was asking. "What are you saying? You want me to follow you? Move to North Carolina?"

"At first, yes. I've signed a contract. I've got to teach this year."

"And you've got your business with your dad. You're tied there. That's where you live. That's where you'll always live."

"Not if it's not the right place for you. All I've ever wanted was a family, a real one. A wife who loves me, who'll grow old with me, and children to raise."

"A wife?" The ice in her stomach turned sharp as a knife. "Jesus, Ty. What are you saying?"

"I want you, Jill. For today, for tomorrow, forever. I love you. I want you to marry me."

She gripped at the throbbing in her temple. He had to stop. Didn't he know he was ripping her apart with his words? "You're asking me to leave my home. My family."

"If it's not what you want, living in North Carolina, we'll move."

"What do you mean? You'd move here? For me?"

"For us, if it's what's best. Or we can live in both places at different times of the year. We can live in North Carolina in the summer. You can train anywhere. We can live out here the rest of the year."

"That..." God, her head was going to explode. "That'll never work." She couldn't think. She absolutely couldn't put one single thought together. "Kids? Are you out of your mind?"

"No. We'd have really great kids."

She could see it, their kids. Tall, athletic, good-natured, and a little bit mischievous. Damn him for putting the image so clearly in her head. "I don't know."

"I'm only asking what I'm willing to give up for you."

"Your family."

"I want you to be my family."

She reached out and touched his cheek. His eyes, the hazel that changed from blue to green, closed at the first brush of her fingers. "You have a family, a very good, tight, oddly functioning family. You're very lucky."

"I wasn't always so lucky. There was a time when I was younger that my parents hated each other. They fought constantly, and not in hushed voices like you see on TV. They think I was too young to remember and I never said otherwise because I know it was a time neither one of them is proud of, but it lives inside me. The feeling of being at fault, of them not loving me enough to stay together, of the anger and the pain. Things are fine with them now, better than fine, but I want what they couldn't give each other. You're the one I want it with."

"But I'd have to walk away from everything here."

"I'm not asking you to walk away from any of it. I'm asking you to walk toward something, something real, something that won't end if you get injured or feel moody or low. I'm asking you marry me, to commit to me, and to trust that everything will work out okay."

"I do trust you, but…"

"I'm not your father, Jill. I'm not going to look for someone else when things get tough. You remember when you asked me if I knew what it felt like to lose the one thing I'd always wanted?"

She nodded her head. "I've trained to be a distance runner my whole life. Every second, every thought was about getting better, and winning, and moving on to the next level. You've only known me a couple of months. How can you be so sure?"

"I've known you for more than a couple of months and I've wanted what you and I can have together for as long as you've been dreaming about setting the world on fire with your legs."

"Wanting it and training for it are two different things."

"What do you think dating is, Jill? Fun and games? It's training for the real thing, so that when the real thing comes along, you know it, you recognize it, and you don't waste any more time on anything else."

She sputtered out a laugh. "You're equating dating with my training regimen?"

He shrugged. "You've trained. I've dated. You know what it takes to win and so do I. I love you and nothing in my life matters more than you."

"Tyler," she fell to her knees, "I don't know what to say."

"You don't have to say anything now. Just think about it. Think about how happy we could be."

The words, held so long in her heart, spilled out of her mouth without thought. "I love you, Tyler. I want you. I'm just so confused. I never thought…I couldn't bring myself to imagine you'd want a future with me."

"Baby." Ty pulled her up and onto his lap. "You're all I want. You're everything to me."

They fell together onto the couch, clutching at clothes, mindless in their need, in their passion. He was here, he was real, and he was hers for only a few more hours until he had to leave.

They jerked apart when the front door slammed. "Oh, for God's sake. Can you two please move to the bedroom?"

"Shut up, Olivia," they both said. Ty held Jill against his chest, shielding her bare breasts from view.

"I do live here," she reminded them as he ushered Jill down the hall and into her room.

Ty pushed the door shut with his foot and then stood staring at Jill. They both burst out laughing. "I guess the gig is up. She knows we're having sex."

"I told her we were having sleepover tea parties, but I don't think she believed me."

Ty let out a shaky breath. "I love you. I know I dumped an awful lot on you tonight. I've been trying to tell you for weeks, but I kept chickening out. I hoped to have more time to ease you into the idea. I've had to mend the line a bit."

"You've had to what?"

"It's a fishing term. You mend the line when it gets ahead of the bait." When she stared at him confused, he said, "You adjust the line according to the current."

"This is one heck of a current."

He lifted a shoulder, dropped it, and cocked his head to the side. "You don't have to answer me now. Think about it. Go run your race and live your dreams and I'll be back. I just want to be with you tonight before I have to go."

"I'll call Tommy," Jill said. "I'll drive you to Springs in the morning."

"I've already arranged for him to take me."

The stab of hurt was quick and painful. "Oh."

"I wasn't sure I could get on the plane if you were there, baby. Don't be mad."

"I'm not mad. But I will be if you don't touch me soon."

He scooped her into his arms and fell with her onto the bed. "I love it when you tell me what to do."

She licked her lips. "You do?"

He nodded and put his lips below her ear, right where he knew it made her quiver. "Um huh."

"Tommy's driving you, right?"

He lifted his head and looked into her eyes, his brows drawn tight. "Yeah."

"Good, because you're not going to get much sleep tonight."

CHAPTER 35

Tommy jerked his head toward Ty and his SUV swerved onto the shoulder. "You asked her to marry you?"

Ty made a grab for the wheel, but Tommy corrected and had them back on the road before Ty had to act. "What did she say?"

"Nothing, yet."

Holy shit, Tommy thought. Ty was in deep. Didn't the kid know that women only led to trouble? "Nothing?"

"I told her to think about it while I'm gone."

Tommy let out a huge breath. "Okay."

"You think we're too young," Ty said. It wasn't a question, but a statement.

"I think it's your life. If you want to get married, if you want to marry Jill, I wish the best for you."

Tommy could feel Ty staring at the side of his face. "You're a cynic. How didn't I know this about you?"

"I'm not a cynic. I just don't think marriage is the end all, be all. It's hard work on both sides and sometimes it doesn't end well."

"Have you ever been married?"

An image of Gretchen flashed through his mind. God, he hadn't thought of her in years. "Almost. I couldn't quite pull the trigger."

"Ahhh."

"What do you mean, ahhh?"

"I mean I get why you're cynical. You come from divorce. I come from divorce, too. I think you either go one way or the other when your parents split up."

"What do you mean?" Tommy asked.

"I mean you either long for a strong, solid marriage and go in knowing it's forever, or you avoid marriage because you think of it as a trap."

"I'm in the latter court."

"And I'm in the former. I love her. I've never been more sure of anything in my life."

Tommy took a deep breath, held it, and let it out slowly. "I'm happy for you, man. I guess you got what you came back for?"

"Not yet," Ty said and looked out the window. "Not quite yet. But I'll be back."

***

"Jill?" Bobbie said with a look of concern when she found her daughter on her doorstep at eight in the morning. Jill tried to wait until later, but she needed her mother now. "What's wrong?"

Jill fell into her mother's arms and drank in her scent. She smelled like Oil of Olay and the hazelnut cream she put in her morning coffee. "I need to talk to you."

Bobbie grabbed her arms and held her out, studying her face. "Oh, dear. Did Tyler break up with you?"

"No, Mom. He asked me to marry him."

Jill felt her mother's hands tighten painfully on her arms before she relaxed her grip and her hands fell to her side. "What?"

Jill closed the door at her back and grabbed her mom's arm, dragging her into the kitchen. She sat down at the table where she'd eaten thousands of meals, done hundreds of homework assignments, and dreamed of the future. Her mom stumbled into the chair next to Jill.

"How?"

"He came over last night to say goodbye—"

"Goodbye? I thought he asked you to marry him."

"He did. Just let me get this out." She took a deep breath, exhaled slowly, and laced her fingers together on the table in front of her. "His dad threw his back out. You know he owns a raft shop. When they were here last week, he left a man in charge who did a horrible job. Ty's dad needed him to come home and run the shop until he's back on his feet."

Bobbie impatiently pushed the hair out of her face. "Okay…"

"So he came over last night to tell me he had to leave. I was upset. I knew he was leaving at the end of the summer and we'd never talked about the future. Ty was all wound up about leaving and he said he's in love with me. He's coming back to get his things and he wants me to think about moving there with him."

Bobbie gasped. "To North Carolina?"

Jill nodded. "He's signed a teaching contract for the year that he can't get out of. He's also starting the fly fishing shop with his dad. He's tied there, at least for a year."

"He wants you to move across the country? After only knowing you for a few months?"

"He said if I didn't like it there, he'd move here, or we could live both places during different times of the year. He's got to be there in the summer."

"Jill," Bobbie reached out and gripped Jill's hands, "are you considering this?"

She couldn't lie to her mom, no matter how devastated she looked. "I love him, Mom."

"What would you do there?"

Her mother had hit on Jill's biggest concern. "Ty said his mom and stepdad are opening a new restaurant. A nice one, nicer than anything the town has now. They want me to help with both places—the pizza place they've owned for years and the new place. His mom hates doing the books and she'll need lots of help running two places."

"Will that be enough? And what about your training? Are you giving up on that for good?"

"No. I've been running. My leg feels strong. I've decided to run in the qualifier in Denver this weekend."

"Have you told your dad?"

Jill shook her head from side to side.

"You know he's taking Charla?"

She nodded. "I know. Do you think he'd let me ride up there with them?"

"Honey, I'm sure all you have to do is ask."

"Good." At least one thing was settled.

"So, what are you going to do?"

"I don't know. I love him. I do. I want to be with him. I can't breathe when I think about not being with him."

"But?"

"But moving away from here, from you…it scares me. What if I hate it? What if I make him move back here and he hates me for making him leave his family behind?"

"That's an awful lot of what ifs." Bobbie stood up, gathered her coffee mug in both hands, and refilled it from the pot. She carefully added her creamer from the refrigerator and rejoined Jill at the table. "Love's the biggest risk of all."

Jill nodded. "Yes. He's the best man I've ever known."

"I could argue your dad's case here, but I doubt you'd see my side of things."

"Let's just say we both love really good men."

Bobbie pursed her lips. "Your daddy's going to be upset."

"I know."

"Sounds like you've made up your mind."

"One minute I think I have, and the next minute I'm all confused." She got up and began pacing. She couldn't think without moving around. "I'm going to run the race this weekend because that's a goal I need to try and achieve first."

"Do you think you'll qualify?"

"My times have been close."

"You know if you do, your daddy's going to say I told you

216

so."

"And he'd be right. But I have to qualify first."

Bobbie got up and stopped Jill in her tracks. "Don't tell him about Ty just yet. He's all keyed up about the race, about Charla, and if he were being honest with himself, about you. He'll be glad you're going. Let him be glad for a little while."

"You think he'll be upset about Ty?"

"That his little girl's getting married? Honey..."

"I haven't answered him yet."

She cupped Jill's face in her palm. "I know this face. You're already gone."

CHAPTER 36

Ty came into the den and plopped in the easy chair with a sigh. His back, after twelve hours on his feet, ached like the devil.

"Long day?" his dad asked from his reclined position on the couch.

"I'm not sure how you managed to go so long without throwing your back out sooner. I'm exhausted."

"That's 'cause I'm heartier than you and the wimps in your generation."

"Whatever," Ty said. He tossed the ledger book on the coffee table within his dad's reach. "There's the books. We had a good day. I think I've managed to reconcile everything from when you were gone."

"Fantastic." His dad turned the volume down on the Braves game.

"What's the score?"

"Braves are up three in the bottom of the fourth."

Ty tried not to nod off. Every muscle in his body ached. Even his brain hurt. "Are the girls in bed?"

"Lita's putting Ella down now. She fights it."

"She's a night owl like her dad."

"It's a wonder I can sleep at all after laying around all damn day. Lita will hardly let me get up to use the bathroom."

"Yeah, it must totally suck to have the woman you love cater to your every need."

Ty's dad didn't miss the sarcasm in his voice. "Have you talked to her?"

Ty sighed and rubbed his aching shoulder. "Yeah. She's working, getting ready for the race. She misses me."

"Has she given you an answer?"

"No, but I haven't asked." When his dad gave him an exasperated look, he said, "I told her to think about it and I'm not going to pressure her. If she loves me enough to give up everything she knows and is familiar with, she'll do it because she wants to, not because I've bullied her into it."

"There's nothing wrong with nudging her along. Do it for me, for goodness sake. I'm sick of feeling guilty watching you mope around here every morning and night."

"Maybe I'll go stay with Mom and Bryce so you don't have to feel guilty."

"Do whatever you want to do."

Lita walked into the middle of the den and stood in front of the television. She folded her arms over her chest. "What's going on in here? I can hear you two sniping at each other from upstairs."

"Somebody thinks I should've hoisted Jill over my shoulder and manhandled her into agreeing to marry me." Ty crossed his arms over his chest and sneered at his dad.

"And somebody thinks sitting around moping is going to magically make Jill move here."

"Neither one of you is right," Lita said. She stared at Jesse with her brows raised. "And someone is forgetting that he did the same thing as his son, presenting his case and then giving me time to think."

"You didn't take a whole lot of time, thank God."

"So you have no idea how Ty is feeling and you might stop feeling guilty and sorry for yourself long enough to have a little sympathy."

Jesse lifted a shoulder, glanced over at Ty. "Sorry."

Ty gave an identical shoulder lift and shrugged it off. "Sorry, too." He stood up and stretched his back. "Maybe I will go stay with Mom. She's been nagging me to come over and it might help to beat up on the boys for a while."

"You can come and go as you please," Lita said. She hugged Ty, rubbing her cheek on his chest. "You know we love having you."

"I know. Under different circumstances, I'd love being here. I'm beat. I'm going to grab a shower and turn in."

He climbed the stairs carefully, being sure to miss the creaky spot that might wake the girls. He closed his door and leaned back against it, staring at his childhood bedroom. On impulse, he took out his phone and snapped a picture of his room.

Maybe Jill was so hesitant because she didn't know what she'd be coming to. He'd never showed her any pictures of the area or his little part of the town. He decided to start that night by sending the picture by text.

Here's the bed I'm sleeping in alone, missing you, dreaming of you. Yes, that is an autographed Chipper Jones baseball on my nightstand. Considering he's destined to be a Hall of Famer, I'm allowed to be a fan. Love you.

***

The phone in Jill's pocket beeped as she worked behind the bar at The Tap. Through the crowd and the music, she didn't hear it and the text went unnoticed until almost eleven when she walked out to her car. She smiled at the double bed with a brown and red quilt, the glassed in baseball on the nightstand, and when she zoomed in on the corkboard on the wall, a picture of her held up with a yellow tack.

She looked at the time. He was asleep by now in that bed. She didn't want to wake him, but she couldn't let his text go ignored. *I love you* was all she wrote. She hoped, in the end, that was enough.

***

With every mile she ran, images flashed through Jill's head. The raft shop along the banks of the Powellachee. The nearly ready to be christened fly shop and the wooden sign that was yet to be hung. His mother's brick house where the twins wrestled in the sprawling yard. His father's picture perfect farmhouse where the girls ran through a sprinkler near the front porch. Ty, with his arm around his grandfather's shoulders. The cabin where they would live until they decided what and where they wanted to be. His mother's restaurant from the outside along the quaint city block. The site of the new restaurant they planned to open in the fall, construction crews already at work.

The pictures played like a movie in her head. The soundtrack was Ty's voice, telling her he loved her and explaining to her his mother's plans for the new restaurant. Kerri Ann needed help and she was more than willing to trust someone who had restaurant experience, someone who cared as much about the success of the businesses as the owners, and someone her son wanted as his wife.

Ty said he'd be waiting at the finish line. She'd thought he hadn't kept his promise, but she understood now that he *was* waiting at the finish line. He was waiting for her to finish one chapter of her life and he was there to help her begin another.

Heedless of her stride or her leg or the time she kept on her watch, Jill ran like a woman possessed along some of Denver's most famous streets and attractions. She crossed the finish line without even noting her time and slowed to a walk. The sound of her father calling her name broke the trance she'd been in for the half marathon.

"Jill!" He grabbed her in a bear hug, lifting her off her feet, and twirling her in the air. "You did it! You qualified."

"I did?" She accepted a bottle of water from a race volunteer and looked back toward the finish line. "What was my time?"

"You beat it by three minutes." He scanned the crowd. "I've got to go look for Charla. She should be close." He gave her a smacking kiss on her forehead. "I'm so damn proud of you. I knew you could do it." He jogged back to the finish line and waited for his runner.

Jill guzzled the water, tossing the empty bottle in one of the many trashcans around the finish area. She kept walking until her heart rate steadied and her breathing calmed. She stretched her quads, calves, and hamstrings before joining her dad and Charla where they stood next to the water station. Charla missed qualifying by twenty-three seconds.

"Congratulations," Charla choked out through gasping breaths. She leaned over and clutched her knees, gulping in air. Frustration bounced off her in waves. Jill felt sympathy for the girl she'd expected to dislike, but found charming and unaffected on the ride up from Westmoreland. Her dad had chosen a good runner with a big and eager heart.

Jill rubbed her back. "You did great. It won't take any time at all to shave off twenty-three seconds."

"I lagged on mile seven," Charla said. "I just kind of zoned out and didn't focus. By the time I realized my mistake, I couldn't make up the difference."

"It's one race," her father said. "There'll be others. Knowing where you dropped the ball is half the battle. Now we know to work on keeping you focused throughout."

Charla nodded and gave Jill a beaming smile. "I guess it's off to Oregon for you."

Jill swallowed and looked away. Her father, bless the man, threw her a lifeline. He thought he was sparing Charla the embarrassment. "We've got plenty of time to talk about Oregon. Let's get you girls to the massage table and work out those kinks before the award ceremony."

CHAPTER 37

Tommy helped Lyle hitch Ty's boat to the back of his truck while Olivia stood brooding, kicking dirt with her sandal and squinting into the bright morning sun.

"I still can't believe you're leaving me," Olivia said. "What in the world am I supposed to do in this town without you?"

"Get your degree," Tommy mumbled out of the side of his mouth. Olivia, with years of eavesdropping experience, overheard him perfectly.

"Besides that," she said.

"It's okay if you miss me," Jill said. "Because I'm going to miss you like crazy."

"So don't go. Make Ty move out here so I won't be all alone with them." She jerked her thumb at Tommy and Lyle where they knelt to secure the lock on the hitch.

"I'm not going to make him do anything, just like he's not making me do anything." Jill gave her a beaming smile. "We're going to make each other very happy."

"You weren't this annoyingly sappy before you fell in love." Olivia put air quotes around the words 'in love.'

"You will be too when it's your turn."

"I guess the good news is that if tall, dark, and handsome ever shows up, my biggest competition will be across the

223

country."

"See," Jill said. "There's my optimistic friend. I knew she was in there somewhere."

"Okay," Tommy said as he walked over and handed Jill the keys. "The boat's secure. Be sure, when you stop for the night, to pull everything into the hotel. If you don't, there's a good chance there won't be anything left when you go back out in the morning."

"My dad already warned me that we shouldn't use the boat for storage for that very reason."

"I can't believe you talked him and your mom into riding with you to North Carolina," Lyle said.

"It was their idea. Since neither Charla nor I are going to Oregon, he had the time and he and Mom really want to meet Ty's family. See where we'll be living."

"And you still haven't told Ty you're coming?" Olivia asked.

"And ruin the surprise?" Jill asked. "No way. I can't wait to see his face when we pull up in his truck."

"I feel like I'm never going to see you again," Olivia pouted.

"I'll be in constant contact. I've got a wedding to plan. I need my maid of honor to help me with all the details."

Olivia squealed. "Oh my gosh, really?" She hugged Jill and began jumping up and down. She spun around and faced Tommy who stood rolling his eyes. "A good brother would send us to New York to find your dress."

"She's marrying the guy who stole my best employee."

"Hey," Olivia said. "*I'm* your best employee."

Tommy ignored her and pulled Jill into his chest. "Be careful. If anything happens to you, Ty'll have my head."

"I will. Thank you so much for everything."

"Go," he said. "Be happy. Come back and visit us sometime."

"Count on it."

Lyle wrapped his arm around Jill's shoulder. "Be careful, Jill. If you all get tired, make sure you switch off or stop for the day. That's a long haul, especially pulling the boat."

"We'll be fine. I'm actually looking forward to spending some time with my parents. Dad was really cool about me forgoing Oregon and I think he and Mom need some time to digest the fact that I'm leaving."

Olivia and Lyle walked arm in arm with Jill to the driver's side. "I hate you for leaving me," Olivia said, "but I'm so darn happy for you."

"I love you," Jill said.

The thin hold on Olivia's emotions broke. "Damn it, you're making me cry. I love you, too."

"Call me when you get there," Lyle said.

"I will."

"Call me from the road," Olivia said. "I'll be so bored here alone."

Jill gave them both a hard squeeze and then hopped into the truck. "I've got a feeling you won't be alone for long."

"Really?"

"Really." Jill blew her best friends a kiss and waved as she pulled out.

Olivia wiped at her tears. "Damn it, Lyle. Why did she have to fall in love?"

"They say it makes the world go round," Lyle said and placed a consolatory arm around her shoulders.

She looked up at him and grimaced. "How would we know?"

He shrugged. "Beats me."

***

"What are you wearing?" Ty asked Jill when she answered her cell phone. He'd stolen a moment for himself in his dad's office while the afternoon groups were gone and the place was quiet. Ty was better when things were busy. During the slow breaks in the day, he missed Jill so much he wanted to jump out of his skin.

"Ahhh, jeans and a t-shirt."

"No, silly. Underneath."

She cleared her throat. "Yeah," she said after a pause. "The weather's beautiful."

"Oh," he chuckled. "I thought you were alone."

"Nope."

"Who's with you?"

After another awkward pause, she said, "Um, Tommy. We were just going over the inventory."

"Put him on for a minute," Ty said. "I want to ask him a quick question."

"Ah…his cell phone just beeped and he's on a call."

"Good. So tell me what you're wearing." He tipped back in the seat and imagined Jill in her office. Naked.

"Oh, gosh, Meredith's here and she needs me in the restaurant. I've got to go."

His chair hit the floor. "Okay. Call me later?"

"Yeah, yeah. Of course."

"I love you," he said before he realized she'd hung up. He sat listening to the dial tone and felt everything in his world start to tip. He was losing her. He'd been gone just long enough for her to realize she didn't need him in her life. He rubbed his chest where it began to ache, just above his heart.

His dad wasn't scheduled to come off bed rest for another four days. Ty could envision living every one of those ninety-six hours on the edge of sanity. He'd never make it.

He shot to his feet and barreled out the door, toward the back where a pile of pebble rock waited to be spread. He tugged his shirt off, reached for the shovel, and put his body to work. No way was he going to sit around and worry for four solid days.

CHAPTER 38

"There it is," Jill said and pointed to the raft shop entrance. "Up ahead on the right."

Her dad eased off the gas and set the turn signal.

"Thank the Lord," Bobbie said from the back seat. "I'm so ready to get out of this truck."

Jill yanked the visor down and scowled when she realized it didn't have a mirror. She turned in her seat to face her mom. "How do I look?"

"Oh, sweetie. You look beautiful. And nervous."

"I am. What if he's not happy to see me? What if he feels bombarded?"

Jill's dad laid a hand on her knee. "In my experience, a man doesn't ask a woman to marry him if there's any chance he's going to change his mind."

"I know, but—Oh, God. There's his dad's car. He's here."

"Isn't that why we just drove fifteen hundred miles?" Gary asked. "Where should I pull this thing?"

"Over there," Jill said. "Out of the way of the main thoroughfare."

Gary stopped and put the truck into park.

"Where do you think he is?" Jill asked.

"You're never going to figure it out sitting here," her mom said. "Get out of the car, Jill, and go find him."

"Yes, ma'am." Jill opened the door, glanced at both of her parents, who looked back at her with expectant faces, and closed the door. She turned around and faced the two buildings. From Ty's pictures, she knew the larger of the two was the raft shop and office, and the smaller housed the restrooms and changing facility. She wiped her sweaty palms on her jeans and carefully made her way toward the larger of the two buildings.

There were a handful of cars in the parking lot, but otherwise the place was quiet. She opened the door and walked hesitantly inside. Two teenaged girls whipped around from where they'd been leaning on the windowsill.

"Oh, sorry," one of them said. "Girl moment." She pointed with her thumb toward the window. "The owner's son is working with his shirt off. His hotness cannot be overstated."

Jill should have been jealous, but she found herself stepping to the counter, leaning over to try and get a peek. "Do you mind if I take a look?" she asked.

They waved her back and made room on the side of the window. Ty stood about twenty yards away, shoveling rocks in low-slung cargo shorts and work boots. His sweat drenched hair was plastered to his neck and the muscles of his back rippled with every movement. "Wow," Jill said. "That is a sight to see."

As if on cue, Ty stood up, wiped his brow with the back of his hand, and tossed the shovel like a spear into the gravel pile. He ambled down to the river, sat on a boulder, and untied the laces of his work boots. He flung the socks to the ground before standing up and easing into the wide and meandering river. Jill's mouth went dry and one of them, she's not sure who, actually groaned.

"Do you have any towels?" Jill asked.

"Towels?" one of the girls said.

She nodded with her head toward the window. "He'll need a towel when he gets out."

"And you're going to take him one?" the other asked as if Jill had suggested she strip naked and join him in the water. The thought had crossed her mind before she remembered her parents.

"If you don't mind."

The taller of the two reached under the counter and tossed Jill a fluffy yellow beach towel. "This I gotta see."

Jill walked out the front door, around the building, and down the slope toward the boulder where Ty's shoes sat abandoned. Her heart beat a steady drum in her chest and the cheerleader in her stomach began practicing her tumbling moves.

At the boulder, she stopped, clutching the towel to her chest, and stared. Ty had completely submerged himself in the thigh deep water and floated on the surface with his eyes closed. He looked so completely at peace she hated to disturb him.

He let out a huge breath, stood up, and shook his hair, spraying water droplets in an arc around him. When he pivoted and took a step to get out of the river, he looked up and saw Jill. He stopped in his tracks, his mouth hanging open, and blinked his eyes twice. When he dropped his hand to his belly, Jill's heart soared.

"Jill?"

"I thought you might need this?" She held out the towel.

He bolted out of the water and up the bank, grabbing her around the waist and hoisting her into his arms. Jill held on with everything she had, soaking her clothes in the process. She nuzzled her lips against his neck, drinking in the scent of his skin.

"What are you doing here?" he asked. "How did you get here?"

He eased her onto her feet, ran his hands through her hair, and kissed her long and deep and so thoroughly she clung to his arms when they came up for air. "We brought your truck back. And the boat."

"We?"

He jerked his head up and around, searching the parking lot. Jill watched the shock register on his face when he spotted her parents, standing arm in arm between the two buildings. "Your parents are here?"

She nodded while the cheerleader stomped in her stomach. "They wanted to meet your parents and see where we'll be living."

His hands tightened on her shoulders almost painfully. "Living? Does this mean...?"

She glanced up and met him stare for stare. "I'm accepting your marriage proposal, if the offer still stands."

She was back in his arms before she even knew what happened, twirling in the air, the sound of his laughter ringing in her ears.

"Oh, God, Jill. I thought I was losing you."

"What?"

"You were so distant when I called. I thought you were pulling away."

"I was lying through my teeth. I've always been a terrible liar."

"No more lies," he said when he set her down. "My heart can't take it."

Jill's mom and dad approached. "Is it safe to say hello?"

"Mr. and Mrs. Jennings." Ty held out his hand after using the towel Jill handed him. "I'm totally blown away. Thank you for bringing Jill here."

"We brought your truck, your boat, and Jill and I packed up all your things from the cabin," Bobbie explained.

Ty's grin went from ear to ear. "I don't know what to say."

"Well," Gary said, "you can tell me you'll make my daughter happy."

Ty tightened his hold on Jill's shoulders. "I'll spend every day of the rest of my life making sure I do."

"That's good enough for me, Bobbie," her father said and turned to look at her mother. "What about you?"

"Is it good enough for Jill?" Bobbie asked.

"It's everything," Jill said as she turned into his arms. "I got everything I've ever wanted."

ABOUT THE AUTHOR

Christy Hayes writes romance and women's fiction. She lives outside Atlanta, Georgia with her husband, two children, and two dogs. Visit www.christyhayes.com for more information.